13/21

The
BLACKBIRD
GIRLS

—

The
BLACKBIRD
GIRLS

BY

Anne Blankman

VIKING

VIKING

An imprint of Penguin Random House LLC, New York

First published in the United States of America by Viking,
an imprint of Penguin Random House LLC, 2020

Copyright © 2020 by Anne Blankman

Visit us online at penguinrandomhouse.com

LIBRARY OF CONGRESS CATALOGING-IN-PUBLICATION DATA IS AVAILABLE.

ISBN 9781984837356

This is a work of fiction. Names, characters, places, and incidents either are the product of the author's imagination or are used fictitiously, and any resemblance to actual persons, living or dead, businesses, companies, events, or locales is entirely coincidental.

Printed in USA • Book design by Nancy Brennan • Set in Harriet Text

1   3   5   7   9   10   8   6   4   2

For my friend Victoria, who lived many pieces of this story;

my husband, Mike, who faced cancer with courage and humor;

and my daughter, Kirsten, who is brave and kind.

(1)

Valentina

VALENTINA WONDERED WHERE the birds had gone.

They weren't waiting on the sill when she went to the sitting room window that morning. All year she had put slices of salami out for them. Blue jays came every day, and blackbirds sometimes, and sparrows least of all. The birds would stand on the sill, their claws black as soot against the gray concrete, and fly away when she unlatched the window, only to flutter back when she set out the pieces of salami.

Today, though, they were nowhere in sight. Valentina leaned out to look. Overhead, no blue jays circled one another, vanishing into the clouds, then reappearing. There were no blackbirds or sparrows, either. All of Pripyat's birds seemed to have disappeared. The sky was empty.

Except for a crimson glow in the distance. Valentina squinted. Usually, at half past seven, the sky was the pale blue of a robin's egg.

Not now. The sky in the south was red. Smoke churned up toward the scarlet-colored clouds. The smoke wasn't black or gray, but a strange, unearthly blue. It was so thick that Valentina couldn't see anything below or behind it: all she could see was the wall of smoke coiling up and up into the red sky. But she knew what stood under that billowing smoke.

The nuclear power station where her father worked.

She whirled away from the window. "The power station is on fire!"

Her mother hurried out of the bedroom, buttoning the cuff of her blouse. "What did you say?"

Valentina pointed at the window. Her mother joined her and gasped. "Oh my God!"

"Where's Papa?" Valentina glanced at the empty kitchen table. Her father worked the night shift at the power station. Usually, he was back in time to eat breakfast, tired and hungry after a long night. Then he would go to bed once Valentina had left for school. When he hadn't been at the kitchen table this morning, Valentina had assumed he was already in the bedroom, asleep.

"He hasn't come home yet." With shaking hands, Valentina's mother latched the window. "Do you remember he said he would have a busy night? The supervisors were planning to run a safety drill. So when he didn't show up an hour ago, I wasn't worried."

She pulled Valentina in close for a hug. "I'm sure he's fine, Valyushka. If he was hurt, someone at the power station would have telephoned us."

Valentina leaned into her mother, breathing in the comforting scent of her violet perfume. Mama had to be right. An accident at a nuclear power station was a statistical impossibility. A one-in-ten-million chance, her father had told her. And in school she and her classmates were taught that nuclear power was the safest, cleanest source of energy in the world. It had brought heat and light for the first time to thousands of citizens in the Soviet Union. But . . .

"Why isn't the smoke black?" she asked.

Her mother held her tighter. "I don't know. Maybe I shouldn't send you to school," she murmured. "But I have to go to work. And if we don't show up, people might talk . . ."

Valentina understood what her mother meant. They mustn't do anything out of the ordinary, *ever*, or they risked attracting attention. And attention was bad. It meant someone was watching you, waiting for you to make a mistake. And mistakes—like saying the wrong thing, criticizing the government, making someone important angry—led the secret police to you. People who were taken away by the secret police, the KGB, often weren't seen again. When Valentina's mother was a university student, one of her classmates had been arrested by the KGB. The last time anyone had seen him was when he was shoved into the back of a car. Valentina's mother had never forgotten it.

"I want to stay home and wait for Papa," Valentina said.

"If Papa was injured, one of the other workers would have let us know," her mother replied. "If we don't carry on as usual, we look as though we don't trust the people at the power station. And we mustn't—"

"Risk attention," Valentina interrupted. She pulled herself free from her mother's embrace. "But what if everybody's hurt and no one can telephone us?"

"Then the hospital workers would call." Her mother gave her a gentle push toward the door. "Papa's fine. Now you'd better hurry or you'll be late."

"Yes, Mama." Valentina grabbed her satchel and rushed out the door. Her mother didn't understand. She never did. She cared more about being safe than anything else. If Valentina did the best in her class on a mathematics exam, her mother said next time she ought to get one or two questions wrong on purpose. "We're Jews," she would say when Valentina complained. "Others are looking for a reason to hate us. Don't give them any."

"Come straight home after school!" her mother called after her. "I have to work this morning, but I'll be home by lunch. I'm sure Papa will be back by then."

"Okay," Valentina called back. Saturdays were half days at school. On Saturday mornings, her mother played the piano during ballet lessons at the culture palace. Many children who were too little for school went there for ballet or swimming instruction. Usually, after her mother finished the lessons and Valentina was done with school, they had lunch together while Valentina's father slept.

Then Valentina would play in the park with her best friend, Larisa, while her mother shopped for groceries. When Valentina would get home, her father would usually be awake, and they'd tinker with different experiments. Last month they had rewired the electrical outlets in their apartment. Currently, they were working on a design for a water heater. Ordinarily, Saturdays were golden, glorious days, but now as Valentina walked down the corridor, she couldn't stop worrying about her father.

The stairwell of their building was full of small children. On the landing, kids played with dolls and jacks. Valentina stepped over them, nearly bumping into her neighbor, Dyadya Sergei. When she was little, she had thought all of her family friends and neighbors were her uncles and aunts, because that was how she had been taught to address them. It wasn't until she was older that she had realized calling grown-ups *dyadya* or *tetya* was a custom, and all these "uncles" and "aunts" weren't blood relations. She still liked calling them the traditional names, though, because she hadn't any uncles and aunts of her own, for both of her parents had been only children.

"Good morning, Valentina," Dyadya Sergei said. He was dressed only in trousers and had a book tucked under his arm. "I'm going up to the roof to sunbathe and watch the fire. Did your father tell you how it started?"

"No, Dyadya Sergei." Her voice trembled. "He isn't home yet."

Dyadya Sergei patted her head. "I suppose he stayed to watch the firemen work. You ought to go down to the station, have a look about. It's the sort of thing one sees only once in a generation."

He sounded as though he thought the fire was some sort of entertainment! "I have to go to school," she said, skirting around him.

His laugh followed her down the stairwell. "Poor Valentina! Having to go to school on such an exciting day is a true misery."

Valentina paused at the landing to look out the window. The sky still flickered red. Below it, the city of Pripyat lay burrowed like a bird in a nest. People walked the streets; under the scarlet dome of the sky, they looked as flimsy as paper dolls. Blocks of pink-and-white plaster-faced apartment towers stretched into the distance. The enormous Communist hammer-and-sickle insignia crowned several buildings, their neon lights dark in the daytime. Beyond them rose the gunmetal-gray domes of the four reactors of the power station where her father worked. The station's proper name was the V.I. Lenin Power Station, but it was usually called Chernobyl, after an ancient nearby village.

Valentina's father said Pripyat was a model city because the station powered electricity for millions of people in the western Soviet Union. Its citizens got the best of everything, like shaving cream from East Germany and toothpaste from Bulgaria, sweaters from Poland and dresses from Finland, and cheeses and chocolates and caviar. They were lucky to live in such a paradise, he often told her. Valentina knew he was right: she remembered the years they had lived in Siberia, where the winters were so cold you could actually hear your breath turn to ice.

Outside the air tasted of metal, not the wild roses and cut grass that Valentina was used to. *No fire should smell like this*, she thought. The scent of soot should carry on the air, but not this hot metal that tickled the back of her throat.

Everywhere she looked, she saw police officers leaning against walls or standing on corners. The city was a sea of blue-and-red uniforms.

She'd never seen so many policemen in her life. What were they doing here? They couldn't all be from Pripyat's police force; there were too many of them. Some must have been summoned from nearby cities. Were they patrolling because of the fire?

Some of the grown-ups walking past sent nervous looks at the policemen. But they kept walking, their eyes going from the police officers to the red sky overhead. Nobody asked the policemen what was going on. Questions were dangerous, Valentina knew.

Children streamed along the avenue, staring at the police officers. Ladies carrying string shopping bags went in and out of stores; young mothers pushed babies in carriages or held toddlers by the hand, guiding them toward parks or nurseries where they would be cared for while their mothers worked. Everybody looked at the blue smoke coiling up into the red sky, and nobody said a word to the policemen.

Valentina's steps slowed. Her father was somewhere behind that wall of smoke. Maybe hurt.

She *had* to know what was happening. Before she could think herself out of the decision, she dashed over to the nearest policeman. "Are you here because of the fire?" she asked.

The man flicked his cigarette into the gutter. "Shouldn't you be in school?"

"I'm on my way." Valentina hesitated. Her parents often said her chattering mouth would get her into trouble. Maybe she ought to keep walking to school. But then she thought of the strange blue smoke enveloping the power station and of her father who was in there somewhere. "Why isn't the smoke black?"

The man narrowed his eyes at her. "There isn't any smoke. That's steam, and you ought to be accustomed to it from living near such a large power station. Now you'd better get on."

"Thank you," she muttered, and walked on, frowning. The policeman was wrong. Steam was thin and gray, not thick and blue, and it didn't turn the sky red: she knew that much from living close to the nuclear station. Was the policeman lying or mistaken?

As she went through the school gates, she saw she had another problem to deal with. And it was waiting for her in the schoolyard.

Oksana Savchenko.

She was leaning against the fence, toying with the white ribbons at the end of her braids. She looked like the perfect Ukrainian girl—blond hair, blue eyes, pink-and-white skin, a porcelain doll come to life.

But Valentina knew there was nothing sweet or doll-like about Oksana.

The other girl caught sight of her. She pushed off the fence and called, "Valentina, come here!"

Valentina's heart sank to her shoes.

She wished she could run home. But she'd get in trouble for playing truant.

Better to get it over with.

Squaring her shoulders, she walked into the schoolyard, where Oksana stood waiting for her.

(2)

Oksana

OKSANA WATCHED VALENTINA Kaplan come closer. Valentina was almost the tallest girl in the fifth grade, second only to Tatiana Gavrilenko. She might look ordinary with her braids and white ribbons, like the other girls in school, but Oksana knew she wasn't.

"All Jews are liars," her father had told her again and again. "They're always watching you, trying to find a way to steal your job away from you or take your place. That's how they've survived as long as they have, by working together and trying to destroy the rest of us. Do you understand?"

"Yes, Papa," she had always said. Valentina's father was the reason her papa hadn't gotten a promotion last year at the nuclear power station.

A wave of pain washed over Oksana. The back of her shoulder ached so badly she had to clench her jaw so she wouldn't groan. It didn't matter. She deserved the pain, for having a saucy mouth.

She focused on Valentina, who had come to a stop a few feet away and was waiting, her expression wary.

"Let's race," Oksana said.

Valentina bit her lip. Oksana knew what she was thinking—that she'd like to say no but didn't dare refuse.

"Okay," Valentina said.

They went to the far end of the yard, where they crouched on the pavement. The other children stopped playing tag or marbles and came over to watch. Their loud voices filled the air. "Run hard, Oksana! You can beat her!"

Oksana looked up at the sky. It was the same shade of scarlet as her mother's silk shawl. She knew the color should make her afraid, but instead it made her want to draw the image inside her mind, so it would never go away. A scarlet sky, dotted with clouds that looked as if they had been dipped in red dye, and above the tops of the brick-and-plaster buildings, columns of blue smoke, the sort of blue you'd get if you mixed pale blue with black, giving you an almost navy.

"You can win, Oksana!" someone shouted.

Oksana flinched. What was wrong with her, daydreaming about colors? She was stupid—stupid and weak.

Crouching on the pavement, she reached forward, pressing the tips of her fingers into the rough surface. She'd win the race. Valentina wouldn't be so foolish as to run fast. And then tonight at supper she could tell her father, and he'd pat her cheek and say he was proud of her.

"Go!" one of the other fifth-grade girls shouted.

Oksana took off. Her feet flew across the cracked pavement. The back of her shoulder throbbed, like a tooth gone rotten. It made the breath hitch in her chest. She could feel herself slowing, her legs stumbling.

"Come on, Oksana!" her classmates cheered. "You can do it!"

Don't stop, she told herself, and raced on. From the corner of her eye, she glimpsed a blur of movement. Valentina. She was surging forward, her brown braids streaming behind her. She slapped the wall of the school building. She had *won*.

Oksana's steps slowed. Automatically, she reached out, her fingertips grazing the rough stone wall. Valentina had won. She had beaten *her*. Valentina hadn't followed the rules they all knew, although no one ever spoke them aloud.

Oksana could never tell her father. Never.

All of her body went hot, then cold. She touched her left shoulder. Through the thin fabric of her school blouse, she could feel the smoothness of a bandage.

She made herself smile, even though her stomach felt sick. "I wasn't really trying," she said to Valentina. "Races are for little kids anyway."

Valentina's eyes narrowed. "You certainly looked as though you were trying. Or are you always out of breath?"

Oksana couldn't think of anything to say. Behind them, someone shouted, "Cheating Jew!"

The girls spun around. The forty other boys and girls in their class stood at the opposite end of the yard, watching them. Everyone looked the same, dressed in their school uniforms: the girls in brown dresses, white blouses, and black pinafores, and the boys in button-down white shirts, black trousers, and black blazers.

Their faces were solemn. Nothing in their expressions told Oksana who had shouted. And they wouldn't say a word to Valentina. Nobody would tattle on a classmate to a Jew.

"I didn't cheat," Valentina said loudly. Her cheeks were red.

"Everybody knows Jews are crooks." Oksana smoothed her hair ribbons, making sure to frown at Valentina. "My papa says your family ought to go back to Israel."

At her sides, Valentina's hands clenched into fists. "That shows what your father knows. We've never even been there."

"That's where your kind belongs!"

Valentina glared. "At least I'm not a baby who whines every time I lose."

"Fight, fight!" the other children chanted.

Oksana froze. This wasn't what she'd meant to happen. She mustn't fight at school. If she did, at best she'd be sent to the headmaster's office. At worst, it meant the headmaster would call her father's supervisor at the power station and Papa would receive a black mark in his work record—for something *she* had done.

"Why would I want to fight Valentina?" she said, inching away. "She'll only cheat."

But her words were drowned out by the other children's shouts. "Fight, fight!" They swarmed around her and Valentina, laughing and waving their arms.

"Stop!" A woman's voice cut through the commotion. It was their teacher, Svetlana Dmitrievna.

At once a hush fell over the schoolyard. The fifth graders looked at one another. Quickly, they formed a line, as they were supposed to do every morning before entering the school. Oksana found herself and Valentina standing at the end.

Keeping her gaze trained on the pavement, she listened to Svetlana Dmitrievna's high heels click closer. She was going to be in so much trouble. Even worse than the time she'd accidentally left her essay at home.

The shoes stopped in front of her. "What," said Svetlana Dmitrievna sternly, "is the meaning of this?"

"It's her fault," Oksana began just as Valentina said, "We got carried away."

"Quiet!" Svetlana Dmitrievna snapped. "Sniveling excuses are unacceptable. I'll deal with the two of you inside. The rest of you—march. Not a word or you lose morning recess."

Oksana could scarcely breathe. What would Svetlana Dmitrievna do to her? Was she going to telephone her father?

Maybe Svetlana Dmitrievna wouldn't be able to reach him or his supervisor. After all, the fire was still burning—wasn't it?

Overhead, smoke drifted like a screen, turning the sky into a patchwork of black-blue and red. The air tasted of metal and something else she couldn't identify, like scorched earth. Surely her father and his supervisor were too busy coping with the fire to receive a telephone call from her school. Tomorrow, Sunday, they didn't have school, so hopefully by Monday, Svetlana Dmitrievna would have forgotten about the almost fight and Papa would never learn about it.

The line inched up the steps into the school. In one of the big plateglass windows, Oksana glimpsed her reflection. The red tie knotted around her neck was the one bright spot. A pin, embossed with the face of Vladimir Lenin, the man who had helped their country become a Communist republic and was now long dead, was clipped to the front of her blouse.

They were proof that Oksana belonged and Valentina never would. Oksana had received them last year, when she turned ten and was accepted as a member of the Young Pioneers.

Valentina hadn't been let in. Jews weren't welcome. Everyone was encouraged to join, of course—all citizens were supposed to be equal, regardless of their background or religion. But, as Oksana's father said, Jews weren't Soviet citizens. They were intruders.

Now Oksana followed Valentina into the classroom. Together they stood against the back wall, waiting for their punishment. Oksana didn't care what it was, as long as it didn't involve her parents. She could handle whatever Svetlana Dmitrievna dished out.

Taking a deep breath, Oksana touched her Young Pioneer pin. Her father had been so proud when she had received it. He had even called her "my angel." She must make him proud again.

She glanced at Valentina, who was staring straight ahead, her face pale and set. Valentina knew the rules, or she ought to by now. Why couldn't she have just let Oksana win?

Oksana wouldn't tell her father about the race. But if Valentina told her own father, and if Comrade Kaplan mentioned it at work, then her father would know. And then she would never forgive Valentina.

Never.

131

Valentina

VALENTINA WATCHED SVETLANA Dmitrievna take a bag of rice from her desk and pour its contents on the floor. Then she dropped her and Oksana's workbooks onto the floor, along with two pencils.

So it was going to be the rice punishment. That wasn't too bad, as punishments went. Far better than the time her first-grade teacher had made her wear a pointed cap and instructed her classmates to point at her and shout, "Dunce!" At least now she wouldn't be made to feel stupid for being a lousy speller.

Without a word, Valentina and Oksana knelt in the rice. The granules dug into Valentina's knees through her tights. She bit her lip so she wouldn't make a sound. She must be quiet. Complaining or reacting would make it worse, for then Svetlana Dmitrievna would smack her hand with a ruler.

Valentina looked around the room, certain the other children would be making faces at her, silently making fun of her for getting in trouble.

But no one was looking at her or Oksana. Her classmates were all staring out the windows. Outside, the sky still flickered red. Far off in the distance, Valentina could see curls of blue smoke.

Papa, she thought.

She had to think logically about this. As an engineer would, like her father. In her mind, she wrote up a list. No contact from Papa. Red sky, blue smoke. Policemen everywhere.

Something terrible must have happened. And no one was telling her, or anyone else, what it was.

Suddenly, she was so frightened that she felt cold everywhere. She wrenched her gaze away from the window, back into the classroom.

Svetlana Dmitrievna rapped a ruler on her desk. "Attention, students! Who can tell me the names of the republics in our great Soviet Union?"

Nobody raised a hand. After a moment, a girl in the front row said timidly, "I beg your pardon, Svetlana Dmitrievna, but what happened at the nuclear power station?"

The teacher glanced at the window, then quickly away. "Obviously, there has been a mishap. A minor accident, one that I'm sure is already being taken care of. Because, children?"

"Because the Motherland protects us," they recited. Valentina, too. She had had to say the words so many times they were practically embroidered on her heart.

"That's correct," Svetlana Dmitrievna said. "Capitalist nations, like America, are full of greedy people who care only about themselves. Here in our great socialist nation, we are always safe. Our government protects each one of us. Now," she said briskly, pointing at the map on the wall, "who can tell me the names of our republics?"

A forest of arms, held at the proper ninety-degree angle,

shot up. Valentina and Oksana kept their hands at their sides. Everybody knew to stay silent during punishments.

Valentina's stomach churned. Why hadn't she let Oksana win the race, as she usually did? She should have. Something about the little smile on Oksana's face, though, when she had challenged her to run had made her want to win.

Svetlana Dmitrievna called on one of the boys, who stood up next to his desk. "The republics are Armenia, Azerbaijan, Belorussia, Estonia, Georgia, Kazakhstan, Kirghizia, Latvia, Lithuania, Moldavia, Russia, Tajikistan, Turkmenistan, Ukraine, and Uzbekistan."

"Correct," Svetlana Dmitrievna said. "And recited in alphabetical order—well done!"

Valentina leaned forward so she could write the date— April 26, 1986—in her workbook, which was lying on the floor in front of her. Today was a Saturday, so Svetlana Dmitrievna would collect their workbooks at the dismissal at noon and mark them tonight.

Valentina knew her workbook grade had better be a perfect five-plus this week to balance the black mark she was sure to receive for arguing with Oksana. She couldn't afford to do poorly. So few Jews were accepted into universities or good professions. Since she wanted to be a scientist, she needed to be better than good. Today's fight might have damaged her future chances.

She swallowed hard. There was nothing she could do to help herself now. Besides, it was hard to care when she was so worried about her father.

The grains of rice felt as sharp as needles. Shifting uncomfortably, she held her breath so she didn't let out a moan of pain.

She had to distract herself or it wouldn't be long before she was begging Svetlana Dmitrievna to let her get up.

She studied the map, where each of the republics was a different color. Russia, the largest, was red, and Ukraine, the second largest and where they lived, was white. The section of the map where she had been born, Siberia, was red, too, for it lay within Russia. When she had first come to Ukraine, she had missed Siberia so much. She had loved the way the steppe seemed to go on forever, and the forests of towering pine trees, and the realization that spring was coming because it was finally warm enough to carry metal coins in your pocket.

"Girls, that's enough." Svetlana Dmitrievna's voice interrupted Valentina's thoughts. "You may return to your seats."

Thank the stars! Valentina staggered to her desk. Her best friend, Larisa, gave her an encouraging smile as she passed. Valentina smiled back.

As soon as they were settled, Svetlana Dmitrievna asked, "Valentina, what's the birth date of our nation?"

She had to stand to answer. Prickles stabbed up and down her legs, forcing her to grip the edge of her desk so she didn't sway. Somebody giggled.

This time, Valentina paid no attention. She mustn't risk getting in trouble again.

"Valentina?" Svetlana Dmitrievna prompted. "The birth date of our nation?"

"Nineteen seventeen," Valentina said quickly. The year wasn't exactly correct, but everybody knew that was the answer the teachers wanted. Their country was centuries old. Only sixty-nine years ago, it had been ruled by a tsar. Then the Bolsheviks—now called the Communists—had revolted, and the country had plunged into civil war. Eventually, the Communists had emerged victorious, and their country had become a republic. Now it was called the USSR, the Union of Soviet Socialist Republics, and it had only one political group: the Communist Party.

"Very good," Svetlana Dmitrievna said. "Valentina, you may sit."

Valentina eased into her seat. She sneaked a hand under her desk to rub her knees. Grains of rice had stuck to her tights, and she brushed them off.

As the teacher droned on, Valentina gazed at the numerals *1917* on the chalkboard. Before then, her parents said, their countrymen had been allowed to follow different religions.

Not anymore. The government didn't approve of any religion, not Christianity, not Islam, not Judaism. Valentina's teachers said religion was a trick that drugged people's minds. The highest power was the Motherland—not faith.

Svetlana Dmitrievna wrote another answer on the board. Once her back was turned, Valentina felt a finger poke her in the back. Oksana.

She ignored her.

Oksana's wooden desk creaked as she leaned forward. "Did your father come home this morning?" Oksana whispered.

That got Valentina's attention. Oksana's father worked the night shift with Papa. Maybe Oksana knew what had happened at the power station.

Valentina shook her head no.

"Mine didn't, either," Oksana whispered. Wood creaked again as she settled back into her chair.

They didn't speak to each other again all morning. When the dismissal bell rang at noon, Valentina joined the throngs of children spilling into the schoolyard.

Smoke wafted across the red sky. The air still tasted of metal and earth. The back of Valentina's throat tickled. She wondered if her father was home yet. She needed to run back to their apartment as fast as she could, to see if he was there.

Larisa came up to her. "I felt so awful when Svetlana Dmitrievna caught you fighting! Are you all right?"

"I'm fine," Valentina said. "The rice punishment isn't too bad."

"You ought to know." Larisa giggled.

Ordinarily, Valentina would have made a face, for Larisa was right: Valentina had been ordered to kneel in rice several times before, when she was caught whispering in class. She had such a difficult time not talking because she had so many big ideas crowding her head all the time, waiting to be let out.

Now, though, she didn't care about getting in trouble. "I need to go home," she said to Larisa. "I have to see my father. He might be hurt."

"You heard Svetlana Dmitrievna," Larisa said. "There was only a little accident at the power station."

The words "How does she know that?" almost leapt out of Valentina's mouth. She swallowed them barely in time. She mustn't say bad things about the teacher, in case someone overheard and reported her.

"I have to go home," she said again.

"All right," Larisa said.

Together they weaved through the crowd. All around them, classmates were making plans for the afternoon. None of them seemed scared anymore; Svetlana Dmitrievna's reassurances must have done the trick. Some of the children said they would play in the schoolyard; others would go to the parks or fish on the banks of the river. Several boys were going to get their bicycles after lunch and ride over to the nuclear station to look at the fire. Oksana and her friends were going to the amusement park, where they would ride the Ferris wheel and drive the bumper cars.

"Do you want to meet in the park after lunch?" Larisa asked. "I'll borrow my sister's jump rope so we don't have to share yours."

"Maybe," Valentina said. All she wanted was to see her father.

She and Larisa reached the pavement. Military vehicles rumbled down the road toward them. Truck after truck after truck.

All of the drivers were wearing gas masks.

The trucks rolled closer. The gas masks made the soldiers look like massive bugs or creatures from a nightmare. Where were the soldiers going? To the power station?

Papa, Valentina thought.

"I've got to go," she said to Larisa.

Understanding flashed across Larisa's face. "Go," she said, and Valentina took to her heels, running as fast as she could, with only one word echoing in her head.

Papa.

(4)

Oksana

AS OKSANA WALKED home from school, she saw policemen everywhere. They slouched against walls, smoking, or stood with their hands in their pockets, watching everyone with wary eyes. The sight sent a chill down Oksana's spine. What were all these policemen doing here? It must have to do with the fire, but she couldn't imagine why: extra firemen ought to be here, putting out the flames, not police officers.

She half listened to her friends chattering about going to the amusement park after lunch. When they reached the block of apartment towers where they lived, she said goodbye and hurried to her building. Maybe her father was home and he could tell her and Mama what was wrong.

The back of her shoulder throbbed. Gritting her teeth, she slipped into the lobby. It was a box of a room, made of dirty plaster walls and chipped linoleum. She trudged across it, making for the stairwell. Along the back wall, a woman was talking on the communal telephone. "Oleg and I are going to Sochi on holiday . . ."

Her voice faded as Oksana climbed the stairs. It was

deserted now; all of the building's little kids must be in their apartments, eating lunch or napping, or at the nurseries provided by their mothers' employers.

Above her, she heard someone talking. "Something's happened at the power station," a girl said.

She recognized the voice. Valentina. Why did it have to be *her*? Oksana would have to walk past her in order to get to her floor.

Sighing, Oksana kept climbing. There was someone else talking now, a man. "Naturally something's wrong at the power station," he said. "It's the biggest fire this city has ever seen. Something to tell your grandchildren about, eh?"

Oksana rounded the curve in the stairwell. On the landing above stood Valentina and one of the men who lived on the second floor, Dyadya Sergei. He wore only trousers. He must have been sunbathing on the roof. Lots of the building's residents went up there to sunbathe or to tend to their garden. Oksana's mother kept several pots of herbs on the roof, and she had told Oksana at breakfast that she planned to pick rosemary and sage today.

"You were white as milk this morning," Valentina said to Dyadya Sergei.

"I've never tanned so quickly in my life," he said, sounding pleased. "There must be something in the air."

It was an expression Oksana had heard many times before. "Love is in the air tonight," her parents said when they saw a young couple out for a romantic evening stroll. Or, "Spring is in the air," they said when wild roses bloomed in the forests outside Pripyat. And, "Winter is in the air," they said when they could smell the sharpness of snow.

Today, though, the words made Oksana uneasy.

"Ah, Oksana," Dyadya Sergei said. "I didn't see you standing there. You're as quiet as a shadow."

Although she wanted to rush past him so she wouldn't have to look at Valentina, manners forced her to put on a smile and say, "Good afternoon, Dyadya Sergei."

"I have to see if my father is home," Valentina said without looking at Oksana. She hurried up the stairs.

"I saw your mother on the roof," Dyadya Sergei said to Oksana. "There was a crowd of us. You ought to go up there before the fire's put out. It's quite a sight! Above the station, you can't even see the sky. It's all smoke, blue everywhere."

That meant Papa was sure to be angry, because the fire was probably someone's fault. Or a machine's. Either way, he would be furious, for the fire would mean filling out loads of paperwork and accident reports. Papa might even be in trouble because the fire had started during his shift.

She started shaking deep inside. Dimly, she heard Dyadya Sergei saying something, but she couldn't pay attention anymore. "I have to go home," she said, and pushed open the swinging door at the landing. She mustn't be late for lunch. The soup would go cold, and Papa must be hungry.

Inside the apartment, her mother stood at the stove, stirring a pot. "Good, you're home," she said without looking up. "Set the table."

Oksana didn't move. "Where's Papa?"

Now her mother did look at her. "He isn't home yet." Her smile didn't touch her eyes. "We'll eat lunch without him."

"Mama, I saw military trucks. The soldiers wore gas masks. And there are policemen all over the place!"

Her mother pursed her lips. "I'm sure the authorities are merely taking precautions. Everything's fine," she added when Oksana didn't speak. "I telephoned the power station, and nobody answered. The workers must have their hands full. The best thing we can do is leave them alone."

Oksana nodded. She hung her satchel on a peg by the door and went into the kitchen area to wash her hands. She loved being home, when it was just her and her mother. Their apartment was far nicer than any of her relatives'. They had two whole rooms—the main living space and a small bedchamber for her parents. They even had their own bathroom, which they didn't have to share with the neighbors.

Old rugs covered the wooden floorboards, and framed pen-and-ink drawings dotted the walls. There was even a bookcase, where she had an entire shelf to herself, and a radio. Her parents had just spent their savings on a television set, too. And Papa had promised that once she brought home a school report full of fives they'd buy her a proper bed and she wouldn't have to sleep on the sofa anymore.

"Set the table," her mother said.

"Yes, Mama." Oksana grabbed a handful of silverware.

After they had sat down and begun eating, her mother asked, "How was school?"

Oksana thought of the footrace and shifted uncomfortably. She hoped Valentina wasn't downstairs in her apartment, tattling to her mother about beating Oksana today. "Fine," she muttered. She dragged her spoon across the bottom of her bowl, creating ripples along the surface of the borscht. It was her favorite kind of soup, because it was the same deep purple as a sky long after the sun had set, before black crept in.

"Valentina said her father didn't come home this morning, either."

Her mother rapped her knuckles with the back of her spoon. "Enough. I already told you not to worry. Did Svetlana Dmitrievna return your essay on Comrade Lenin?"

There had been a 3 scrawled across the front of her paper. Oksana felt her cheeks warm. "No," she lied.

There was a knock on the door.

"Eleonora, I must speak with you," called a woman's voice.

Eleonora was Oksana's mother. With a sigh, she got up and opened the door. Valentina and her mother, Galina Yurievna, stood in the corridor. Valentina was still dressed in her school uniform and clutched a burlap sack to her chest.

The Kaplans had never come to their apartment before. What could they possibly be doing here?

"May we come in?" Galina Yurievna asked.

Oksana's mother hesitated. "Of course," she said after a moment, and ushered them into the main room. "Please sit down," she added, but Galina Yurievna shook her head.

"I have news about the fire," she said. "A friend just telephoned me. She's a nurse at the hospital. She said there was an accident at the power station last night."

"Yes, we know about the fire—" Oksana's mother started to say, sounding impatient, but Galina Yurievna interrupted.

"It isn't only a fire. Reactor number four exploded."

Reactor number four was where Papa worked! Was he hurt?

"Something went wrong during the safety drill," Galina Yurievna went on. "There was an explosion. And now the whole building's caught fire."

Oksana's mother had gone white. "The men—"

"Are at the hospital," Galina Yurievna said.

Thank the stars! Oksana took a shaky breath. Her father would be fine. The doctors would fix him, and he'd come home and everything would be all right.

"We're leaving for the hospital now," Galina Yurievna said. Oksana noticed that her hand rubbed Valentina's shoulder absently, as if she didn't notice she was doing it. As if the movement were automatic.

Oksana glanced at her mother. But Mama didn't touch her. Instead, she tapped her lips with her finger, as she always did when she was thinking. "We'll go with you," she said. "Oksana, pack Papa's medicines."

Oksana knew what her mother meant. Every child in Pripyat knew about radiation poisoning. It was a sickness you could catch from working with nuclear power. Thankfully, it was easily cured. All you had to do was drink milk or mineral water and eat plenty of cucumbers, and you'd be well in a day or two.

She found two cucumbers and a glass bottle of milk in the refrigerator. Quickly, she wrapped the cucumbers in wax paper and slid them into her mother's string shopping bag. Then she realized what Valentina must be carrying in her burlap sack: her own father's medicines.

Together they all went down the stairs. The mothers walked ahead, talking in low voices. Hurrying a few paces behind, the girls were silent. Oksana sneaked a look at Valentina, whose face was pale and anxious. Valentina didn't look back.

Good, then they were ignoring each other. Oksana held the string bag tighter. The medicines would help Papa, and he would be so glad she'd brought them. He would kiss the top of her head. *You saved me*, he'd say, smiling at her. *You're a good girl.*

Not that he'd ever said those words to her before. He called her an angel when he was in a good mood, a brat when he wasn't. But never "good."

That was all right, though. She already knew she was bad. She didn't need anyone to call her good, because it would be a lie.

In the lobby, they found Dyadya Sergei slumped on the floor. A puddle of vomit was spreading across the linoleum tiles. "I don't know what's wrong with me," he whispered. "I'm so dizzy."

His face was now a faded brown. The whites of his eyes were bloodshot.

Oksana's mother placed a hand on his forehead. "You're burning up, Sergei. You need to go to the hospital."

While she used the communal telephone to call for an ambulance, Galina Yurievna knelt at Dyadya Sergei's side. "Help is on the way."

His eyes flickered open and closed. Oksana couldn't tell if he had heard. She remembered his earlier words: *something in the air.* She thought of the soldiers' gas masks and the strange, metallic taste in her own mouth, which she had felt while playing in the schoolyard.

"Galina Yurievna," she said, "is there something in the air that can hurt us?"

"Of course not," Valentina's mother said quickly. But from the way she didn't look at Oksana, Oksana knew she was lying.

(5)

Valentina

THE LADY ON the telephone told Oksana's mother that they couldn't spare an ambulance to pick up Dyadya Sergei, so the girls' mothers bundled him into the back seat of the car of their only neighbor who owned a vehicle. The neighbor volunteered to drive them all to the hospital, so they piled in.

From the back seat, sandwiched between Oksana and Dyadya Sergei, Valentina watched the long, straight streets of Pripyat roll past. How badly hurt was Papa? What was wrong with Dyadya Sergei? He looked so different. *Everything* looked different.

Smoke filled the sky. It cast shadows across the city. In the dimness, policemen patrolled and women walked hand in hand with their children, and men went into shops. A trio of soldiers wearing gas masks strode down the pavement. At a sidewalk restaurant, a crowd lifted their glasses in a toast, and a young woman in a white dress blushed. It was a wedding reception. People were celebrating, and Valentina's father was in the hospital. Nothing felt real.

At Pripyat Hospital, a nurse whisked Dyadya Sergei away.

The girls' mothers went to the reception desk to ask about their husbands.

Valentina hugged the bag of cucumbers to her chest. For a moment, she and Oksana stood without speaking until Valentina couldn't bear the silence anymore. There were too many questions in her head, crowding to get out. "What did you bring for your father?"

Oksana didn't look at her. "Why do you want to know? So you can steal it?"

Heat rushed into Valentina's cheeks. "I don't want your stupid medicine."

"Why not? My medicine isn't good enough for you?"

"Th-that's not what I meant," Valentina stammered. "I'm not a thief."

"My father says your kind is always trying to steal from us." Oksana started to say more, then closed her mouth. Their mothers were coming back.

"The nurses won't tell us anything," Oksana's mother said quietly. "Come along. We're sneaking upstairs to find your fathers."

They took an elevator to the top floor. When the doors opened, a wall of noise roared out at them.

The corridor was a jumble of confusion. Doctors and nurses ran to and fro, carrying charts and glass bottles and trays lined with syringes and needles. A doctor in a white lab coat talked to a man in a dark business suit. The man must be a Communist Party official—Valentina saw a pin, embossed with a hammer and sickle, in his lapel. In the middle of the corridor, a group of women talked loudly. Some of them were crying. One of them, who had a big, pregnant belly, sobbed, "Leo, my Leo!"

"I don't recognize those women." A hopeful note hung in Valentina's mother's voice. "Perhaps they're from one of the villages. Maybe there's been an accident, a farming accident, and that's why they're here—"

"No," Oksana's mother interrupted. She nodded at the pregnant woman. "I know her. Her husband's a fireman in Pripyat. All of these ladies are probably firemen's wives."

Valentina seized on her words. The firemen must have been hurt while fighting the blaze. Her papa was probably resting in one of these hospital rooms, eager to be discharged and home with them again.

Her mother grabbed the arm of a passing nurse. "We're looking for our husbands. They were on duty at reactor number four last night."

"They might be in the dormitory," the nurse said. "You can come with me. I'm going there now." She caught Valentina looking at the clear glass bottle in her hand and said, "Vodka. One of the best cures for radiation sickness." She beckoned for Valentina and the others to follow her through an open doorway.

Valentina took two steps into the room and froze.

The smell was horrific: vomit, blood, and excrement, and something else, something that smelled like hot metal.

Dozens of men lay on cots. Their pale faces glistened with perspiration. Some were sitting up and mumbling to themselves, while others lay motionless under thin white blankets. Where was Papa? She didn't see him anywhere.

A nurse rushed over to Oksana and Eleonora Ivanovna. She hugged Oksana's mother, murmuring something Valentina couldn't hear. They must be friends. Then the nurse led Oksana and her mother out of the dormitory. Valentina guessed Oksana's papa must be in another room.

She looked away to scan the rows of cots. Where was her father? He had to be here somewhere.

Then she saw him. He was in a cot by a window. He lay still. So still. The blanket covering his chest barely rose and fell. His eyes were closed.

Beside her, her mother gasped. *"Nicolai."*

Valentina unfroze with a jerk. She raced across the room to her father's bedside. "Papa!" she said, but he didn't wake up. She laid her hand on his shoulder. Through the fabric of his hospital shirt, the heat of his body pumped into her hand. He was so hot she thought he would burn her, but she didn't move away.

Her mother leaned over him, smoothing his hair away from his sweaty forehead. "Nicolai," she said shakily.

He looked different from the man who had kissed Valentina good night only hours ago. His face was as pale and thin as paper; she could see the veins in his temples. Sweat had darkened his hair, turning the strands from brown to black.

What was wrong with him? He didn't look as though he had been burned in the fire, and he couldn't be sick from radiation poisoning, for everyone knew that was easily cured. So what had happened to him?

His eyelids fluttered open. For an instant, they focused on Valentina. "Red stars in the sky," he muttered. "Black pebbles on the beach."

What did he mean? He wasn't making any sense. Had the explosion damaged his brain?

The strong odor of drink wafted from him. Valentina guessed it was from the vodka the nurses had been giving him, to ease the radiation sickness. He sounded as though he were drunk, not ill. Perhaps he wasn't badly hurt after all. Maybe he only needed to sleep away the alcohol.

"Papa," she said, bringing her mouth to his ear, "can you hear me? It's Valentina."

His eyes blurred. She saw his lips moving, but she didn't hear any words coming out. "Papa!" she cried. "Please answer me!"

An arm wrapped around her waist and held her tight from behind.

She twisted in the person's grip, craning her neck to see his face. She caught an impression of a man's cheek dotted with stubble.

Before she could say anything, the man hauled her out of the dormitory. Her mother rushed after them. "Let go of my daughter!"

The man paid no mind to her mother. In the corridor, he released his hold on Valentina. She moved back from him, staring. He wore a doctor's white coat, and his brown hair was sprinkled with gray. His eyes were angry.

"Who the devil let you into the dormitory?" he demanded.

"A nurse." Valentina's mother squeezed her hand, a warning to hold her tongue. "Why did you take my daughter?"

"I removed this girl," the doctor said, still sounding upset, "for her own good. The men are under quarantine. That means they're being held separately from other people," he added to

Valentina. "You mustn't see your father. Do you understand?"

She shook her head no.

He bent down to her level and spoke slowly. "When the reactor exploded and released radiation into the atmosphere, the plant workers absorbed that radiation. Their bodies have become dangerously radioactive. If you hug your father or eat something he has touched or spend too much time with him, you might absorb some of his radiation." The doctor's gaze remained steady on hers. "Your father's body could make you very sick or kill you. You must get away from here as quickly as possible."

Valentina didn't believe it. "Can't he drink milk and eat cucumbers and be cured?"

The doctor sighed. He looked tired. "I'm sorry, but no."

"But that's what we've been taught!" Valentina said. When the doctor didn't reply, she asked, "Then how are you going to make him better?"

Her mother squeezed her hand harder. "Hush, Valya." Her face looked pale. "You mustn't talk like that in public."

"But, Mama—"

"That's enough." Her mother turned to the doctor. "If this were true, you would be telling the other wives, too," she said quietly.

The doctor took off his spectacles and pinched the bridge of his nose. "I wish I could. I'm not permitted to because our officials are concerned about starting a panic. But when I saw your daughter, an innocent child, in danger . . . Go now, both of you."

Still Valentina's mother made no move to leave. "What do we do?" she asked him.

"Did your husband teach you what to do if there was a nuclear disaster?"

"Yes, but he said it would only happen once in ten million years."

"That's what the government ministers said, too," the doctor said. "It looks like this is that one time. You must return home at once and follow your husband's instructions."

What did he mean? And why wouldn't he say how he was going to heal Papa? There was always a solution—that's what Papa said; you just had to fail and keep trying until you discovered it.

Valentina opened her mouth to ask when a fireman's wife rushed over to them. "Doctor, I heard a rumor that our husbands are being flown to Moscow tonight. Is it true?"

The doctor looked pained. He raised his hands. "Ladies, ladies!"

At once the firemen's wives silenced. Valentina's mother placed a hand on her shoulder, showing she wanted to stay and listen to the doctor, too.

"Your husbands are being flown to a special hospital in Moscow," the doctor said. "They will receive the best possible care. The clothes they were wearing when they were at the power station have been burned. If you would like to help your husbands, then I suggest you return to your homes and gather spare clothing for them."

Some women burst into tears. Others gasped, while a few said, "Yes, we'll pack their things," as though they were pleased to have something to do. Relief washed over Valentina. The doctors in Moscow must have special medicine or medical machines that would heal her father and the others.

"Come." Her mother walked toward the elevator. "We must go home and collect Papa's belongings. The hospital in Moscow might be cold. He'll want his warmest sweater."

When they got outside, they found the trolleys weren't running, so they had to hurry on foot to their apartment. In the distance, blue-black smoke churned above the broken reactor. In spots, the streets were white with foam; it looked like thick, soapy water. Valentina wondered where the foam had come from. Was it part of the radiation? She knew she couldn't ask out here in the street.

Policemen stood on every corner. Children rode bicycles, skipped rope, and played marbles or dolls on front stoops. Some laughed and slipped in the foam. Valentina's friend Larisa was dancing in it with a group of girls. She caught sight of Valentina and waved. "Isn't it splendid? Papa says they'll evacuate us and we'll camp in the forest!"

Valentina waved back at Larisa. "My papa's going to a hospital in Moscow, and they'll make him better."

"Hurrah!" Larisa shouted.

"Come," Valentina's mother said, and they kept hurrying through the white foam that ran in rivulets down the road.

At home, they threw some of Valentina's father's possessions into a suitcase: two wool sweaters, a pair of trousers, underpants and socks, and a couple of his favorite books so he wouldn't get bored.

Then it was back outside, where red light fell softly everywhere and the foam glistened white and the smell of smoke and metal weighted the air. The stink was so strong that Valentina's eyes stung. The back of her throat tickled, no matter how many times she coughed. She'd look at her father's textbooks tonight. Maybe she could learn more about radiation. And she and her mother ought to eat lots of cucumbers, despite what the doctor in the corridor had said.

By the time they reached the hospital, the sun was sinking below the horizon. A crowd had gathered in front of the building. Against the lighted windows of the hospital, the people looked like a black mass writhing up the steps. Several soldiers had formed a line at the doors. People screamed at them, demanding to be let in.

Her mother clutched Valentina's shoulder. "My God, what now?" she murmured to herself. She pushed her way through the crowd, clamping one hand on Valentina's wrist. Valentina had to jog to keep up.

As they reached the steps, the same doctor from before came out the door. The soldiers fell back to let him through, then took up their positions again, barring the way inside. The doctor raised his hands for silence.

Slowly, the crowd quieted. From the lights shining through the hospital windows, Valentina could see most of the people gathered at the door were women. Tears shone in their eyes.

"Thank you for bringing your husbands' belongings," the doctor said loudly. "Unfortunately, the airplane for Moscow has already departed. Your cooperation is appreciated."

A huge gasp rose from the crowd. All Valentina could think was: *Papa*.

The doctor scuttled into the hospital. The door hadn't even closed behind him when the women started shouting.

"How dare they take my Andrei without me!"

"They tricked us! They sent us to get our husbands' clothes so we wouldn't make a scene when they took our men away!"

"Monsters! Give me my husband! Let me see what has been done to him!"

There were so many wails of grief and rage that the air seemed to echo with them. Valentina's mother stood still with her hand over her mouth. She hadn't said a word.

Valentina moved closer to her. "Why is everyone so upset? Because we didn't get to say goodbye?"

Her mother's hand fell to her side. "Yes. And they're afraid the doctors are trying to hide the truth from us."

"What do you mean?" Valentina asked. "The doctor already told us they're going to a special hospital in Moscow. They'll be healed there."

"Yes," her mother said again, wrapping Valentina in an embrace. "They'll be fine. We all will be."

But her voice shook, which was how Valentina knew she should be frightened.

16

Rifka

"**HIDE IT AWAY**, Rifka," her mother said.

Rifka Friedman looked at the flute in her hand. It was the most wonderful gift she had ever received: smooth and silver and made of three pieces that fitted together perfectly. Mama and Papa had gotten it for her twelfth birthday in March. For years, she'd had to make do with borrowing her neighbor Reuben's, and he'd insisted she do his mathematics homework in exchange for thirty minutes every day with his flute. Then at last, she'd had her own.

Every single night since her birthday, she'd played. The music took her outside of her mind, away from bombs and bread lines. When she played, all she felt were the notes. Someday she wanted to be a professional flutist in an orchestra, and maybe even compose her own music. Her flute was the only thing that always made her happy, no matter how much she missed her father, who was away fighting in the war, or how badly her empty stomach ached.

And now she had to give it up.

"Please, Mama," she said. "Let me keep it. I'll be careful with it, I promise!"

Her mother's eyes filled with tears. "I'm sorry, my love," she said in a choked voice. "But we must hide all of our treasures so the Germans won't find them."

The Germans. How Rifka had grown to hate them! When war had broken out two years ago, Germany had been allies with her country. Then, this past June, the Germans had invaded the Soviet Union. Rifka's teacher had explained why to her and her classmates: Germany, and its Nazi leader Adolf Hitler, wanted to take over the world.

"Maybe the German soldiers won't come," Rifka said to her mother.

Sighing, her mother took the Shabbat candlesticks off their special space on a shelf. They were silver and covered in intricate carvings. The two candles symbolized the warmth and light of Shabbat, the Jewish holy day. Mama lit them every Friday night. But she did it with the curtains drawn, and Rifka's family whispered the prayers instead of saying them aloud. The government disapproved of religion.

"The Germans are coming, Rifka," her mother said. "You know they'll be here soon."

Rifka did know: the German army had been racing across the Russian countryside, crushing anything in its path. The soldiers drove their tanks across wheat fields, destroying the crops. They stole from people's homes. They burned villages. And all summer they had come closer and closer to Kiev. Soon—no one knew when—they would encircle her city.

Rifka looked around the room, which served as their parlor and kitchen. It appeared as it always did: the big wooden table dressed in Mama's best lace tablecloth, the old stove in the corner, the sink where her brothers' cloth diapers hung over the lip, drying, and the best place of all, the shelf where they kept the Shabbat candlesticks and a stack of books.

Someday soon it would be overrun with German soldiers. They could take whatever they wanted. They could burn the apartment building to the ground. They could leave the Friedmans without a home, without food, without any possessions at all. And that was if Rifka and her family were lucky. She had heard the rumors in the streets: the German soldiers also shot children and women and old folk.

She shuddered. What would happen to her and Mama and her two little brothers when the Germans reached Kiev?

"Hurry," her mother said. "Your brothers should be waking from their nap any moment, and I'll need your help making supper."

Biting her lip so she wouldn't cry, Rifka slid the flute's pieces apart. Then she laid them in a wooden box. Gently, she pulled up the loose floorboard. Unlike the others, it wasn't nailed down. She had seen her mother remove the nails last night, her face red from the effort, her pregnant belly getting in the way. She had offered to help, but her mother had said no, children shouldn't have to do grown-ups' work.

Silently, Rifka placed the box beneath the floorboard. She took the candlesticks her mother handed her and put them beside the box. Then she eased the floorboard into place.

"Here." Her mother gave her four nails. "You'll have to do it. I—I need to rest."

Rifka's head snapped up. Her mother sank onto a chair. She rubbed her stomach, her face contorted in pain.

"Are you hurt?" Rifka asked.

"It's the baby," her mother gasped. "I think it's coming."

"Now?" Rifka cried. Her mother had told her the baby probably wouldn't be born for another two weeks.

"Babies arrive on their own schedule." Her mother heaved herself out of the chair. "Help me to the bed. Then fetch the midwife."

Rifka guided her mother into her parents' bedroom. Only her mother slept here now, for her father had been drafted into the Soviet army soon after the war began. Last winter, he had come home on leave—and thanks to that visit, now there would be another Friedman. Another mouth to feed. Another body to clothe. Another child to care for, when they already hadn't enough food or clothes for themselves. Rifka didn't know how they would manage. Her mother said with love, they could always find a way, but Rifka wasn't so sure. Love didn't bake bread or sew clothes.

Once her mother was settled on the bed, Rifka glanced into the other bedroom, which she shared with her little brothers, Isaac and Saul. She twitched aside the curtain she had hung between their beds to give herself privacy, and saw the boys were still asleep. Good.

She hurried into the kitchen, put the kettle on to boil, and found a stack of clean towels and sheets in a cupboard. Then she rushed out of her apartment, down the winding stairs, and into Dorohozhytska Street.

A few months ago, the street had been busy, full of babush-kas and mothers walking into shops or standing about their apartment building's front steps, gossiping and laughing. Children used to play in the street, throwing jacks or playing tag. Horse-drawn carts, filled high with wares for market days, would clip-clop past.

The whole neighborhood was Jewish, although as far as Rifka could tell, she and her neighbors didn't seem much different from the Ukrainians who lived elsewhere in Kiev. She went to a nearby school, where all of her classmates were Jewish, and she rarely ventured into other parts of the city, so she didn't know anyone who didn't share her religion. But the Ukrainians she saw in the streets looked like her and her neighbors: the women and girls in dresses, the men in suits or tradesmen clothes, and the boys in short pants, much mended, with patches to hold together pieces of threadbare fabric. The Ukrainians had fair hair, of course, but other than that, Rifka didn't see any differences.

Now the street was quiet. Most of the men were gone, conscripted into the army. So many of the children and wives they had left behind had fled to escape from the coming Germans. Those who remained holed up in their apartments, fearing that at any moment the German soldiers would appear.

The ones who had left were smart, Rifka's teacher had said. They knew how much the Germans hated Jews. Rifka and her classmates hadn't asked the teacher why the Germans hated them—so many Ukrainians hated them, too, after all. Nor had Rifka asked her mother why they hadn't left Kiev. Mama's pregnant belly was answer enough.

Rifka hurried along Dorohozhytska. The midwife lived down the street, near the Viis'kove cemetery. Rifka could get there and back home in minutes. Mama and the boys wouldn't be alone for long.

But she couldn't help pausing to look at the sky. It stretched above the cramped apartment buildings, a canvas of even blue. It looked so peaceful. No warplanes. No bombs. No smoke.

When would that change? And how would they survive once the Germans came?

The questions made Rifka's heart race. She mustn't think of the future. Somehow, they would be all right. Mama had said they would be fine because they were a family, and families took care of one another no matter what.

But the whole time she ran to the midwife's apartment, she thought of that perfect sky and how different it would look soon.

(7)

Oksana

OKSANA SAT ON the parlor sofa. She should have made up her bed for the night long ago—it was nearly ten, past her bedtime—but her mother hadn't told her to.

In fact, her mother hadn't said much of anything since the nurse at the hospital had taken her into an office and shut the door, leaving Oksana alone in the corridor. When her mother had finally come out, her eyes were red, but she hadn't told Oksana what had happened. She'd only said they had to go home, straightaway, without talking to another soul.

When they'd reached their apartment, her mother had locked the door. Then she had gone into the bedroom, closing the door behind her. Alone, Oksana had sat on the sofa, not knowing what to do.

She tried to read, but the words jumped around the page. She got one of her old school notebooks that she kept hidden in the trunk, under a pile of blankets. Her father didn't know about the notebooks. No one did. At the end of every school year, she held on to the notebooks that weren't filled. Those clean pages were precious.

She fetched a pencil from her satchel and curled up on the sofa to draw. The picture had been building in her mind all day, until her fingers ached. She *had* to let it out.

Quickly, she began to sketch. The line of Papa's jaw. Short, light hair. Pride in his eyes.

She had never forgotten how he'd looked when she had placed first in her school's spelling contest last year. He'd laughed and kissed her on both cheeks. "Such a clever girl," he had praised, and she hadn't been able to speak around the lump in her throat. The moment had been perfect. She had wanted to preserve it forever, like an insect in amber.

Her pencil felt clumsy in her fingers. She couldn't capture the delight in Papa's eyes. It was impossible. How could she show an emotion without color, or paints, or lessons? And her parents would never pay for her to learn how to draw. She'd asked them once, when she was younger.

"A daughter of mine, prancing about with a paintbrush?" Her father had smacked her, so hard she lost her breath. "Too fancy to take after me, is that it?"

"No, Papa," she had said quickly.

"You'll learn a useful profession," he had told her. "Become an engineer, like I am. You're good at it."

She was good at it. She always earned fours and fives in science and mathematics.

And she hated the subjects.

She ran her fingers lightly over the drawing. It wasn't too bad. She'd drawn the proper lines of Papa's face; it actually looked like him.

The eyes, though, were flat. Papa might have been feeling anything.

Oksana crumpled up the paper and threw it in the bin in the kitchen. It didn't matter. She'd never be an artist.

The bedroom door opened. Hastily, Oksana moved away from the bin. She didn't want her mother to ask what she'd been doing and find the drawing. Her mother came in, her hair disheveled, her eyes still red. She had changed into her dressing gown.

In her slippers, she shuffled into the kitchen. She took a glass out of the cupboard and turned on the faucet. The sound of the water splashing into the sink was loud.

She turned off the faucet. "What if the water's contaminated? Without Ilya, I don't know what to do!"

Ilya was Oksana's father. She opened her mouth to ask her mother how badly he was hurt, then thought better of it. Mama said polite children didn't ask questions.

"There's no one to help me anymore," her mother said in a choked voice. For a moment, she stared at the glass in her hand. Then she heaved it at the wall. It shattered. Then she slid to the floor, where she sat sobbing, her head in her hands.

"Please don't cry, Mama," Oksana said.

Her mother pulled her down onto the floor beside her. She flung her arms around Oksana, holding her close. Oksana could scarcely believe what was happening: her mother was *hugging* her. She hugged her mother back, as tightly as she could.

"We're alone now," her mother cried. "Ilya is gone."

Oksana froze. Surely she couldn't mean—

"That's what the nurse at the hospital told me," her mother went on. "When she came to fetch us in the dormitory and took me into the doctor's office and you waited in the corridor. Last night during the safety drill, your father was in the southern main pumps circulating room. The force of the explosion brought debris tumbling down on him. They think he must be buried under the wreckage of the steam separator drums. They can't get him out. They can't see him. But they have no doubt. He's gone."

For a long moment, Oksana sat still. The inside of her mind felt blank, like a fresh sheet of paper without any drawings on it. She couldn't think or move. All she could do was sit, still and small in her mother's arms.

Dead. Her father was dead. Buried inside the ruined reactor. It must be so dark and hot there, with the fire still burning and the smoke filling the air. She could see it in her mind's eye, the flames flickering red and reflecting off the piles of melted metal and broken stone. And Papa beneath it all, trapped.

Memories tumbled inside her head, so fast she couldn't grab hold of any of them. Sitting on the banks of Pripyat River with her father, his surprised laugh when she caught a fish. Curling up next to him on the sofa while he watched ice hockey on television. Eating in the kitchen, his quick grin when he tasted the cake she had baked on her own. His smile felt like sunlight. And now he was gone. Forever.

"Oh, Papa," she cried out.

Her mother let go of her. She brought her knees to her chest, hugging herself. "I can't live without him," she said.

"Mama," Oksana managed to say through her tears. She reached for her mother, but Mama stood up.

"I'm all alone," she said. She began to cry again, softly this time.

Oksana watched as her mother shuffled back into the bedroom, closing the door behind her. She didn't say a word. She didn't ask questions. She would be good and quiet, and surely Mama would return.

Slowly, she swept up the broken glass. Then she sat down, folding her hands neatly in her lap. She waited for Mama to come back to her, but her mother never did.

(81)

Valentina

FIVE STORIES ABOVE Oksana's apartment, Valentina watched her mother get four tablets out of the medicine chest in the bathroom. She and her mother had barely spoken since they'd walked home from the hospital a second time. They'd slipped and nearly fallen in the foam, and her mother had made her leave her dirty shoes out in the corridor, even though somebody could steal them. Mama said it didn't matter, and whoever was foolish enough to want contaminated shoes was welcome to them.

She and Mama had each taken a shower, and then Mama had thrown the clothes they had been wearing into the corridor as well. Now she dropped two tablets each into a glass of water. They quickly dissolved.

Valentina knew what they were: Papa had bought iodine tablets when he'd begun working at the power station. Just in case, he'd said, and they'd laughed because they'd thought nuclear accidents didn't happen.

Her throat tightened with tears.

"Drink this." Her mother pushed the glass into her hand. "You need to take two tablets every hour."

Valentina drank. Every time she swallowed, it hurt. "How are the doctors in Moscow going to heal Papa?"

Her mother's breath hitched. "I don't know. But the government wouldn't fly him and the other men to Moscow if they didn't think they could fix them."

Valentina nodded. She knew her mother was right; the government would do what was best for her father.

Her mother guided Valentina out of the bathroom into the kitchen. "We must stay low to the ground. Papa taught me that radiation rises. We have to stay here, out of the poisoned air outside, until the government comes to rescue us."

She pulled Valentina under the kitchen table. Valentina's mind worked furiously. The soldiers had worn gas masks. And Dyadya Sergei hadn't gone near the power station; he had been on the roof, sunbathing, until he fell ill. When the reactor had exploded, the doctor at the hospital had said it released radiation into the atmosphere—which meant they were breathing it in all the time.

The walls and closed windows would only help a little. She and her mother had already been outside off and on all day, breathing in the radiation. And staying low wouldn't do anything; after all, they lived on the ninth floor of their apartment building! What about Papa? He'd been inside the reactor for who knew how long until he'd been sent to the hospital. How much poisoned air had he breathed?

She grabbed her mother's arm. "Are we going to get sick, too? Is Papa going to be okay?"

Her mother held her close. "I don't know. We must have hope."

They lay together on the cold floor. The walls were so thin, Valentina could hear her own shallow, rapid breathing and the neighbor's clock, ticking in the darkness.

Valentina's mother woke her every hour to give her more iodine. Eventually, the mineral water ran out, and she had to use the faucet. At midnight, Valentina noticed her mother had stopped dosing herself.

"We only have ten tablets," her mother said. "You need them more than I do."

"But Mama—"

"Don't argue. I couldn't bear it if I took medicine that you ought to have."

Valentina curled herself into a ball. Her mother lay next to her, holding her hand. As Valentina drifted to sleep, she sensed her mother's fingers interlaced with hers.

When she woke, she was alone.

■　■　■

Valentina crawled out from under the table. In the dark, she could barely see the outlines of the kitchen cupboards and the sofa. The room was silent and still. Only furniture. No Mama.

Valentina started to get up, then remembered what her mother had said about radiation rising. She must stay low.

On all fours, she crawled to the bathroom. The door had been left ajar. The curtains hadn't been drawn, and the window glinted red and black. The reactor was still burning.

Where had Mama gone?

Valentina crawled across the main room to her parents' bedchamber. "Mama, are you there?"

Nothing.

Should she leave the apartment and look for her mother? Mama had said they must stay indoors, safe from the contaminated air.

A door creaked open. Valentina sat up. "Mama?"

Heels clicked on the floorboards. "Valya?" Mama's voice.

Valentina crawled into the main room. "I'm here."

"Thank goodness!" Mama dropped to her knees and pulled Valentina into an embrace.

"Where were you?" Valentina demanded.

Her mother hugged her tighter. "I couldn't stop thinking about what the doctor at the hospital told us. About how dangerous the explosion is. It isn't fair that other people don't know, too. So I went to warn our neighbors about the radiation. None of them believed me."

"Why not?"

Sighing, her mother released her. "Because we've been taught to have faith in our government. To believe our Motherland will protect us. But it's easier for people like us to doubt."

"People like us?"

"Jews," her mother said softly. "For many years, we've known we aren't welcome in our own country."

Valentina shifted uncomfortably. "But . . . if the government really didn't want us here, wouldn't they send us away?"

Her mother gave her a searching look. "There are many ways to hurt people besides exiling them. Why do you think I don't teach at your school?"

Valentina had never thought about it before. Her mother gave private piano lessons; that was the way it had always been. She shrugged.

"I have a teaching degree in music," her mother said. "I'm as qualified as any of your teachers. But I've never been able to get a proper teaching post because of our religion."

"That's silly," Valentina objected. "We don't even go to a synagogue."

That was true. Nobody did, as far as Valentina knew. None of her schoolmates went to church, either. It simply wasn't done. Valentina didn't know anything about Judaism: the beliefs, the holidays, or the customs. Nothing.

"Our traditions were stamped out after the Communist revolution," her mother said. "Your father and I grew up without religion, too. But we are branded as Jews all the same."

"Then why has Papa been able to get such good jobs?" Valentina asked.

"Jews have an easier time in the technical professions. Your father, though, still had to put in his time in Siberia before he was assigned here."

They had all put in their time in Siberia. The place where she had been born and where she had lived with her parents until she was five was a secret city. It didn't have a proper name, and it didn't appear on any maps. Most people didn't even know it existed. The city housed a nuclear power station and other facilities where mysterious experiments were carried out. Her father had taken a post there because once he worked for five years in Siberia, the government was required to assign him to a better location.

And the better location had turned out to be Pripyat. Her

parents had danced around their old apartment when they had gotten the news.

Valentina's mother stroked her hair. "Communism is supposed to be paradise. And there aren't mistakes in paradise. The explosion at the power station was a mistake. Our government can't admit to the world that we're responsible for an accident. They're trying to cover it up."

She framed Valentina's face with her hands. "Everyone in Pripyat is now part of the mistake. We've all received radiation. I won't lie to you and pretend I know what this means for our futures. I don't know if we'll become ill, too. I do know, though, that whatever happens, I'll do anything to keep you safe."

Valentina leaned against her mother. "I'll keep you safe, too, Mama."

"Thank you, my love. But that isn't your responsibility," her mother said.

From outside came the *whump-whump-whump* of helicopter blades. Valentina sat upright. Who was there? What were they doing?

She started to go to the window, but her mother held her back. "Stay away from the windows," her mother said. "Radiation might travel through glass."

So Valentina had to lie on the floor, watching firelight flicker red in the gaps where the curtains hadn't been drawn fully together and wondering what was happening outside—and what would happen next.

19

Oksana

AFTER BREAKFAST, OKSANA'S mother turned on the radio to listen to the news. The announcers talked about the upcoming May Day celebrations. May Day was a holiday across the Soviet Union. Schools and businesses closed, and in every city people took to the streets to watch a military parade.

Ordinarily, Oksana loved May Day: the red banners hanging from the buildings and the red ribbons pinned to people's shirts, and the trumpets and drums. Best of all, her father loved May Day, too. When she was little, she used to sit on his shoulders to see the tanks and soldiers. For the last few years, they had held hands and he had given her a rose to throw to the troops as they marched past.

Now he was gone. No more hand to hold. No more happy May Days.

She had to swallow hard so she didn't burst into tears.

Her mother twisted the radio dial, silencing the announcers' voices. "They didn't say a word about the accident." She looked so tired. "We won't even get Papa's body back. For burial. If they can remove it from the nuclear reactor, they'll have to bury him someplace remote, in a lead coffin."

Something twisted inside Oksana's chest. She didn't want to think about her father lying in a box, beneath layers of grass and soil. She wanted him back, sitting here at this table with them, skimming through the newspaper as he always did on Sundays, which were his day off.

Without another word, Oksana's mother got up and went into the bedroom. Oksana heard the door shut with a click.

Oksana looked at the dirty breakfast dishes. She knew what was expected of her.

After she had washed the dishes, she went to the sofa, where she folded her bedding and put it away in the trunk. Her hand hesitated over her notebook. No. There was nothing she wanted to draw.

The hours passed with agonizing slowness. Oksana didn't have school. There was nowhere for her to go, nothing for her to do except push her tears down inside, so deep they couldn't possibly come out. The whole time, her shoulder ached. Sometimes it throbbed so badly she had to grit her teeth. She wondered what her mother was doing in the bedroom. Sleeping? Crying silently? And why wouldn't she call out to Oksana and ask her to come inside?

Oksana choked back her sobs. She had never felt so alone.

Suddenly, from outside, a woman's voice boomed: "Attention, comrades!"

Oksana listened.

"An unsatisfactory radioactive situation has occurred at the Chernobyl power station," the woman continued. Her voice sounded tinny. The loudspeakers in the streets must be broadcasting her message.

"As a temporary precaution," the woman continued, "it has been decided to evacuate people from Pripyat today."

The bedroom door burst open. Oksana's mother rushed out. In silence, she and Oksana listened to the rest of the announcement. A helicopter was already dropping leaflets with instructions over the city. All residents must be outside promptly in two hours. Anyone who remained in their apartment would be removed by soldiers.

Oksana's mother stood in the middle of the room, her hands fluttering at her sides. She was still wearing her dressing gown. From the pillow creases lining her cheeks, Oksana guessed she had been asleep. "If only Ilya could tell me what to do!"

A wave of impatience washed over Oksana. "Mama, we have to pack and get out of here. So we don't get sick," she added when he mother didn't say anything.

"It doesn't matter." Her mother sank onto the sofa. "Nothing does, without Ilya."

Don't I matter? Oksana wanted to ask. Tears burned in her eyes, and she had to look away from her mother.

A knock sounded on the door. Her mother didn't move, so Oksana went to answer it.

Their next-door neighbor stood in the doorway. "I heard about your father," she said, giving a blue sheet of paper to Oksana. "You have my sympathies, my dear child. I suppose your mother is dithering about as usual?"

Oksana didn't know what that meant. "My mother's on the sofa."

The neighbor snorted. "Naturally. Eleonora," she called over Oksana's shoulder, "you'd better hurry or the soldiers will make you evacuate. By force," she added, then walked back to her apartment.

Oksana read the blue sheet. It was their evacuation orders. They were allowed to bring one suitcase each and three days' worth of clothes. Nothing more. The authorities must expect them to be able to come back soon. Perhaps the fire had already been put out.

Oksana went to the window. At the horizon, smoke rose above the power station. When the veils of black smoke parted, she could see the roof of the ruined reactor. It was mostly gone. Flames leapt out of the opening. Men were up there, throwing things into the gaping hole. She wondered if they were flinging bags of sand or dirt to smother the fire. Above the building, a helicopter flew back and forth in slow arcs.

The fire still blazed, and even inside the apartment a metallic taste clung to her mouth.

"Start packing." Her mother sounded exhausted. "And bring your schoolbooks, too. Wherever we go, I expect you'll continue with your schooling."

She vanished into the bedroom. Oksana thought of her clothes, neatly hung in her parents' wardrobe, and of her schoolbooks, tucked into her satchel. If she brought a few pieces of clothing and her work, she should still have some space left in her suitcase.

Quickly, before her mother could come back into the room, she opened the trunk and pulled out her drawing notebook. She'd put it at the bottom of her suitcase, under her clothes. Her mother wouldn't see it.

■ ■ ■

Two hours later, they left their apartment. As Oksana waited in the corridor, her mother locked the door and pocketed the key.

"Mama," Oksana said, "you don't need to take the key with you. Nobody's going to come here and steal our things while we're gone."

"Maybe not." Her mother put a hand to her temple, as if she had a headache. She had finally gotten dressed in the smart dress and heels she wore to her job as a lawyer's secretary. "I wonder where they'll send us. Someplace nice, I'm sure, to make up for the accident. Perhaps it will be one of those fancy resort spas on the Black Sea."

Oksana hoped so. She had never seen the ocean.

She and her mother joined the orderly procession of people streaming down the stairwell. Everyone was quiet. Small children held on to their mothers' hands, and older kids clutched their bags. Nobody laughed or made a joke.

Outside the air still tasted of metal, and this time, of soot, too. On the far side of the city, smoke hovered above the buildings, throwing long shadows across their brick-and-white-plaster faces. In Oksana's street, buses lined the curbs. The drone of helicopters muffled people's voices.

Doctors in white coats and soldiers in uniforms shouted instructions: "Form lines! Quickly!"

Oksana and her mother got into place behind a dark-haired woman. The woman turned to smile at them, and Oksana saw it was her teacher, Svetlana Dmitrievna. She held a cat in her arms.

"Hello, Oksana," Svetlana Dmitrievna said. "This will

be an adventure, won't it? An unexpected holiday of sorts. You can't tell me you're sorry to miss the mathematics exam tomorrow!"

How could her teacher make jokes when Papa was dead? She didn't know, Oksana realized. It felt as though the world should have ended, because Papa was gone, but for everyone else, it hadn't. Only for her and Mama.

"No," she heard herself say. "I don't mind missing the exam."

Up ahead, doctors held small gadgets next to the first person in each line. The gadgets emitted a series of clicks. The doctors nodded and directed the first people toward the waiting buses.

"They're checking us with dosimeters," Svetlana Dmitrievna explained in a whisper. "They want to see how much radiation we've received."

"Won't we all have gotten the same amount?" Oksana asked.

"People who live close to the power station probably received more than we did."

Buses stood in a long line on the opposite side of the street. Between them, Oksana could see patches of the plaza. The grass was the pale green of early spring, but the leaves and needles of the poplars and evergreens looked strange. Oksana squinted.

The leaves and needles were dark red.

Had radiation done that? Was it killing the trees from within? What was it doing to her and everyone else in Pripyat?

She pictured the inside of her body, as she had seen it

drawn in her schoolbooks: the white spokes of her rib cage, the pulsing mass of her heart, the twin kidney beans of her lungs. Were they changing within her? Was she going to die, like Papa?

Suddenly, she could scarcely breathe.

It was Svetlana Dmitrievna's turn. A stern-faced soldier pointed at her cat. "You'll have to leave your pet."

"Why?" Svetlana Dmitrievna asked. "She's a good cat."

"I'm sure she is," the soldier said, "but animals aren't permitted to evacuate."

"My Zhulka won't be a nuisance, I promise," Svetlana Dmitrievna said. "I'll keep her on my lap for the entire drive to—well, to wherever you're taking us."

A doctor came over. "What's the delay?"

"This citizen doesn't want to leave her pet behind," the soldier explained.

The doctor turned to Svetlana Dmitrievna. "The amount of radiation these small animals' bodies have received has overwhelmed them. We have to contain all animals here. If they're permitted to roam freely, they could wander huge distances and sicken people across the Soviet Union."

Oksana's heart beat faster. Were all of them like the animals of Pripyat—so overburdened with radiation that they had to be contained so they didn't make others sick? Was that the real reason they were being evacuated—not so they could be saved but so they would be held somewhere and wouldn't infect anyone else?

She crept to the doctor. "Are we contagious like the cats?"

"Get back in line!" he barked.

"I beg your pardon." Oksana's mother grabbed her. "I'll make sure she doesn't trouble you again."

"See that she doesn't," the doctor snapped. "I have thirty thousand people to evacuate, and I don't have time for one impertinent child's questions."

"Yes, I know. I apologize." Gripping Oksana's shoulder, her mother guided her into place behind Svetlana Dmitrievna. "What were you thinking?" she whispered. "You know better!"

"I know. I'm sorry." Oksana fell silent as the doctor beckoned Svetlana Dmitrievna forward. Slowly, her teacher set the animal down. It purred, rubbing between her ankles. She held her arms out for the doctor to wave the dosimeter over her body like a wand. When she was cleared, she went into the bus the doctor indicated, leaving the cat meowing on the pavement.

It was Oksana's turn. Obediently, she lifted her arms and waited as the doctor scanned her with the dosimeter. The device clicked loudly when it was held at her shoulder. That meant she had the poison inside her, she thought, trying to fight a rising wave of panic. It was part of her, and she couldn't wash it away like dirt or bandage it like a cut. There was nothing she could do.

"Your level is acceptable," the doctor said.

Oksana let out a shaky breath. She stepped aside so the doctor could wave the dosimeter over her mother's arms. *Click-click-CLICK!* He frowned and made a notation on his clipboard.

"Your radiation level is too high." He pointed to the far end of the street, where a line of ambulances waited. "You must go to a hospital immediately."

"I can't be sick," Oksana's mother gasped. "I don't work at the power station!"

"Your radiation level is too high," the doctor repeated, sounding annoyed. "Get in an ambulance."

Oksana's mother took a hesitant step forward, then stopped to look at Oksana. "Do what they tell you, and be a good girl."

"Mama!" Oksana shouted as her mother began walking away. "No! Please don't leave me!"

(10)

Valentina

FROM ACROSS THE street, Valentina heard a girl scream.

Valentina whirled around. Through the long lines of sad-faced people, she glimpsed Oksana, her arm gripped by a soldier.

"Oh no," Valentina's mother said. "Valyushka, stay here. I'll find out what's happening to the Savchenkos."

Valentina wanted to ask her mother why she cared. Her mother knew that Oksana teased her mercilessly at school. She had always told Valentina to ignore anyone who made fun of her.

And now she was hurrying away to help that bully Oksana and her mother. Valentina would never understand grown-ups.

Should she go, too? Her mother had said to stay, but she didn't want to let Mama out of her sight for an instant. No matter what, they mustn't be separated. What if they were accidentally placed on different buses?

That made her decision. She rushed after her mother. Together they reached the Savchenkos and the soldier.

Oksana's mother had gone pale. "I can't imagine what's wrong with me, Khusha," she said to her daughter, using Oksana's nickname. "Maybe I shouldn't have spent so much time gardening on the roof yesterday."

"Mama, don't leave me!" Oksana cried.

Her mother stepped away. "You'll be fine. Your teacher can look after you."

"Where are you taking her?" Valentina's mother asked the soldier.

"Minsk," he replied, stone-faced. "She received a high dose of radiation and must go to the hospital immediately. Go," he added to Oksana's mother, who nodded and looked at Oksana. Her face was pale and strained.

"Be a good girl, Khusha," she said.

Oksana's eyes filled with tears. "Please don't leave me!"

Her mother didn't respond. The soldier marched her to one of the waiting ambulances at the end of the street. Oksana ran after them. The ambulance stood with its back doors open. Oksana's mother climbed inside, then turned to look at Oksana. She said something Valentina couldn't hear.

"Poor girl," Valentina's mother murmured. She squeezed Valentina's shoulder. Despite her dislike of Oksana, Valentina couldn't help feeling a twinge of sympathy.

Oksana tried to climb into the ambulance, too. The soldier pulled her out. She kicked and scratched at him, but he didn't let go.

A man in a white uniform slammed the ambulance doors shut. The vehicle sped away from the curb.

Oksana slipped out from under the soldier's arms and

raced after the ambulance. It picked up speed, turning the corner and vanishing from view.

"Stop her, Valyushka," Valentina's mother said. "She mustn't make trouble."

Valentina handed her suitcase to her mother, then raced after Oksana. Around the corner, down a deserted street where white powder dusted the pavement, perhaps the remnants of yesterday's foam. Oksana was far ahead, but Valentina quickly closed the distance between them. She yelled at Oksana: "Stop!"

"I can't—my mother—" Oksana panted.

"You'll never catch up," Valentina said, running alongside Oksana.

The ambulance had already become a black speck beneath the red sky. Oksana halted, bracing her hands on her knees and gasping for breath.

"We have to go back," Valentina said. "Now, Oksana," she added when Oksana didn't move.

"No." Oksana's eyes were wet. "I can't go anywhere without my mother."

"Well, she's gone somewhere without you," Valentina said impatiently, and tugged on Oksana's arm. "We have to get out of here. We don't want the buses to leave without us."

Oksana jerked her arm out of Valentina's grasp. Then she started walking in the direction from which they had come. Valentina walked alongside her, her shoes kicking up white powder with each step. Wasn't that just like Oksana: no thank-you, no conversation, only a stony silence.

When they reached their street, Valentina's mother rushed

over to them. Behind her, more people inched forward in lines, holding out their arms for the dosimeters. Everyone, even small children, spoke in hushed voices. Dogs, turned loose by their owners, ran through the street, barking.

"We must get on the bus to Kiev before it leaves," Valentina's mother said. "Oksana, you come with us. I have a friend in Kiev who we can stay with."

Valentina winced. Didn't Mama know how mean Oksana was? Besides, the Savchenkos must have dozens of friends in Pripyat who would let Oksana travel with them. This was a terrible idea.

Oksana looked panicked. "I'll get on Svetlana Dmitrievna's bus. She'll help me."

Valentina's mother bent down, locking eyes with Oksana. "I've been listening to the soldiers. Your teacher's bus is headed to temporary lodgings about twenty kilometers away. That's not very far from the power station. Radioactive fallout will easily be carried there on the wind. And once the people on your teacher's bus are quarantined, there's no telling when they'll be let out. If they'll be let out at all."

Valentina sucked in a breath. What her mother had just said was dangerous—she sounded as though she were criticizing the government. Oksana could report her for this.

But Oksana didn't run to the soldiers to tattle. Her chin quivered, as if she were trying to hold her tears inside. "Mama wouldn't want me to go with you."

"Your mama wants you to be safe," Valentina's mother said firmly. "You must forget your fears about our people. All that matters now is surviving."

Oksana bit her lip. "Okay," she said at last. "I'll go with you."

Valentina didn't understand. How could her mother be so kind to Oksana when she knew how nasty Oksana had been to her? Why did they have to be responsible for Oksana when she had plenty of friends who would take care of her instead?

"Come along, Valyushka," Valentina's mother said.

Reluctantly, Valentina followed her mother and Oksana to the buses at the end of the street. They went into the third bus, which smelled of wool and gasoline and metal.

People already crammed the seats. It was noisy: babies cried, children laughed and chattered, and grown-ups spoke to one another in low, worried tones.

Valentina found two empty seats in the back. She thought her mother would sit with her, but she sat down next to one of their neighbors and gestured for Oksana to sit with Valentina.

Frowning, Oksana settled down beside Valentina. She scooted over to the edge of the seat, tucking her skirt about her legs, taking care that not even their clothes touched.

Valentina's cheeks went hot. Fine, then. If Oksana was going to go on being mean, then Valentina would ignore her.

Without speaking, they waited. Valentina held her suitcase handle tightly. She didn't dare let go of it for an instant. Not now that it contained the only things she had in the world.

When she and her mother had heard the evacuation announcement, she had gone to the trunk that contained her bedding. Beneath the blankets was where she kept her treasures. Drawings of her inventions, a robot figurine she had molded out of clay, a dried rose preserved in a sleeve of wax paper, and—the most important—her father's old watch. It was broken, and she was determined to fix it.

There was also an envelope full of loose snapshots, mostly

of her and her parents. She had glanced at them, pausing at a photograph of an old couple. They were smiling, squinting in the sunlight. The man had gray hair and wore a dark suit; the woman was in a blue dress and had pulled her hair into a bun at the nape of her neck.

Gently, Valentina had traced their faces with one finger. Her grandparents, Mama's mother and father. Valentina had never met them. She didn't know why. Her grandfather had died years ago of a heart attack, but her grandmother was still alive and lived hundreds of kilometers away, in Leningrad. Once Valentina had asked her mother why they didn't talk to or visit her grandmother. Mama had looked sad and said, "Your grandmother does dangerous things." She wouldn't tell Valentina more.

The bus started with a lurch. Its tires kicked up clouds of dust. Once the dust fell to the earth again, Valentina saw that Svetlana Dmitrievna's cat stood in the street, watching them go. Its head was cocked to one side, as if it wanted to ask why it was being left behind.

A lump rose in Valentina's throat. Poor cat. Poor everyone.

To her left, the tall apartment buildings of Pripyat speared toward the sky. Beyond them, the Communist hammer-and-sickle signs atop the buildings in the main square were lost behind a curtain of smoke. Then the bus rounded a curve in the road, and everything was hidden from Valentina's view except for the red gleam of a sky lit by fire and a seemingly endless parade of army tanks driving past her into Pripyat.

(11)

Rifka

THE BABY WAS a boy. Of course. Rifka sighed as she went into the kitchen. Maybe someday she'd have a sister.

If the war ever ended and her father could come home.

Night had turned the window black. Hours had passed since she had fetched the midwife and her newest brother had begun his journey into the world. Little wonder she felt so tired.

But there was work still to be done. She mustn't rest yet.

She went down the apartment stairs to check on her other brothers, who were being minded by a neighbor. Saul and Isaac were asleep, bless them, and the neighbor said it was silly to disturb them and she'd send them back in the morning.

Then it was upstairs again to boil more water. When the kettle whistled, she dumped the water into a wooden tub. She washed the sweat- and bloodstained sheets from her parents' bed, stirring them with a ladle. Once they were clean, she hauled them downstairs to hang them from the laundry lines strung between the chestnut trees behind her building. She had to work by feel—she hadn't thought to bring a candle—but her hands had performed the task so many times they knew what to do.

Up the rickety wooden stairs once more. From her mother's bedroom, she heard the cries of her new brother. He must be hungry. Well, her mother could take care of *that*. Rifka could finally go to bed. She didn't hear the midwife, which meant the lady must have left, for she had a voice like a trumpet.

Rifka started for her room, but her mother called, "Rifka, come here!"

She thought longingly of her bed. The straw mattress lay beneath the large window overlooking Dorohozhytska Street. Countless times she had sat there, doing schoolwork, playing her flute, or daydreaming about Lev, the bookseller's son. He had brown eyes like a doe's, Rifka had decided, although she'd never seen a deer up close and had no idea what their eyes looked like. She'd read the description in a book, though, and had liked it. Unfortunately, Lev was also three years older than she was. When he saw her in the street, he smiled and tugged her braids. As though she were a child.

"Rifka!" her mother called again.

"Coming, Mama." Rifka trudged through the kitchen to her mother's bedroom.

The midwife had left a candle burning on the table. By its weak light, Rifka could see her mother lying in bed, cradling her baby brother. He was asleep.

Her mother smiled at her. "Would you like to hold him?"

No. She was sick of little brothers. Calming them after temper tantrums. Cleaning their hands sticky with crumbs and milk. Playing games she had outgrown long ago. Wiping bottoms and washing clothes.

But her mother smiled at her so hopefully . . .

"Yes," she said, holding out her arms.

Her mother handed her the baby. He was the ugliest baby she had ever seen: red-faced and wrinkled and skinny. The few dark hairs on his head went every which way. Hs mouth was screwed up in a pout, as though he didn't like his dream. He smelled of sour milk.

He was perfect.

Something pulled at her heart. She couldn't stop herself from grinning down at him. "What's his name?"

"Avrum," her mother said.

Avrum had been one of her mother's brothers. Rifka had never met any of them, for they had been dragged away before she was born, forced to serve in the tsar's army and never seen again. Her mother didn't know what had happened to them.

Rifka smiled at her new brother. "He looks like an Avrum." It was a lie, for right now he looked like every new baby— although he was the most ugly-beautiful baby ever. But she said it because she knew her mother would like hearing the words.

Her mother smiled again and reached for Avrum. Rifka gave him back.

"Sit down," her mother said. "I have to talk to you."

Swallowing a yawn, Rifka brought the room's only chair to her mother's bedside. "Yes, Mama?"

"The midwife brought news." Her mother looked steadily at Rifka. "There are rumors the Germans will be here in a month. Maybe less. There isn't much time left to escape."

Rifka shifted uncomfortably. Why were they talking about

this again? They already knew they had to stay; the boys were too small to travel, and her mother couldn't in her condition. "I know."

"The boys and I can't go." Her mother glanced down at Avrum, who was sleeping peacefully. Then she looked up at Rifka. "But you can."

Go. Alone. Without her mother and brothers.

"No," she said. "Mama, I won't leave you—"

"You must." Mama readjusted her hold on Avrum so she could reach for Rifka's hand. "It's the only way. I won't let you stay here because of me and the boys. You have a chance to get out. You have to take it."

"But . . . where will I go?" Panic seized hold of her. "I can't!"

Her mother squeezed her hand. "You can, and you will. You're a strong girl, and clever, and tough, much tougher than you realize. Yes, you are," she insisted when Rifka opened her mouth to argue. "Could a weak girl have gotten good marks in school and helped me care for the boys and missed her father, all without complaint? No. And now I'm going to ask you to be even tougher."

The room blurred. Rifka tried to blink away the tears, but they fell faster and thicker than she could manage. "Please, Mama, don't make me go! Don't you love me anymore?"

Her mother laid Avrum on the bed beside her. Then she framed Rifka's face with her hands. "My Rifka," she said, "it is because I love you that I am sending you away."

(12)

PRIPYAT, UKRAINE, SOVIET UNION

APRIL 1986

Oksana

OKSANA LOOKED OUT the bus window, watching the landscape change. The bus rumbled over a bridge lined with street lamps, then onto a long road that cut through the forest where she and her classmates went on hikes. They liked to pluck cherries and plums or pause in pockets of green-black shadows to gaze at the towering pines.

Now the trees were colored reddish brown. Dead sparrows and blackbirds littered the sides of the road. A breeze kicked up, ruffling the mulberry bushes, and Oksana saw their leaves were dotted with black spots. How far had the radiation already spread? And how much longer until they escaped from it?

Valentina leaned close to her, whispering, "Do you see the birds? The radiation must have already killed them because their bodies are so small."

Radiation. Papa buried under the debris in the pumps room.

Oksana pressed a hand to her roiling stomach. She felt as though she might get sick right here.

"Did you bring your schoolbooks?" Valentina asked. "My mother made me. I don't think we'll have to bother about school, though, at least not for a long time."

Oksana couldn't bear another word. "I don't care about school. My father is *dead*."

Valentina blinked. Her mouth opened and closed. She didn't say anything.

Oksana turned away from her. She stared at the floor, which was covered with a jumble of suitcases and bags. She was suddenly aware of how noisy the bus had become: babies cried, children chattered, and grown-ups spoke to one another, their voices muffled. Somewhere, a mother warned her sons that if they didn't stop poking each other this instant their father would whip them once they reached Kiev. A man scolded his wife for packing pickling jars instead of clothes, and she insisted he'd be glad of the jars once they got to her mother's house and were able to fill them up.

"I'm sorry about your papa," Valentina said quietly.

Oksana shrugged. She didn't want to talk to Valentina. She didn't want to talk to anyone except her mother.

Through the dirty bus window, she could see they had emerged from the forest into farmlands. Late-afternoon sunlight slanted across fields where men in pairs swung scythes. Peasant huts stood in clearings where women in head kerchiefs weeded vegetable gardens. A small wooden building whose steeple was topped with a cross stood alongside the dirt road. The sight was so unexpected, Oksana had to look twice to be certain her eyes hadn't played a trick on her.

It was a church. Her mother had said there were still

churches in some villages, where the old ways hadn't been erased.

She wished she could visit one, so she could sit in the silence and pray for her father. Perhaps, though, this way was better. If she went inside a church, she would have no idea how to talk to God.

It was dark when they reached Kiev. The driver let them off at a bus station. For several minutes, the passengers milled about the street, unsure where to go or what to do. Oksana stood off to the side. Her heart thumped painfully in her chest.

What should she do? Who would help her? She couldn't stay with the Kaplans. Her father hated them.

Only Papa wasn't here anymore.

She looked around desperately. The people from the bus milled about. Some she recognized from the shops or the streets of Pripyat, others she didn't know at all. There was no one here who would take her with them. What was going to happen to her?

"Isn't there a shelter or someplace the government will send us?" a woman asked.

"It looks as though we've been forgotten about," a man replied.

Tall buildings rose like sentinels in the night. Street lamps cast white pools of light onto the pavement, which was littered with strips of colored paper. Ticker tape, Oksana saw when she bent down to look. Had there been a parade? But it wasn't May Day yet.

"There was a bicycle race," Valentina's mother said. Beside her, Valentina peered into the darkness, her face white and anxious. "I heard about it on the radio this morning," she went on. "There must have been thousands of people outside all day long. Breathing in the air . . ."

She broke off, sending a wary look at the people standing around the bus. "I wasn't criticizing the government," she said quickly. "They have their reasons for keeping things quiet. Come along, girls. We'll take the subway to my friend's apartment."

Oksana didn't understand. "*Me*, Galina Yurievna?"

Valentina's mother patted Oksana's hand. "Of course, my dear. You must come with me and Valentina. We'll get a good night's sleep at my friend's and sort everything out in the morning."

Stay with Jews. In the same room. Eat the same foods. Sleep under the same ceiling.

She glanced at the dark sky. Her father's soul might be up there somewhere, looking down. Watching.

"I can't." She stepped away from Valentina's mother. "I have some money. I'll take a train to my mama's hospital."

That was what she should have done in the first place. She'd been so stupid!

"Minsk is more than five hundred kilometers from here," Valentina's mother said. "A child your age shouldn't make such a long journey on her own. In the morning, I'll call the hospitals in Minsk. We'll find out your mother's condition and figure out what to do next. I'm sure she'll recover soon."

Oksana thought of the men in the dormitory at Pripyat Hospital. They had lain so still, their faces pale, their eyes feverish. Water, milk, cucumbers, and vodka hadn't seemed to make any difference for them. What could the doctors in

Minsk do to cure her mother? Or would they not be able to help her?

Oksana's heart sank. She was going to be alone in the world.

"Look," Valentina whispered, catching Oksana's attention.

Nearby, a couple of workmen in coveralls were hosing off the sides of the bus. Water cascaded down its sides, dripping onto the pavement. In the light from the street lamps, the puddles gleamed yellow and green, as though someone had poured paint in them. Oksana had never seen water shine with that strange luminescence before.

A woman gasped. "Radiation!"

"But we're so far away from Pripyat!" a man objected.

"It's from the dust covering the bus," another woman said, shuddering. "And the radiation will most likely get worse. There's no telling how far the wind will carry radioactive clouds."

People let out cries of dismay. Oksana could barely breathe. They had carried the radiation with them! And it was floating on the air, poisoning everything it touched . . .

"We must get inside," Valentina's mother said. She beckoned to Oksana and Valentina.

All Oksana wanted was to get away. Alongside Valentina and her mother, she hurried into the darkness flooding the street, searching for the neon lights of a Metro station sign.

■ ■ ■

They took the subway to Dimeezskaya Street, where Valentina's mother's friend from university, Masha Petrovna, lived. Valentina's mother had met her when they were studying to become teachers.

The avenue was dark and deserted. Oksana heard nothing except their footsteps echoing on the pavement.

Masha Petrovna's apartment was in a five-story brick building. There were several nameplates next to the front door buzzer. Valentina's mother found one marked M. KRAVCHENKO and rang the bell.

For several minutes, they waited. Although the April night was warm, Oksana couldn't stop shivering. When could they get inside, away from the contaminated air?

At last the door opened to reveal a woman in a gray dressing gown. Blinking blearily at them, she pushed her disheveled blond hair out of her face.

"Galina!" she exclaimed. "What are you doing here?"

Before Valentina's mother could reply, Masha Petrovna ushered them inside. The lobby smelled of turnips and cigarette smoke. Oksana put a hand over her nose.

"What's happened?" Masha Petrovna asked Valentina's mother in a low voice.

"There's been an accident," she whispered back. "We can't discuss it here."

Masha Petrovna's face tightened. "Upstairs," she said, leading them to a concrete stairwell. "Quickly, before anyone sees you."

In the apartment, the women gave Valentina and Oksana buttered bread and milk and sent them to eat in the corner. There wasn't anywhere else to go—the apartment was one room. The girls sat on the floor next to the refrigerator while the women perched on the sofa and spoke in hushed tones.

Food had never tasted so good. Oksana gobbled her bread in seconds. She couldn't remember the last time she had eaten. Maybe breakfast, which seemed like days ago.

The back of Oksana's shoulder ached so badly she had to bite the inside of her mouth so she wouldn't whimper. She mustn't think of the reason it hurt. If she did, she feared she would cry and never stop.

Valentina's mother told Masha Petrovna everything that had happened since yesterday morning.

Masha Petrovna didn't interrupt once. She listened with her head bowed, lamplight shining on her fair hair. When Valentina's mother finished, she said, "My dear friend," and opened up her arms. With a sob, Valentina's mother went into them.

Tears tightened Oksana's throat. She had no one to hug her. No one to rescue her.

No one but two Jews.

(13)

Valentina

THE LONGER HER mother and Masha Petrovna talked, the more impatient Valentina became. They ought to be doing something, not sitting about, crying. Back home, Mama had made her throw out her clothes and take a shower to get rid of the contamination. Shouldn't they do the same now? They needed to find solutions, not talk and fret.

And still her mother and Masha Petrovna spoke in low, worried voices. Oksana sat quietly, fiddling with a loose thread on her sleeve. Valentina knew it was rude to interrupt an adult—she'd been smacked by teachers often enough for talking out of turn—but finally she couldn't bear it anymore. She stood up.

Her mother and friend stopped speaking and looked at her.

"We need to wash," Valentina said. She hesitated. She didn't know if it was safe to talk about contamination in front of Masha Petrovna. "We're dirty from traveling," she added, looking at her mother.

"Yes, we're terribly dirty." Her mother scrambled up. "Masha, I'm afraid our clothes are in a bad state. Do you have anything we can borrow?"

Masha Petrovna stood, too. "I'll find something. You girls go ahead and wash up first. I'll get towels and soap."

"But we won't have anything to wear." Oksana clutched the front of her dress. "I don't want anyone to see me without clothes."

Valentina rolled her eyes. Leave it to Oksana to complain. What a princess.

"Better to be naked than to wear dirty dresses," Valentina's mother said quietly.

Oksana nodded, swallowing hard.

Then Masha Petrovna fetched soap and towels, and led the girls out of the apartment to the communal shower at the end of the corridor. Oksana trailed far behind, which made Valentina grit her teeth in annoyance.

"Quickly," Masha Petrovna chided, nudging Oksana into the washroom. Valentina followed and found herself in a green-tiled room with a single shower nozzle.

"There aren't any curtains." Oksana sounded panicked.

"For pity's sake, this is hardly a time to be modest!" Masha Petrovna shoved the towels and a cake of soap at the girls. "Leave your clothes in the corridor. Your mother will take care of them."

"Thank you," Valentina said. She expected Oksana to say thank you, too, but Oksana didn't say anything.

Masha Petrovna didn't seem to notice. She slipped from the washroom, the door clicking shut behind her.

Valentina avoided looking at Oksana. Hastily, she unbuttoned her blouse. The longer she waited, the more time the radiation had to sink into her skin. But washing ought to fix that.

When she had finished undressing, she took Oksana's clothes from her outstretched hands, balled them up with hers, and chucked them into the corridor.

By the time she turned back, Oksana already stood under the spray, washing her hair.

Thick, ugly black bruises scored Oksana's bottom. A red patch of skin marred the back of her left shoulder. A few black dots lay scattered across the damaged flesh.

Valentina gasped. "The radiation hurt you!"

"No." Oksana didn't turn around. She kept washing her hair with rapid strokes. "It's from before the accident. I'm fine."

Water beat down on her head, sending bubbles sliding down the strands of her hair onto her too-thin back. Valentina could see the knobs of her spine through her skin. What had happened to her?

Her eyes trained on the floor, Oksana stepped out of the shower nozzle's range and handed the soap to Valentina.

Ducking under the shower spray, Valentina began scrubbing her skin hard. Should she tell her mother about Oksana's back? If Oksana was ill from radiation and trying to hide it, she could be endangering them. She ought to be under quarantine at a hospital. If she had been hurt in another way, though, it wasn't any of Valentina's business. Or was it?

"I'm fine," Oksana said, as if sensing Valentina's thoughts.

Draped in a towel, she walked to the door. "Don't tell anyone about my back."

There was a pleading note in her voice Valentina hadn't heard before.

"All right," Valentina heard herself say. "I won't."

Together, wrapped in towels, they left the washroom. Oksana clutched the front of hers, holding it up to her neck and hiding the red patch of skin on her shoulder.

Valentina's mother, also wrapped in a towel, was waiting in the corridor. "I burned all of our clothes in the incinerator in the cellar," she whispered. "The clothes in our suitcases, too. I'm afraid they all might be contaminated. The suitcases themselves and our other things ought to be safe. We don't wear them next to our skin, after all. Anyway, I told Masha Petrovna that our clothes were too badly stained to wear again. She'll find new outfits for us tomorrow. In the meantime, we'll have to wear her things."

Inside Masha Petrovna's apartment, the girls found faded flowered dresses laid out for them on the sofa. No underthings—they'd have to do without slips or underpants or tights until she could lay her hands on some, Masha Petrovna told them. For now, the best thing they could do was go to sleep. They'd need their rest to deal with whatever came next.

Straightaway Valentina changed into the dress, while Oksana waited until Masha Petrovna had gone into the kitchen area. Quick as lightning, she whipped off the towel and wriggled into the dress.

"I'm afraid your accommodations will be a bit rough tonight," Masha Petrovna said, coming to the sofa with her arms full of blankets. "You'll have to sleep on the floor."

"Can we go home soon?" Oksana asked.

Masha Petrovna handed them each a blanket. "Probably. That's enough questions for now, girls. Go to sleep."

Valentina's mother came into the apartment, padding across the room on bare feet. She kissed Valentina, wished Oksana a good night, and then joined Masha Petrovna on the sofa. The women curled up on opposite corners.

After rolling the blanket around herself like a cocoon, Valentina lay on the floor. The curtains had been left open a crack. The nocturnal lights of the city showed through the gap, tracing gold and red lines on the ceiling. She closed her eyes.

But sleep wouldn't come. She remembered the dead birds on the side of the road and the forest of red-leafed trees. Could she and her parents ever go back home?

There had to be ways to clean up Pripyat. Her father had never discussed them with her—after all, nuclear power was supposed to be clean and safe. That was what the government had said.

They had been wrong, Valentina thought. And now Papa was sick. Anger rose within her, so red and hot that she had to sit up to catch her breath.

Papa would be all right. The doctors in Moscow would fix him. And somehow the government would decontaminate Pripyat.

To calm herself down, she decided to figure out decontamination methods. First, workers would have to put out the fire. Then they would have to wash everything off. What couldn't be cleaned—like the dead birds—would have to be buried.

She felt her heart rate slowing. Yes, there were always ways to fix problems. Even scary ones.

She touched the glass face of her father's watch. There was no reassuring tick as the minute hand made its revolution; the mechanism had broken long ago.

She kissed the watch. Somehow she would fix it. And she would wear it every day until she could give it back to her father in person.

(14)

Oksana

IN THE MORNING, Masha Petrovna was gone when Oksana woke up. Valentina and her mother were still asleep. The sun was shining; Oksana could see it had turned the yellow curtains white.

She used the toilet down the hall, then wandered back into the apartment. She was hungry, but she didn't dare help herself.

A note lay on the kitchen table. *Rang a hospital in Minsk*, it read. Masha Petrovna must have left it. Oksana kept reading. *Receptionist couldn't tell me much over the telephone, only that Oksana's mother is a patient. I'll be home in the evening, and we'll decide our next step.*

Next step? Oksana wondered. What did that mean? Her mother would be well soon, and they would go home to Pripyat. The government had only let them take three days' worth of clothing—even though Valentina's mother had burned them—but the government must know the radiation wasn't so bad, if they expected Pripyat residents to be gone for merely a few days. It was only Papa's bad luck that walls had fallen in on him.

Her heart began to race. She mustn't think of her father. In a few days, she and Mama would be in Pripyat, and Mama would work at her job at the lawyer's office and she would go to school, and everything could be almost normal.

And she wouldn't have to wonder all the time if she was going to make Papa angry. If he would take something she said the wrong way. If he would hit her.

She let out a deep breath, feeling her muscles relax. With Papa gone, no one would hit her ever again. She wouldn't have to be scared.

No! She was a horrible girl for thinking such a thing! Weak and stupid and mean. Papa had been wonderful. Handsome and clever and quiet and laughing—

She couldn't breathe. Waves were crashing over her, again and again, and dragging her to the bottom of the ocean. She was drowning.

"Steady," said Valentina's mother from behind her.

Oksana felt strong arms holding her in place. "It's all right," Valentina's mother said in her ear. "Breathe, Oksana. You're safe."

Oksana concentrated on her breath whooshing in and out of her lungs. She imagined the photograph of lungs in her science textbook, pink, shaped like twin beans. If she painted them, she would use pink and white paints, swirling them together to make a softer shade. She would make the brush marks small and precise, to mirror the orderly way the lungs worked.

Her heart slowed down. She sucked in a deep breath. She was a bad person. But she could make herself better. And she would never be so disloyal to Papa again.

"Good," Valentina's mother praised. She eased Oksana into a chair, then sat down next to her. She smiled. "Are you all right now?"

Oksana ducked her head. Her cheeks were on fire. "Yes," she murmured.

Valentina sat up, the blankets puddling in her lap. She rubbed her bleary eyes. "What's wrong with Oksana?"

"I'm bad," Oksana said before she could stop herself. Her cheeks went even hotter.

"Not bad." Valentina's mother looked startled. "Sad and worried, Oksana, but not bad. What on earth put that idea in your head?"

Oksana didn't know what to say. She shrugged.

Valentina's mother gave her a long look. "Let's have breakfast," she said at last. "Food ought to help."

But it didn't. The buckwheat cereal felt like a stone in Oksana's stomach. She forced each bite down while she, Valentina, and Valentina's mother listened to the radio.

The announcers didn't say a word about the explosion.

"If the news had been made public," Valentina's mother said, "it would have been the top story. The government is still keeping it a secret. They won't help us, not if they're trying to hide evidence of the accident. We're on our own, girls."

"What about Oksana?" Valentina asked.

"She must have relatives who can take her in." Valentina's mother stood up. "Now that we're far from Pripyat, we have time to figure out what to do next." She carried her bowl over to the sink. "Oksana, whom may I telephone for you? An aunt? A grandmother?"

"My relatives live in a village near Pripyat." Oksana hadn't even thought of them. All she had wanted was her mother and to get away.

She thought of her mother's family. Her mother's parents were dead, and she hadn't seen her mother's sisters and their families in years because her father didn't like them. "They're always trying to turn you against me," he would say to her mother when she mentioned visiting them. As for her father's parents . . . She couldn't stay with them.

"Oksana?" Valentina's mother's voice broke into her thoughts. "Shall we telephone your relatives for you?"

Oksana pressed a hand to her stomach. She felt as though she was going to be sick. "Yes," she managed to say. "Thank you."

"Valyushka, please clean up the kitchen," Valentina's mother said. "Oksana, come along."

Together, they went downstairs to use the communal telephone in the front hall. With each step, Oksana felt sicker. What was she going to do? She couldn't stay with her father's parents; she *couldn't*.

When her grandfather was sober, he was kind. He hadn't even been annoyed when he'd been teaching her how to milk a cow and she'd dropped the pail.

But when Dedulya drank, he became someone else. Someone cruel and angry. On those nights, she hid under the bedcovers, her hands over her ears. She could still hear him, though, cursing and breaking dishes. In the morning, her grandmother would bustle around the table, pouring coffee and smiling. Sometimes she had a black eye, sometimes a bruised cheek, once a missing tooth. Dedulya would pick wildflowers for her, and she would laugh and kiss him. And Oksana's parents had always acted as though everything her grandparents did was perfectly ordinary.

"Here we are," Valentina's mother said brightly as they reached the telephone. She picked up the receiver and held it out to Oksana.

Oksana didn't take it. She couldn't. She couldn't telephone Dedulya. He was too scary.

Valentina's mother gave her a strange look. "Don't you want to talk to your family?"

Oksana couldn't tell her the truth. She forced herself to smile, even though her lips felt like rubber. "Yes, of course I do."

She took the telephone receiver. After the operator had connected her to the village where her grandparents lived, she listened to the phone ring and ring. Finally, she hung up.

"Is there another telephone number to try?" Valentina's mother asked.

Oksana shook her head no. "There's only one telephone in the village, in the post office." She glanced at the clock on the wall. It was half past nine. "The postmistress should be there by now, and she always answers the telephone and takes messages."

"You said they live close to Pripyat?" Valentina's mother asked.

"Yes. About twenty kilometers."

"Perhaps they were evacuated, too. And if they were, then we have no way of knowing where they are now."

Relief flooded Oksana. Thank the stars! She wouldn't have

to stay with any of them, at least for the time being.

"I'll go to Minsk," she said. "I can take the train."

"Certainly not." Valentina's mother looked thoughtful. "In Minsk, there wouldn't be a soul to take care of you, for your mother can't, not until she's released from the hospital." She squeezed Oksana's hand. "We'll figure something out."

Oksana nodded and tried to smile. She followed Valentina's mother upstairs. What should she do next? She couldn't stay with these Jews, not forever, and there was no one else she could go to.

She was alone.

■ ■ ■

The windows were deep blue, darkening to black, when Masha Petrovna returned. "Clothes," she said triumphantly, dropping a parcel wrapped in brown paper on the table. "One of the other teachers gave me these castoffs of her daughter's."

"How kind!" Valentina's mother undid the brown paper, pulling forth skirts, blouses, and light wool coats. The buttons on one blouse were cracked, and the skirts' hems had been let out and resewn again in mismatched thread. Dirt streaked the front of the dove-gray coat, the other's collar was ripped, and the third was missing all of its buttons. There were two pairs of battered children's shoes and a pair of heeled pumps, along with a few sets of underwear that might have once been white but were now faded to gray.

Oksana's cheeks warmed. She had never worn such ragged clothing before. Although she didn't have many dresses or blouses, the ones she had owned were neat and tidy. In these, she would look poor.

"Thank you," Valentina's mother said, looking pointedly at Valentina and Oksana. "This is very generous of your friend."

"Yes, thank you," the girls echoed.

Waving a dismissive hand, Masha Petrovna dropped into a chair. She kicked off her high heels, sighing. "Ah, that's better. That smells delicious," she added, nodding at the dishes on the kitchen table.

Oksana and Valentina and her mother had made supper. Masha Petrovna's larder had been nearly empty, so they had made do with canned vegetables and soup.

After they changed into their new clothes, they sat down to eat. Oksana's skin itched. The blouse smelled musty, and the skirt was too short. She had to keep pulling on it to cover her knees. And she was wearing *someone else's* underpants.

"Any news about the accident on the radio?" Masha Petrovna asked.

"No," Valentina's mother said.

"Well, that's hardly surprising, is it?" Masha Petrovna looked at the girls. "Can they keep their mouths shut?"

"Of course," Valentina's mother said.

"Good." Masha Petrovna fiddled with the radio dials. A woman's voice speaking in another language filled the room.

Now Oksana understood Masha Petrovna's question. Listening to foreign radio stations was illegal.

"What's she saying?" Valentina asked.

Masha Petrovna's eyebrows knitted together. "High levels of radiation were detected at a Swedish nuclear power plant this morning," she translated. "Workers confirmed their plant wasn't emitting radiation. They realized it had to come from another source." She paused, listening. "Swedish nuclear experts traced the weekend's wind currents and determined the radiation originated from the Soviet Union."

In her mind, Oksana pictured a map of Europe: the mass of the USSR and to the north, across the Baltic Sea, the slender raindrop of Sweden. The wind had carried radioactive clouds farther than she had imagined possible: thousands of kilometers and over water.

"Our government denies it," Masha Petrovna said. "Countries all over the world are demanding our leaders admit what has happened."

For a moment, the only sound was the announcer's voice. Oksana's thoughts whirled. With every breath she took, every bite she ate, every sip she drank, she was absorbing more radiation. Was she going to die? And what about her mother? What would happen to her?

"My God," Valentina's mother said in a hollow voice. "All the way to Sweden . . . This is far worse than I thought."

Masha Petrovna gasped. "The radiation is so strong it went all the way to Sweden—it must be inside your bodies. You must be sick."

"The doctors checked us with dosimeters," Valentina's mother said. "They wouldn't have let us go if we weren't healthy."

But Masha Petrovna was shaking her head. "I'm sorry," she said in a choked voice. "But I must ask you to leave."

"Please, take pity on us," Valentina's mother begged. "We've lost our homes. We have nowhere to go."

"I wish I could let you stay." Masha Petrovna's eyes shone with tears. "But I can't risk you getting me sick. Please, go."

Slowly, Oksana, Valentina, and Valentina's mother went

to the corner of the room, where they had left their suitcases. Oksana's hands shook so badly it took her two tries to fasten the buckle on her bag. Where could they possibly go? Would she have to find her grandparents and live with them after all?

"I'm sorry," Masha Petrovna said softly, and opened the door. The three of them trudged through it. Oksana turned around in time to see it slam shut behind them.

In the darkened corridor, they looked at one another. "What do we do?" Oksana asked.

Valentina's mother squared her shoulders. "We go far away from here. Then I'll figure something out. Come, girls."

■ ■ ■

Gripping their suitcases, they descended the stairwell. The lobby was empty, the bulbs in the overhead lamp flickering. When they reached the street, the warm April breeze washed over them.

"The weather's lovely," Valentina's mother said. "We can spend the night outside, if we have to."

"Like vagrants?" Oksana had never slept outdoors before. She couldn't imagine sleeping outside in a *city*.

"We'll be adventurers," Valentina said.

The stars hadn't come out yet, and the sky was black velvet. By the glow of lighted windows, Oksana could see men in business suits and women in dark dresses walking the avenue, heading home after a long day at work or an evening at a restaurant. Some strolled arm in arm, chatting and smiling. Up ahead, boys played with a dog, and girls made their dolls march up and down a building's front steps. Across the street, classical music spilled into the air through an open window. It was like a painting.

Maybe sleeping outside wouldn't be so bad, in a city that was as pretty as a piece of art. Oksana readjusted her grip on her suitcase and followed Valentina and her mother down the street.

"Where are we going?" Valentina asked.

"The train station," Valentina's mother said. "We're going to Leningrad."

Leningrad was even farther away from Minsk than Kiev! How would Oksana ever get back to her mother?

"We should go to Moscow," Valentina objected. "And see Papa."

Her mother stopped walking and looked Valentina squarely in the face. "We can't. You heard what the doctor said about Papa being contagious. I won't risk you getting sick from him. Or you, Oksana," she added. "I have to keep you both safe. So we're going to Leningrad."

Oksana couldn't catch her breath. Everything was happening too fast. She had never been there. She had heard it was one of the most beautiful places in the Soviet Union. It was a city of ice and palaces, a former swamp built on a series of canals. It was located in the republic of Russia, but that didn't worry her: Like most Soviets who lived in Ukraine, she had learned to hop from one language to the other, speaking Russian at school or in the streets and Ukrainian at home. What frightened her was the distance. It lay on the edge of the Arctic Circle, over a thousand kilometers away.

"Why are we going there?" Valentina asked.

"Because the one person who might be willing to take the three of us lives in Leningrad." Valentina's mother resumed walking, taking such long strides that the girls had to run to keep pace with her. She took a deep breath. "My mother."

Oksana couldn't do it. Spending a night with Jews was one thing, but how long would she have to live with them once they got as far from home as Leningrad?

"I can't," she said quickly as Valentina said, "But, Mama, you have nothing to do with your mother! I've never even met her!"

"I'm not giving either of you girls a choice," Valentina's mother said shortly.

The girls stopped walking. Valentina's mother kept going. Left behind on the pavement, Valentina and Oksana stared at each other. Neither spoke.

"Hurry, girls," Valentina's mother called over her shoulder. "It won't do for us to be on the streets late at night."

Oksana wondered if the fear on Valentina's face was mirrored on her own. They had nowhere to go. No one to rescue them, except for a stranger in a city one thousand kilometers away. They had no one else.

"Come," Valentina said, and together they followed her mother into the encroaching darkness.

(15)

Valentina

THEY SPENT THE night in a park. It wasn't as bad as Valentina had expected: the air was soft, and the bench where they sat was sheltered by the branches of a chestnut tree. Her mother said the girls should sleep and she'd stay awake to act as their lookout. Valentina tried to rest, but her mind kept tickling her into wakefulness.

What was her grandmother like? When Valentina had asked about her before, her mother had said sharply, "She does dangerous things. We can't have anything to do with her or we'll find ourselves in trouble."

Dangerous things . . . Was her grandmother a criminal? A political agitator? Whatever she did, it must have been terrible for Mama to cut her own mother out of their lives.

And yet now they were going to her. Would they find themselves in trouble, too, as Mama had warned?

Although the night was warm, Valentina shivered.

Every time she woke, she looked up to see if it was day yet. Although her father's watch was broken, she was able to keep track of the passing hours by watching the sky. At first, it was a black blanket. Later, it turned gray. The stars winked out one by one. Dawn had come.

Her mother shook her and Oksana's shoulders gently. "It's time to leave for the train station," she said.

Oksana sat up, rubbing her bleary eyes. "I've only just gone to sleep."

"That was hours ago." Valentina's mother stood, casting a wary look around the park. It was still deserted; the hour must be too early for people to walk to work or school. Valentina heard the clanging of a trolley bell and the roar of far-off traffic. Kiev was waking up. Soon the first trains of the morning would depart the city.

The central train station was a short walk from the park. It was a massive building of pale stone. Inside, arched ceilings soared high overhead, and dozens of people rode the escalators. In the middle of the cavernous space, small boys and girls sat on suitcases, eating sticky buns, and teenagers stood in clumps, talking. Babies cried in their mothers' arms. A few men in business suits were kissing their children's cheeks.

"What are all these children doing here?" Valentina didn't understand. Today was a Tuesday, and the children should have been in school.

Her mother shook her head; she didn't know, either. She went to one of the ticket counters, where a kindly looking gray-haired gentleman stood. Valentina and Oksana kept close to her heels.

"I beg your pardon," her mother said to the man. "Why are so many children here?"

"Same reason as you are, I expect," he said, blinking owlishly at them through his spectacles. "Evacuation."

Evacuation! Did that mean the government had finally announced news of the accident? Valentina thought of the illegal radio station they had listened to last night. Or had all these people here in the train station listened to foreign broadcasts, too?

The man tapped the side of his nose, the signal they were to keep quiet. "You're lucky you're leaving today. Once the official news gets out—or I should say, *if* it does—the train and bus stations and airports will be flooded with people desperate to get away from here. Tickets will be hard to come by, if not impossible."

So the government hadn't yet told the public about the accident. Valentina's heart sank. That meant she and her mother were still on their own.

"Where are you traveling to today?" the man asked.

"Leningrad," her mother said.

The man busied himself with the papers at the counter. "Leningrad, is it? You'll have to take the eight a.m. to Moscow. At Moscow, you'll board the midnight train to Leningrad, which should get you there by tomorrow morning."

He handed over two tickets.

"I think you've made a mistake," Valentina's mother said. "We need three."

"Two is all I have left."

"You don't understand." Valentina's mother put a hand on each girl's shoulder. "The three of us are traveling together."

"Two is all I have, and two is all you'll get." The man drummed his fingers impatiently on his desk. "We can't have a panic."

A knot in Valentina's stomach loosened. Only two tickets!

So Mama would find a safe place for Oksana to stay, and then she and Valentina could go on to Leningrad. It was better than Valentina could have hoped.

Her mother handed the man several bills, then ushered the girls away from the ticket counter. Her hand on Valentina's shoulder was shaking. "I'm sorry, girls. You'll have to go on without me. I'll follow on a later train."

Valentina went cold. "Mama, you can't!"

"Hush," her mother said. "You mustn't make a scene. I'll meet you in Leningrad. It will be fine. You'll see."

Valentina looked around the crowded station. All these people milling about couldn't be getting on the same train. Surely there were extra seats on the eight a.m. to Moscow.

"I know what you're thinking," her mother said. "There might be room on the train for me. But the man at the ticket counter was trying to tell us that he's only permitted to sell a certain number of tickets. The government wants to prevent a mass panic, so they're creating a ticket shortage. That will force most people to remain in their home cities."

Valentina stared at Oksana, silently willing her to offer to go on a different train. Or better yet, to go to her mother in Minsk.

But Oksana didn't. She didn't say anything at all. She stood with her arms wrapped around her chest, hugging herself. Her face was pale and anxious.

"Come, girls." Her shoes clicking on the tiled floor, Valentina's mother strode across the lobby. Valentina followed her to the third platform, her thoughts spinning. This couldn't be happening. Mama couldn't be about to send her away with

Oksana. There must be something she could do to change her mother's mind—

"Do you have your papers?" her mother asked.

"Yes, Galina Yurievna," Oksana said.

Oksana held up her passport for Valentina's mother to see. It was an internal passport, to be used for traveling within the Soviet Union. Ordinary citizens weren't permitted to travel outside the country; Valentina had never seen an external passport, although she had heard they existed.

On Oksana's papers, under the heading marked NA-TIONALITY, the word *Ukrainian* was typed. Valentina's face warmed. Although she had been born in Siberia, her papers didn't identify her as Russian. Instead, under NATIONALITY was typed the word *Jew*.

"Valyushka?" her mother prompted. "Do you have your papers?"

Valentina held up her passport, keeping her thumb over the section about her background. She could imagine how Oksana would snicker if she saw it.

"Mama," she said desperately, "can't Oksana go on a different train? She doesn't even want to come with us! She should—"

"Hold your tongue," her mother interrupted. She bent down so they were face-to-face. "I know this is hard, but you and Oksana must go. You are children; you can't take care of yourselves. And you both deserve to get as far away from the radiation as quickly as possible."

"So do you." Tears burned Valentina's eyes. Angrily, she rubbed them away with the back of her hand.

"I promise, I'll be fine," her mother said firmly, then turned to Oksana. "I'll write to your mother's hospital in Minsk," she said. "That way, she'll know where you're going. As soon as she's well, I'm sure she'll fetch you."

Oksana nodded, her head bowed so her hair fell forward, curtaining her face. Valentina wondered if she was trying to hide her tears. She knew she would cry if one of her parents was dead and the other ill, and she were sent to live with a stranger.

Not that she felt sorry for Oksana. Not that she would *ever* feel kindness toward her.

The shrill whistle of an incoming train sounded. Valentina shoved her passport into her suitcase.

Her mother pulled her close. "I wish I had more time," she said. "There's so much I want to tell you about your grand-mother."

"Why is she dangerous? Why haven't I ever met her?"

"There isn't much I can tell you here in the open," her mother replied. "When I was pregnant with you, I decided we would no longer see her. I had your safety to consider, too, you see. I was afraid if we continued to see her, we might get in trouble with the authorities."

She gave Valentina a quick hug. "Stay close to Oksana. Once you reach Moscow, make sure you get on the proper train to Leningrad. If you need help, ask a conductor."

Before Valentina could ask her mother another question, the train pulled into the station, coasting to a stop alongside their platform. Parents and children pushed toward it, jostling Valentina and her mother. Valentina had to grab her mother's hand so they wouldn't be pulled apart.

"I'll send her a telegram so she knows to meet you at the station." Her mother shouted to be heard above the din. "Wait for her at the statue of Lenin."

She pushed Valentina forward into the crush of passengers boarding the train. "Hurry! You don't want to be left behind!"

Valentina tried to turn around, to look for her mother, but the passengers were packed so tightly together that she couldn't. The wave of people carried her toward the train doors. She looked from side to side, searching for Oksana. To her right, she glimpsed the other girl's blond hair. She was only a few feet away.

Most of the passengers were children. The littlest ones had papers pinned to their coats, with names and addresses written on them. Their destinations, Valentina guessed. Those children must be too small to be able to tell the conductors where they were supposed to go. Many of them were crying. Valentina climbed the train's steps, her suitcase knocking into her knees. Inside, a couple of harried-looking women led a group of toddlers down the train corridor; the children held hands, forming a chain.

Someone poked her in the back. "There are too many people here." It was Oksana's voice. "There can't be enough room for everyone. We need to find seats. They won't make us leave if we have a place to sit."

Valentina nodded. Together they hurried down the train corridor until they found two empty seats. They dropped down onto them, not bothering to stow their suitcases on the rack over their heads, but holding them on their laps instead.

Through the window, Valentina saw a handful of grown-ups pacing up and down the platform. Her mother walked among them, her arms crossed over her chest as if she were holding herself together. Miserable. Valentina could see it in the tightness of her face. She was scanning the windows. When her eyes met Valentina's, she smiled and blew a kiss.

A lump lodged in Valentina's throat. She blew a kiss back.

The train lurched forward, picking up speed until her mother was only a blur of red and black. Then it rounded a curve, and she was gone.

■ ■ ■

At the next station, Valentina opened the window in their train compartment and poked her head out. This place was crowded, too, with lots of children and parents. She watched as a group of boys and girls tried to board her train. A conductor barred the way.

"Please, we have money!" the parents begged. "We can pay for tickets, no matter the cost!"

Valentina leaned out farther. The conductor stood on the train steps with his arms crossed, stone-faced. "There are no more tickets," he said. "The train is full."

He was lying! Only half of the seats were occupied; she had seen when she had gone down the corridor earlier to use the lavatory. They must not have let many of the passengers at the station in Kiev board the train.

Quickly, she wriggled back into the compartment and shut the window. Oksana sent her a questioning look.

Valentina studied the people sitting around her. Other children, reading books or sucking on sweets; a young, tired-looking mother with two little boys; a couple of men in business suits. No one was paying attention to her, but still . . . she'd better be cautious. She mustn't sound as though she were saying anything bad about the government.

She put her mouth next to Oksana's ear and whispered, "The conductor isn't letting anyone on. He's saying there aren't any seats left."

Oksana looked as scared as Valentina felt. Everything was wrong. Grown-ups were lying to children. The government wasn't permitting people to escape from the radiation. The government was *deliberately* letting its citizens get sick.

They didn't say anything else to each other for a long time. Valentina pressed her nose to the window, watching the landscape change. At first, the sights were familiar. Scattered clusters of oaks, pines, and hornbeams flashed past. Sometimes, Valentina saw hawks and eagles in the sky. At least these birds were alive. Maybe the contamination hadn't spread this far. Yet.

In the late afternoon, an old lady rolled a tea cart into their car. Valentina and Oksana bought tea and rolls for a few kopecks. While they ate, Valentina returned to looking out the window. The flat steppe had changed into rolling hills. The sky had turned to lead. Fir and spruce trees grew along the horizon. They must have reached Russia.

By the time the sky turned black, Valentina's eyes ached from exhaustion. Fields had given way to a city: dilapidated factories, blocks of apartment towers, and trash-strewn streets. They must be on the outskirts of Moscow—where Papa was.

Did she dare leave the train to search for the hospital where her father had been taken? The doctor in Pripyat had said the men had been flown to a special hospital, but not which one. Maybe she could go . . .

But when they pulled into the Moscow station, she saw it was already ten o'clock. The train to Leningrad left at midnight. If she tried to find her father's hospital, there was no guarantee she would locate the right one, nor that she would get back in time to board the train. She had to keep going— Mama wanted her to get as far away from Pripyat as possible.

Her throat felt tight with tears. She had to go on. *I'm sorry, Papa*, she thought, looking around the crowded train station. She was afraid she would burst into tears, so she ran her fingers over the watch fastened around her wrist. The worn leather strap and glass face were comforting. They reminded her of home.

The tears were a ball inside her chest now, but at least she thought she could talk without crying. She asked a conductor for help—Oksana seemed afraid to talk to anyone, so she was useless—and he gave them directions to the proper platform.

On the train, they had to share a sleeping compartment with two teenage girls whose parents had evacuated them from Minsk.

Minsk! That was where Oksana's mother was recovering. Valentina waited for Oksana to ask the girls how bad it had gotten in Minsk. But she didn't. Fully clothed, she climbed onto the top bunk. Valentina guessed she didn't want to change and have the teenage girls see her bruised back.

Valentina washed in the bathroom at the end of the corridor. She wished she could change into a nightdress, but all she had were the blouse and skirt Masha Petrovna had given her. Everything she owned in the world was in her suitcase, and she wasn't certain if she should throw it away, too. Were the rest of her things poisoned, like her clothes?

She set the case on the bathroom floor and carefully went through it. Her school textbooks. The sketch pad where she had drawn ideas for inventions. An envelope of photographs.

Opening the envelope, she riffled through the snapshots. She and Mama laughing in the kitchen, Mama's arms around her waist, a plum cake on the counter beside them. That had been taken two years ago, on her ninth birthday. Her and Papa on a sleigh beneath a starry Siberian sky, bundled in furs. And here were her parents on their wedding day, smiling, standing in front of a taxi whose grille was bedecked with ribbons. Mama held a bridal doll and a teddy bear, the symbols that she and Papa wished to have children someday.

Valentina's chest tightened. She couldn't throw these out. *Never*, she thought, touching the wedding day picture. She loved these things too much to let them go.

(16)

Rifka

"DO YOU HAVE everything?" Rifka's mother asked.

Rifka checked her supplies again. Her knapsack contained a woolen shawl, a loaf of bread, two apples, and a chunk of cheese wrapped in a kerchief. She had wanted to pack her winter coat as well, but it was too big to fit in her knapsack so she was wearing it. She was already sweating.

"Yes, Mama," she said.

Her mother stood in the parlor, holding the new baby in her arms. Rifka's two little brothers Saul and Isaac were supposed to be asleep, but they stood in the doorway, watching Rifka with wide eyes.

Everyone in the apartment was dressed in their nightclothes. Except for her. Because she was going away.

Tears gathered in her eyes. "Mama, please don't make me leave—"

"Stop," her mother said in a choked voice. "We've been over this. You have to escape Kiev."

A knock sounded on the door. Her mother opened it,

revealing Rifka's cousin Nathan standing in the corridor. "Come in," she said quietly. "Rifka is ready."

Nathan trudged into the parlor. Rifka tried not to make a face. Nathan was fifteen—only three years older than her—but he always acted so superior, as though she were just a small child. It didn't help matters that she was short and he towered over her at six feet and had enormous hands and feet to match.

He carried a knapsack, too, and wore a dark woolen coat. Lines of perspiration slid down his face. "It's time to go," he said. "We want to leave when it's dark."

Her mother set baby Avrum on a blanket on the floor. Then she and Rifka hugged. Rifka breathed in her mother's familiar scent of soap and yeast.

"Have courage," her mother said in her ear. "And know that God is with you."

Blinking back tears, Rifka nodded. Then she hugged her brothers, first Isaac, then Saul. They began crying, clinging to her, and her mother had to pry them off her legs.

Rifka wanted to say goodbye, but her throat felt stuck. She went to the door with Nathan, then turned for one last look.

Saul and Isaac were still crying and tugging at their mother's nightdress, begging to be picked up. On the floor, Avrum had begun to wail. How could she possibly leave her mother alone to care for all three of them?

"I'll be fine," her mother said, as if sensing the reason for Rifka's hesitation. "Go, Rifka. You have a chance to escape. You must take it."

Rifka nodded. "Goodbye," she managed to whisper. Nathan echoed her farewell.

Then Nathan was tugging her out of the apartment and into the corridor, and then down the stairs. "Come," he said impatiently, pulling harder on her wrist. "We need to be far out of the city before dawn. We don't want anyone to see us."

"I *know*!" She yanked her arm free.

"Good," he said. "Then since you're so smart, you know to keep your mouth shut and follow me."

Without another word, he slipped out the front door. Glaring at his back, Rifka hurried after him.

Dorohozhytska Street was dark. The stars overhead did little to break apart the blackness. Despite the lack of light, Nathan moved quickly. Rifka had to break into a light jog to stay at his side.

"You're going too fast," she panted.

"If you can't keep up, I'll leave you behind." By his grim tone, she knew he was serious.

From then on, they didn't talk. Her eyes adjusted to the darkness, and the buildings and shops took shape, becoming black masses. The streets widened; the houses grew bigger. They had left the Jewish quarter.

Rifka concentrated on the next step, and then the next, and then the one after that. Tears stuck fast in her throat. She mustn't cry. She had to be brave. She had to think of something that would make her feel stronger.

She listened to the wooden creaking of houses settling, and the rustle of wind through chestnut trees. The thud of her feet on cobblestones, the rasping of her breath. It was like music. She hadn't been allowed to bring her flute, but she could still hear music all around her. It was there, all the time, waiting for someone to notice it. The thought made her smile.

At last the buildings grew smaller and farther apart until they disappeared altogether. The road turned from cobblestones to dirt. Rifka smelled wildflowers and earth. The countryside. They had made it!

"Look." Nathan pointed.

In the east, the sky was flooded pink and orange. Dawn. Thank heavens, now they would be able to see where they were going.

But Nathan's face was grave. "We have to be especially careful now. If the German soldiers see us, they'll shoot us. And some of the Ukrainian farmers will want to kill us. They might even try."

The August morning was warm and her coat heavy; sweat slicked Rifka's blouse to her skin. Despite the heat, she shivered. "Why would the farmers want to kill us? We've done nothing to them."

Nathan threw her a scornful look. "We're Jewish. For some people, that's reason enough."

A sick feeling hollowed out her stomach. She knew he was right. "But how would they know we're Jewish? As long as we don't tell anyone, we should be safe."

Shaking his head, he began walking again. She fell in step beside him. The sky was turning to rose and gold, brightening everything beneath it. Now she could see farm fields feathering out in all directions and, in the distance, a forest.

"They can guess," Nathan said. "We're dark-haired, we're on our own, and we're obviously running from the German army. They'd be fools if they didn't suspect. Let's go to the forest," he added, nodding at the jagged outline of trees on the horizon. "We can hide there and get some rest."

They reached the woods without seeing anyone. Nathan laid his coat on the ground as a blanket and rested his head on his knapsack. Rifka did the same. She stared up into the canopy of trees. Branches stretched toward one another, blocking out the sky so all she could see were slivers of reddish gold.

She doubted she would sleep. Her thoughts spun like leaves in a windstorm. Mama. Her brothers. Papa, fighting somewhere on the front. The dark streets of Kiev. Ukrainian farmers, with their hunting rifles and knives.

She started to shake. A hand touched her arm. It was Nathan, sitting up. "Don't be scared," he said, his brown eyes intent on hers. "I'll keep you safe. I promised our mothers I would."

Something about the quiet way he spoke made her believe him. She closed her eyes and slept.

(17)

Oksana

THE CENTRAL TRAIN station in Leningrad was enormous. Weak gray light filtered through the large windows, touching the floor where Valentina and Oksana perched on their suitcases, waiting. They sat beneath the bust of Lenin, as Valentina's mother had told them to.

Oksana scanned the crowds. The station was crowded: men in business suits, women in dresses, university students carrying knapsacks, everyone in a tremendous hurry. Red banners dripped down the walls. Oksana supposed they had been put up for May Day, which would be celebrated across the Soviet Union tomorrow. It had been Papa's favorite holiday.

"You're lucky," she said to Valentina. The words seemed to burst out of her mouth before she could stop herself. "You got to say goodbye to your father. In the hospital dormitory," she added when Valentina looked at her.

"I don't think he knew I was there." Valentina looked sad. "Most of what he said was nonsense. He seemed drunk."

"You're still lucky," Oksana muttered. She rubbed her shoulder. Why did it have to hurt so much? And why, *why* had she talked back to her father? That had been the last time she'd seen him, and he had been so angry with her. It had all been her fault. She ruined everything.

She had to stop thinking of that evening or she would start crying right here in the middle of the train station. In front of Valentina, who would probably laugh at her.

"My father said something about black pebbles on the beach," Valentina said suddenly. "I think he was talking about the Black Sea! We were supposed to go there on holiday this summer."

"So he did know you were there." Oksana tried to ignore the twinge of jealousy in her chest. "He was trying to talk to you about happy times."

Valentina's face lit up. "That's lovely! Thank you for figuring that out."

Oksana ducked her head. Her father would say that gratitude from a Jew was a poisoned gift. That they were liars, all of them.

Except . . . Valentina hadn't looked as though she were lying when she had thanked Oksana. She had looked happy.

"Valentina Kaplan and Oksana Savchenko?" a woman's voice said.

Oksana looked up to see a lady in an elegant blouse and skirt. Her dark hair, which was pulled back in a severe bun, was streaked with silver.

If this was Valentina's grandmother, she looked nothing like the gray-haired lady Oksana had expected. Oksana didn't know many old folks—few elderly people lived in Pripyat, but there were several babushkas whose job was to sweep the streets. Oksana had often seen them on her walk to school: bent with age, white hair escaping from their head scarves, dressed in black. She had thought all grandmothers resembled them. Her own grandmother did.

"Valentina and Oksana?" the woman asked again. "I hope the journey hasn't robbed you of the ability to speak."

"I'm Valentina, and this is Oksana." Valentina scrambled to her feet. She dipped into a curtsy, which her grandmother acknowledged with a curt nod. "Thank you," Valentina said, "for letting us stay with you"—she hesitated, clearly not sure what to call her grandmother—"Rita Grigorievna," she finished.

"Yes, thank you very much." Oksana curtsied, too.

Valentina's grandmother sniffed. "There's no need to use formal terms, as we're going to be living with one another. Tetya Rita will do," she said to Oksana, instructing to call her *auntie*. Then she turned to Valentina. "You, of course, will call me Babulya."

Oksana was glad she didn't have to address this aloof lady as "grandmother." She watched as Valentina forced a smile, saying, "Yes, Babulya."

"That's settled, then. Are those bags all you've brought with you? Well, I suppose that's a small mercy, as my room isn't large. Come along, girls."

She strode across the station's main hall without looking to see if they were following. Clutching their suitcases, the girls scurried after her.

"Did she say *room*?" Oksana whispered.

"I think so," Valentina whispered back.

Maybe they had misunderstood. Oksana hoped so. Three people squeezed into one room sounded awful.

They stepped out of the station, and the city exploded all around them: buses trundled past, belching exhaust; a tram rumbled closer, its cables shooting off blue sparks; and automobiles sped by, sleek lines of gleaming metal. Enormous buildings spread themselves along the avenue. Some of them were made of yellow stone; others were pastel, as pretty as iced cakes. Oksana hadn't known buildings could be painted pink or green or blue. She had never seen such color.

And the *people*. Pedestrians everywhere: whistling, chatting arm in arm, digging through their pockets for spare change. Children circled an old man and his ice cream cart. A couple of mangy cats slunk between the children's legs, hoping someone would spill.

"It's beautiful," Oksana gasped.

"It certainly is," Valentina's grandmother said. "This street is called Nevsky Prospekt. I wanted your first sight of Leningrad to be of the most famous street in the city. That's enough sightseeing for now," she added briskly. "Come along. We need to catch the next train to my neighborhood. Your neighborhood now, too."

Oksana didn't want to move. She wanted to stay there forever, drinking in the street. She wished she dared to take out her notebook and sketch the scene. But Valentina and her grandmother would laugh at her. Art was what people did who hadn't talent for anything else.

"Come along," Valentina's grandmother said again, and they went back inside the train station to take a subway ride. Valentina's grandmother said she lived in Avtovo, an area on the outskirts of Leningrad and one of the final stops on the red line.

When they reached Avtovo, Oksana understood why Valentina's grandmother had wanted them to see Nevsky Prospekt first. Avtovo's narrow streets were lined with apartment towers. The buildings were little more than piles of bricks and mortar that had been thrown together; in several places, bricks had fallen off, exposing the plaster beneath. Wire-mesh awnings were fastened to many buildings to catch the bricks before they fell to the pavement.

Here there were no pastel houses, no ice cream carts or shiny automobiles. The roads were rutted, the curbs lined with mud. A couple of passersby waved at Valentina's grandmother, but no one stopped to chat. Oksana shivered in her thin spring coat. Leningrad felt colder than Pripyat.

"This is your new home," Valentina's grandmother said at last, stopping in front of a six-story brick building. Its walls were streaked with soot. The smell of cigarette smoke drifted through an open window.

Oksana didn't understand. All Jews were rich. So why would Valentina's grandmother choose to live in such a shabby place?

"It looks lovely," Valentina said quickly.

"Yes, thank you, Tetya Rita," Oksana said. Maybe the building was nicer inside.

Valentina's grandmother snorted. "I'm glad to see your mothers taught you some manners. It isn't lovely, but it'll keep the snow off your shoulders."

She unlocked the door and led them into a dingy entrance hall. "Here's the kitchen," she said, ushering them through a second door. They found themselves in a room where a large wooden table stood in the middle. An enormous stove took up most of one wall.

"This burner is ours," Valentina's grandmother said, pointing to one on the far right. "Don't use the others—they're reserved for the lodgers in the rest of the apartments. You'll have your breakfast and supper down here. I have a hot plate in our room, which we'll use sometimes. Lunch will be at school."

A piece of paper had been affixed to the front of each padlocked cupboard. Babulya tapped the one marked GOLDMAN. "This is where I keep our groceries. Don't try to open any of the other cupboards. You'll get a tongue-lashing if you do."

Oksana couldn't believe it. Valentina's grandmother didn't have her own kitchen. She shared with everyone else in the building. But why?

Valentina looked as confused as Oksana felt. "Excuse me, Babulya," Valentina said, "but is this kitchen for everyone in the building?"

Her grandmother sighed. "I forgot you've been spoiled in Pripyat. This is a *kommunalka*. A community apartment," she added. "There aren't many of them left. The government started cutting down on them thirty years ago, but there's so much demand for housing in the cities that they haven't been able to get rid of all of them yet. We share a kitchen, bathroom, and corridors with the other tenants. I'll show you which light switches in the hallways are for us to use."

She strode out of the room. Oksana followed her. A *kommunalka*. Only the lowliest people lived there, didn't they? So that must mean that Valentina's grandmother was poor. But

Papa had always said Jews were secretly rich and hid their wealth.

Oksana looked around the entrance hall. It was small, and water stains had traced brown shapes on the ceiling. The walls were made of beige tiles that hadn't been washed in a long time. This place certainly didn't seem like the sort of place a secretly rich Jew would live. It looked like a poor person's home.

Had her father been wrong?

"The elevator isn't working." Valentina's grandmother's voice interrupted Oksana's thoughts. "It hasn't worked in fifteen years, so get accustomed to going up and down stairs."

In silence, they climbed to the top story. Three doors flanked the dimly lit corridor: one for them, one for their neighbors, the Kozlovs, and one for the communal toilet and shower.

"You may store your washing-up things in the bathroom," Valentina's grandmother said. "Nobody takes anyone else's toothpaste. But don't leave our kitchen cupboard unlocked. I'm sure the people on the third floor stole two cans of beets from me last year, but I can't prove it."

She unlocked the door to her apartment. Inside was a box of a room. The furniture was simple: a bed in an iron frame, a sagging sofa, a wardrobe, and a table. A shelf held a hot plate, a few cups and bowls, and a teapot. A porcelain sink jutted out from the wall.

Valentina's grandmother must have been doing her washing when she had come to fetch them at the station, for laundry lines were strung across the room. Skirts, blouses, underclothes, and tights were clipped to the white strings.

This room didn't belong to a secretly rich Jew. It belonged to a poor person.

Her father *had* been wrong.

Oksana felt as though she were going to be sick. Quickly, she turned away from Valentina and her grandmother, so they couldn't see her face. Her cheeks were on fire.

Had Papa been mistaken about Jews? Or had he lied to her? He had told her, again and again, that Jews were thieves. He had said Valentina's father had stolen his promotion at work by spreading rumors that he was a bad worker. He had said Jews cheated to take others' jobs or earn the best marks on a test. He had made her promise to be on her guard against them.

No! Papa hadn't been a liar. She was awful for even thinking such a terrible thing.

Valentina's grandmother closed the door behind them. "Ever since I finished work yesterday, I've been sewing so I could have some clothes ready for you when you arrived. Your mother didn't tell you I'm a seamstress?" she asked Valentina, who shook her head no.

Her grandmother pursed her lips. "I suppose she hasn't told you much of anything about me. Never mind," she said briskly. "During the day, I manage a grocery shop. Ordinarily, I'd be there now, but I took the afternoon off to get you girls settled."

She pointed at the blouses and skirts hanging from the laundry lines. "At night, I sew clothes to make extra money. Luckily, I had saved enough leftover pieces of fabric from old jobs to make each of you girls a blouse and skirt. I see I'll need to sew more clothes for both of you. You can hardly go anywhere in those ratty things!" she added, nodding at them.

"Thank you for the clothes," Valentina said. "That was very kind."

Oksana ran a finger down the front of a white blouse, lingering over the plastic buttons. A Jew had made this for her. She didn't know what to think. "Thank you, Tetya Rita," she said softly.

"It was no trouble." Valentina's grandmother busied herself with hanging her purse on a hook. Before she turned away, however, Oksana saw her smile, and she knew she was pleased.

Valentina stood by the door, gripping the handle of her suitcase. "Did Mama tell you if she's on her way yet?"

"She rang me last night." Valentina's grandmother took the suitcases from the girls' hands and set them on the floor beside the bed. "She'd already sent me a telegram yesterday morning, to let me know you were coming. When she telephoned me, she said she couldn't get a ticket. The train station had tripled their prices, and there aren't any tickets to be had anyway. She doesn't know when she'll be able to leave Kiev."

Valentina's face fell. "But she doesn't have much money left! She spent almost all of it on our train tickets. What's going to happen to her?"

Her grandmother reached out as if she meant to touch Valentina, then let her arms fall to her sides. "She'll do whatever she has to in order to get to you," she finally said. "She told me that she has another friend from her university days who she can stay with for a few days. She'll do everything she can to raise money and find someone who can get her a ticket."

Oksana didn't understand. Nothing made sense anymore. Valentina's mother was so poor she couldn't buy a train ticket, and her grandmother lived in a poverty-stricken building. These Jews had less than her family.

Valentina's grandmother helped them unpack their things and store them in the wardrobe, and even though Oksana tried to smile and make the proper responses, all she could think over and over was one thing: Papa had been wrong about Jews.

Which maybe meant he had been wrong about other things.

Something loosened around her chest, like a band that had been released. For the first time since the explosion, she felt as though she could breathe. And even though she didn't understand why she felt that way, she was glad for it.

(18)

Valentina

FOR SUPPER, BABULYA showed them how to make *pelmenyi*, which were dumplings with butter and onions. They were Valentina's favorite food, but she'd never made them before. When she and Oksana burned the onions, Babulya scolded, "My gracious! Didn't your mothers teach you how to cook?"

Oksana looked terrified. Babulya laughed and shooed them away from the smoking stovetop. Afterward, when they ate the dumplings and drank their tea, Valentina felt full and warm.

By the time they had finished eating, families from the other apartments had trickled into the kitchen. Soon the room was crowded and fragrant with oil and herbs. Babies crawled across the linoleum; women bent over their pots, stirring soups; and men lounged at the table, smoking or reading newspapers. In the corner, a few children sat on the floor, playing cards.

"Go on, join them," Babulya said, nodding at the children. "I'll do the washing up." She beckoned Valentina and Oksana closer before they could walk away. "Don't mention you've come from Pripyat," she whispered. "If anyone asks, say you traveled here from Kiev. Then it isn't a lie."

Valentina swallowed hard. Of course—if others knew she and Oksana had come from the city where the nuclear accident had occurred, some of them would be frightened. Even though news of the explosion hadn't been made public, so many people seemed to know about it. They would wonder if she and Oksana were contaminated.

She looked at her hands. They appeared normal. She felt normal, too. She thought of the dosimeters the doctor had used to check her for radiation. Perhaps she could make her own. Then she could periodically test Oksana and herself, to make sure they were still all right.

No, that didn't make sense. They'd already received radiation from the explosion; they wouldn't get more. Maybe they should perform other tests on themselves, like how long they could hold their breath, to see if their lung capacity had been affected—

"Valentina, are you listening?" Babulya asked. "I told you not to mention Pripyat."

Valentina jumped. Sometimes her mind was so busy with thoughts, she forgot where she was. "Yes, Babulya, I promise I won't."

As she and Oksana crossed the room, she noticed one of the men sitting at the table was staring at her. He wore spectacles and was smoking a cigarette. "Rita," he called to Babulya, who was washing their dishes in the sink, "who are your guests?"

"My granddaughter and her friend." Babulya plunged

her hands into the soapy water. "Oksana's mother isn't well, and my daughter's in Kiev at the moment, so I've taken the girls in."

"Interesting," the man said. Valentina felt his eyes on her as she sat down with the other children. Did he suspect her grandmother wasn't being completely honest? If he learned she and Oksana came from Pripyat, would he demand they move out? Or maybe he was a member of the KGB, the secret police. She'd heard they had spies everywhere. You never knew if they were watching you.

Kommunalkas weren't only uncomfortable and overcrowded, she realized with a shiver.

They could be dangerous.

Babulya insisted the girls share the bed while she took the sofa. Tomorrow was May Day, so schools would be closed for the holiday. The follow morning, on Friday, she said she would take them to the middle school to register them in the fifth grade. Schools were set up in the same way here in Leningrad as they were in Pripyat: first through third grades were in the primary school, fourth through seventh were middle, and eighth through tenth were high school. That made moving somewhat easier: at least they wouldn't be sent down to the primary grades. Still, with only a few weeks left before the summer holidays began, Valentina thought it hardly seemed worth the trouble of registering and going to school, but she knew better than to say so.

She was asleep when something woke her. For a moment, she lay still, listening. Floorboards creaked. Someone was walking across the room.

She sat up. In the darkness, she could see a shadow moving toward the door. It was Oksana—she recognized her outline. What was she doing?

Oksana opened the apartment door. By the fluorescent glare of the corridor lights, Valentina could see she was gripping her shoulder. Valentina remembered what she had seen in the shower in Kiev. Was Oksana still hurt?

Valentina glanced at her grandmother. She was asleep on the sofa. Valentina didn't want to wake her to tell her Oksana was in pain. For all she knew, Babulya would be angry at being woken.

The door closed behind Oksana. Once again, the room was dark. Valentina shut her eyes. In the street below, a car trundled past. Somewhere outside something shattered, like glass breaking, and someone shouted a curse. Valentina put her pillow over her head.

Oksana had been gone for a long time. Valentina thought of how tightly Oksana had been holding her shoulder.

She sat up again. Maybe she should check on Oksana. She got out of bed and went to the bathroom at the end of the corridor.

Oksana was standing in the middle of the room. She had peeled her nightgown away from her shoulder and was craning her neck, trying to look at herself in the mirror.

Valentina gasped. Oksana's shoulder was now swollen and red. A line of pus dribbled from a dot in the center of the wound.

Was this radiation sickness? Oksana had said it wasn't, but what if she was wrong? What if Oksana was contagious, and Valentina and her grandmother grew sick from being near her?

Valentina stumbled backward.

Oksana's tear-filled eyes met hers in the mirror. "I kept hoping it was getting better. But it feels worse. It hurts all the time."

Valentina found her voice. "We have to tell my grandmother. Right now."

Oksana hung her head and burst into tears.

■ ■ ■

Babulya told the girls to bundle into their clothes straightaway. They were going to the hospital.

They caught the last train of the night. At the hospital, they waited in the emergency area. When Oksana's name was called, she and Babulya vanished down a corridor, leaving Valentina alone.

She didn't know what to do. Silently, she began reciting multiplication tables in her head, which she often did when she was nervous. She had gotten all the way to the fourteens when her grandmother returned.

"Come with me," Babulya said. "I don't want you staying out here by yourself." Her face was gray, her lips a thin line. She looked so exhausted that Valentina didn't dare ask her anything.

Together they went down the corridor into a small examination room. Oksana sat on a table, dressed in a hospital gown. The gown was open at the back. A doctor was studying her bare shoulder.

"It isn't radiation," he said. "It's a burn. If I had to hazard a guess, I'd say it was caused by a cigarette."

Babulya looked startled. "A cigarette did this? But how . . ." She trailed off.

"I can think of only one way a wound like this would occur." The doctor glanced at Oksana, his expression softening. "It was deliberate."

For a long moment, Valentina stared at Oksana. Somebody had hurt Oksana on purpose. That was what the doctor meant. Somebody had pressed the burning tip of a cigarette into her skin. Somebody had *wanted* to harm her.

"Oksana," Babulya asked gently, "who did this?"

Oksana ducked her head, letting her hair swing forward to hide her face. "My father," she whispered.

Valentina remembered Comrade Savchenko. He had had blond hair, like many Ukrainians, and blue eyes. Sometimes she had seen him in the stairwell of their apartment building, or in the street. Once he had spit on her, when she was little and had bumped into him on the stairs. "Watch where you're going, rat," he had said. She had run away, crying. That was the only time he had spoken to her. Her father had warned her to keep clear of him.

Babulya let out a sigh. "Oh, Oksana, my poor girl."

"It wasn't his fault," Oksana said quickly. "He only wanted the best for me. That's why he had to punish me, so I could learn."

"Nonsense," Babulya said. "Hurting someone is never acceptable, no matter the reason."

The doctor bent down to look Oksana in the face. "You

must be honest with me so I can properly treat your wounds. Do you understand?"

Avoiding his eyes, she nodded.

"Good. The wound on your back was caused by a cigarette, wasn't it?"

Still not looking at him, she nodded yes.

"Often," the doctor said, "cigarette burns heal on their own. I suspect some loose ashes worked their way into the wound, which is how it became infected. You're fortunate this lady brought you in tonight. If an infection like this is left untreated, skin tissue can die. Your injury could have become very serious."

Valentina couldn't stop staring at Oksana. She knew plenty of their schoolmates were spanked or hit with a belt when they misbehaved. But to have a father who burned you with a cigarette on purpose . . . She couldn't imagine how horrible that would feel.

"I'll incise and drain the skin around the wound," the doctor said to Babulya. "She'll need to have the dressings changed once a day for at least a week. If it looks worse or begins emitting pus again, bring her here immediately."

Valentina couldn't understand his manner. He acted as though it didn't matter that Oksana's father had burned her. "Aren't you going to do something about her father?" she asked him. "He ought to be arrested!"

"For disciplining his child?" The doctor looked startled. "I hardly think so, young lady. Now move back. I have work to do."

Reluctantly, Valentina stepped away from the examining

table. Oksana sat hunched over, picking at the frayed hem of her hospital gown. While the doctor scribbled on a chart, Babulya took Valentina aside.

"You're so upset I think you've forgotten that Oksana's father is beyond punishment," she said quietly.

Valentina *had* forgotten. "It isn't right. He got away with this."

"My dear girl," Babulya said, "no one gets away with anything. By hurting his daughter, Oksana's father will never have her love. He may have thought he did, but he didn't. Not in life or in death. I hope Oksana learns that someday. You'll understand when you're older."

Maybe, but she didn't understand now. Crossing her arms over her chest, she watched the doctor set out metal instruments, a tube of ointment, and a roll of bandages on a tray. Oksana stared at the floor, her eyes vacant. Valentina recognized what she was doing. She was retreating into her mind, to someplace where nothing could hurt her. Valentina had done the same thing when she was called a dirty Jew.

Babulya guided Valentina out of the room. "You don't want to see what he has to do to Oksana. It's best if you wait out here."

Valentina watched the door close after her grandmother, leaving her alone in the hallway. She had thought she knew Oksana, after being classmates for six years, but it turned out she hadn't known her at all.

Closing her eyes, Valentina leaned against the wall, letting the iciness of the painted cinder blocks seep through her clothes into her skin, keeping her awake.

(19)

Oksana

THE METRO TRAINS had stopped running for the night, so the doctor let them stay in the exam room. Oksana had a hard time falling asleep. What must Valentina and her grandmother think of her now? They knew she was bad—such a bad person that her father had had to hurt her, to help her improve. They must hate her.

And what was happening to Mama? Was she getting better or was she going to die, too? Tears seeped out from under Oksana's eyelids. She brushed them away, hoping no one had seen.

The hospital was noisy: machines beeped, voices hummed, and gurneys squeaked in the hallways. And her shoulder still ached, like a rotting tooth. It took her a long time to fall asleep. When she woke in the morning, she felt as though she hadn't slept at all.

After they left the hospital, she saw red pennants hanging down the sides of buildings. Crowds lined the streets, talking and laughing. Almost everyone wore a red ribbon pinned over their heart. It was May Day, Oksana realized. Because of everything that had happened, she had forgotten about the holiday.

If she were still at home, she would have had the day off from school. She would have gone to the main square to watch the parade, and Papa would have held her hand—

No. She mustn't think about that. Home didn't exist anymore. And neither did Papa.

Her chest grew tight. Head down, she followed Valentina's grandmother through the throngs. She supposed they were going to the nearest Metro station, where they would take the red line back to Avtovo.

But Valentina's grandmother stopped in front of an ice cream cart. "Two vanilla cones," she told the vendor, then glanced at the girls. "Unless you prefer chocolate."

Ice cream for breakfast? Oksana bit her lip. "My parents don't like me to have sweets."

"We all need extra sweetness sometimes," Valentina's grandmother said. "Two vanillas," she told the ice cream man again. "And a chocolate cone for me."

And that was how they wound up eating ice cream in the slanting sunshine while all around them Leningraders cheered and threw red flowers on the pavement. Dozens of tanks, decorated with red bunting, and hundreds of people wearing red ribbons streamed through the streets. The city had the biggest May Day parade Oksana had ever seen. She and Valentina shouted, "Hurrah!" until they were hoarse.

When the last tank had disappeared from view, Valentina's grandmother asked Oksana how she felt.

Oksana's cheeks warmed. She didn't understand why she felt so ashamed. "Fine," she mumbled.

"Very well." Valentina's grandmother said, and dropped a handful of coins into Valentina's hand. "This ought to cover your expenses for the day. Get back for supper by six o'clock. The Summer Garden is lovely this time of year—that's where I'd start, if I were you."

"Aren't we going back to Avtovo with you?" Oksana asked.

"Certainly not." Valentina's grandmother said in Ukrainian. Oksana couldn't help smiling a little—hearing the familiar language again was comforting. "After last night, what you girls need more than helping me around the apartment is fresh air and fun. Explore Leningrad and have an adventure. And, Oksana, the instant you start feeling tired or ill, come directly back home, all right?"

Oksana's heart beat faster. A whole day in a new city with a pocketful of coins and no grown-ups! It was like a dream. But what if they got lost?

"Do you think you can find your way back?" Valentina's grandmother asked.

"Yes," Valentina said quickly.

"Then have a lovely time," her grandmother said.

"Thank you, Babulya," Valentina said, and pulled Oksana into the crowd with her before Oksana had a chance to object.

"Wait!" Oksana panted. "What if we can't figure out how to get back to your grandmother's apartment? Or run out of money? Or get in trouble for playing truant?"

Valentina rolled her eyes. "No one will think we're truants. Schools in Russia close for the holiday, too, just like back in Pripyat. We won't run out of money because I'll be careful. And if we get lost, we'll ask for directions. Let's go!"

They asked a nice-looking lady in front of a bakery how

to get to the Summer Garden. They took a couple of wrong turns, but every mistake was part of the adventure, and when Oksana saw Valentina wasn't worried, she began to relax.

They saw enormous buildings painted pastel pink and ice blue. They bought roasted chestnuts from a street vendor. They pressed their noses to the window of a fancy shop whose shelves were lined with food Oksana hadn't seen before: glass bottles of Coca-Cola, canned caviar, plastic-wrapped packages of cookies, and other items she couldn't identify because their labels were printed in foreign languages.

"Orange soda," she said longingly. "I've always wanted to try it."

Valentina jingled the coins in her pocket. "Let's go in," she said.

"Oh, no! We shouldn't."

"Don't be silly. Of course we should."

Valentina hurried toward the shop, Oksana trailing after her. Orange soda would be frightfully expensive, she was sure of it. Valentina's grandmother would be furious when she found out they'd wasted her money.

Oksana started to shake. "Valentina, I don't want to go—"

"It will be fun!" Valentina interrupted.

A big man in black stood in front of the shop door. "Papers?" he barked at them.

"Papers?" Valentina looked surprised. "Why do we need to show you our identity papers to go inside?"

The man frowned. "This shop is for foreigners only. Show me your papers." His eyes narrowed. "Or do I need to telephone the police to report two troublemakers?"

"Valentina," Oksana whispered, "we need to go."

Valentina flashed the man a big smile. "We were just leaving."

Together, they hurried away. When they got to the corner, Valentina looked back and shouted, "Your orange soda is probably made from pee anyway!"

Then she started to run. Oksana raced after her. Around the corner, down another street, then around another corner and along an embankment overlooking the river. Finally, they stopped in front of an enormous wrought-iron fence whose black spokes were topped with gold leaf.

"That was awful!" Oksana clutched at her heart. "Do you think the guard will find us?"

Valentina laughed. "No. He can't leave the shop."

Oksana took a steadying breath. They were safe.

Through the fence railings, she saw parkland stretching out for what seemed like forever. This must be the entrance to the Summer Garden, for she couldn't imagine there was another park in Leningrad so large or so beautiful.

The gates were open. Oksana and Valentina went inside and dropped onto the nearest bench. For a moment, they didn't say anything. Then Oksana asked, "Did you really say their orange soda is made from pee?"

Valentina made a face. "Yes."

There was a beat of silence.

Then Oksana giggled. Imagine telling that big, mean-looking man that his shop's soda was made from pee!

She felt Valentina looking at her. Then Valentina laughed, too. "I know I shouldn't have said it," she said. "My mother is always telling me my mouth will get me into trouble."

Smiling, Oksana offered the bag of chestnuts to Valentina. "Want some?"

"Thanks." Valentina took a few.

They crunched in companionable silence. At last, Oksana asked, "How did you think to say that to the guard?"

Valentina shrugged. "It just came out."

"It must be marvelous to be able to come up with cutting insults," Oksana said. "I wish I could do that."

"I'm sure you could . . ." Valentina broke off. She glanced at Oksana, then away.

Oksana knew what she was thinking. There had been many times over the years that she had said cutting insults to Valentina.

Her papa had been wrong about all Jews being rich. Maybe he had been wrong about Jews in other ways. Oksana thought of how Valentina had summoned her grandmother after she had seen Oksana in the bathroom last night. How Valentina's mother had given up a seat on the train for her. And how Valentina's grandmother had given them money for the day, even though she didn't have much to spare.

This was too confusing. She didn't want to think about it anymore. "Let's explore the gardens," she said quickly.

"Fine," Valentina muttered.

They started to walk. The pathways were lined with marble statues, which glimmered in the sunlight. Flower-dotted grass spread in all directions. The place was lovely, but Oksana was too miserable to enjoy it. Valentina must despise her—that was why she had stopped talking. And somehow, for reasons she couldn't quite understand, Oksana didn't want Valentina to hate her.

"It's beautiful here," Oksana said at last. "I like the statues."

"My mother told me about them," Valentina said in a grudging tone. "In the winter, they're stored in boxes to protect them from the snow and cold. Every year for May Day, city workers uncover them."

"They're pretty," Oksana said.

The statues stood under the protective branches of greening trees. Each was different: some were characters from fairy tales, others from Roman myths, and a few were long-dead kings and queens. There must have been a hundred of them.

Oksana tried to imagine what it would feel like to have a block of stone or marble in front of her and to form something beautiful from it. She wondered if the art was trapped within the stone, and if it took an artist's talent to free it.

"Which statue is your favorite?" she asked, and then, naturally, they had to look at every one before they could pick which they liked best, and before long Valentina was smiling again. Neither of the girls could decide, although Oksana preferred the queens, while Valentina loved the Roman gods and goddesses.

They were sitting on the edge of a fountain, dragging their fingers through the cool water, when Oksana asked, "Why does your grandmother speak Ukrainian?"

"She does?" Valentina sent her a surprised look.

"This morning in the street," Oksana said. "You didn't notice?"

Valentina shook her head no.

"You're from Siberia, aren't you?" Oksana asked. At Valentina's nod, she said, "Then you probably won't understand. Most Ukrainians resent having to speak in Russian at work or school. My parents say we ought to speak the language of our ancestors."

Russian was the official tongue of the Soviet Union, and its citizens were supposed to speak it at school or at their jobs, regardless of the language that had originally been spoken in their republics. Valentina's grandmother was from Leningrad, which meant she was Russian and there was no reason for her to know Ukrainian. Yet this morning she had spoken it so fluently, Valentina hadn't noticed what language she was using. Oksana wondered how Valentina's grandmother had learned Ukrainian in the first place.

Valentina didn't seem interested, though, and suggested they go for a walk. As they ambled alongside the canals, the sun rose higher, gilding the windows in the elegant buildings, turning them into sheets of golden glass. They were like a sort of art, Oksana thought. Even ordinary windows could be beautiful, if she looked at them the right way.

For lunch, she and Valentina bought meat-and-potato dumplings from a street cart. After they ate, they went to Decembrists' Square to see the famous statue of Peter the Great called the Bronze Horseman.

In the sunlight, the bronze looked black. Peter sat astride a horse rearing on its hind legs, his face turned to the right, his sword hanging at his side. His left hand gripped the reins, and his right was flung out, as if he were reaching for or pointing at something in the distance. Oksana imagined he had ridden to the shore and was looking out across the Neva River, picturing the city he would build that would become St. Petersburg—and which would be renamed Leningrad after the Communist revolution.

When she finally turned away from the statue, she felt as light as the soft spring air all around her. "Are you ready to go home?" she asked Valentina.

"Okay."

Together they reached the embankment. The river flowed alongside them, its surface sparkling with sunlight. It looked as though diamonds had been tossed across the blue water. Oksana thought it was beautiful, and it was *hers*, hers to see and enjoy.

She felt something rise up in her chest, as delicate as a plume of smoke. She recognized the feeling. It was the same way she felt when she finished a drawing or saw something lovely and sketched it in her mind.

Joy.

(20)
Valentina

THE NEXT MORNING, Babulya walked Valentina and Oksana to the middle school to register them for the fifth grade. With every step, the knots in Valentina's stomach tightened more. Maybe this school would be different from her old one. Nobody here, except Oksana, knew she was Jewish, and perhaps Oksana wouldn't say anything. Maybe here she could feel as though she belonged.

The building looked like the one in Pripyat. In the classroom, about forty children, dressed in black-and-white uniforms, sat in orderly rows of desks. A large portrait of Lenin hung on the wall.

The teacher, Yekaterina Federovna, was covering the Great Patriotic War. In Pripyat, Svetlana Dmitrievna had been about to teach it, too. Svetlana Dmitrievna had said it was called World War Two in other countries. Everything seemed the same, and the knots in Valentina's stomach ached.

But when the teacher introduced her and Oksana to the class, several of the girls smiled at them. Valentina felt herself smiling back. Maybe this school would be all right.

At recess, though, a boy from her class planted his feet in front of her and said loudly, "Your last name is Kaplan."

Valentina looked up. She and Oksana had been drawing squares on the pavement with chalk for a game of big bear's den. The first square had to be big enough for several children to fit inside. Within the first square, she had been drawing a smaller square, which would be the bear's den. One child would stand in the den while the others waited in the outer square for the "bear" to try to tag them.

"Your name is Kaplan," the boy said again.

"Yes," Valentina said. To her ears, her voice sounded calm, but her heart had started beating hard. She knew what the boy would say next. It was starting—the sly looks, the insults, the name-calling. She hadn't been able to escape after all.

The boy loomed over her. She thought his name might be Andrei, but she couldn't remember for sure. "Kaplan's a Jewish name."

Valentina didn't say anything. Maybe if she ignored him, he would stop. In Pripyat, sometimes that had worked. Her hands shook as she drew the inner square. The lines came out wobbly. Oksana stopped drawing and looked up at the boy.

"I know all about your kind," he continued.

Valentina drew over the wobbly lines, trying to make straight edges for the square. Her face felt hot. Why couldn't he leave her alone? But even if he did, there would be other children to take his place. It had been the same at every school she had gone to. Nothing ever changed.

"Why don't you go back to Jerusalem, where you belong?" the boy said. "Nobody wants you here."

Oksana stood up. "Nobody wants *you* here. Why don't you shut your mouth?"

The boy's eyes narrowed. "What did you say to me?"

A hush fell over the schoolyard. Children stopped playing to stare at Oksana.

"You heard me." Oksana fisted her hands on her hips. "Leave Valentina alone."

Valentina couldn't believe her ears. She stayed crouched on the ground, unable to move.

"I know who you are," the boy said. "You're one of those Chernobylites. My father says you're all contaminated and you'll turn into rabid dogs."

Oksana shoved her face into the boy's. "He's right. I think I'll take a bite out of you." She clicked her jaws, and the boy jumped back. She shouted, "You'd better run away! Next time I might bite your face."

"You're crazy!" The boy dashed across the schoolyard.

The girls clustered around the chalk squares cheered. "Well done, Oksana! Andrei's a bully. We've all wanted to tell him off forever."

Oksana's face was red. She put her hands to her cheeks. "I can't believe I did that," she whispered.

Valentina couldn't believe it, either. This couldn't be the same girl who had mocked her at their old school.

But it *was*. She stood there, her face flushed, smiling a little. It was the first time Valentina could remember someone at school other than Larisa or a teacher defending her.

Oksana looked at Valentina. "Are you all right?"

Slowly, Valentina took the hand Oksana offered. She stood up. She knew she should let go of Oksana's hand, but for some reason she didn't. They stood awkwardly, not looking at each other. Valentina wanted to say thank you, but the words stuck in her throat. Oksana seemed to understand, though, for she didn't let go, and while they played big bear's den they held hands the whole time, even though they weren't supposed to.

■ ■ ■

When Valentina was a small child in Siberia and the autumn evenings turned cold and misty, her parents liked to say, "The moon has put on his furs."

Instead of using a refrigerator, she and Mama hung food in bags outside their window. Their drinking water was hauled to their apartment in solid chunks of ice sawn out of the river. She wore reindeer-fur-lined boots and carried her shoes in her satchel to change into when she got to school. On days when the thermometer dipped below minus-sixty degrees, the schools closed, and she stayed home with her mother, snug and cozy behind their three-panes-thick windows.

May in Leningrad was the opposite of October in Siberia. The moon shed its furs and shone like a silver coin. The last traces of snow melted, and the frozen patches of earth in the courtyard behind Babulya's apartment turned to mud. Leningraders stopped wearing coats.

Babulya told the girls that the days would grow longer and longer until the sun would set for only a few hours every night. Those were called White Nights, and they were like magic. Sailboats glided on the Neva River, swans swam the ponds in the Summer Garden, and the scent of linden trees carried on the soft breeze. Valentina could scarcely wait to see it for herself. She hadn't heard of White Nights before, not even in Siberia, where the sun seemed to shine forever during the summer.

Her mother still hadn't been able to get out of Kiev. Tickets were impossible to come by unless you had special connections, and she had none. For now, she was staying with the second university friend.

She had spoken on the telephone with a doctor at the special hospital in Moscow. He said Valentina's father and some of the other survivors would receive bone marrow transplants. "They're taking excellent care of him," Valentina's mother had promised, then had to hang up because long-distance telephone calls were expensive.

Valentina didn't know what bone marrow transplants were. Babulya and Oksana didn't, either. The next day at school, instead of going out to recess with the other children, she lingered in the classroom to ask her teacher about them.

"Marrow is a sort of tissue deep inside your bones," Yekaterina Federovna explained. "It makes blood cells. People need transfusions to replace dying or damaged bone marrow."

"Can a transfusion cure someone who's sick?" Valentina asked.

Yekaterina Federovna put her arm around Valentina's shoulders. "Absolutely. Now go out and play. Put some pink in those cheeks."

"Thank you!" Valentina rushed outside. The whole time she played in the schoolyard, she felt as though she were floating instead of running. Papa would be cured! It couldn't be long now until he was released from the hospital, and somehow he and Mama would get train tickets and make their way to Leningrad. They'd be a family again.

"What did you talk to Yekaterina Federovna about?" Oksana asked. "You look so happy."

"Nothing." Valentina wiped the smile from her face. She didn't want to tell Oksana the doctors were healing her father. Not when Oksana's father had died.

And Valentina didn't want to hurt her. Not anymore. Something had changed between them. She wasn't sure when it had happened—after they had spent the night in the hospital, maybe, or had wandered the city together, or had dealt with that bully Andrei at recess. They weren't friends exactly, but they weren't enemies anymore, either. Valentina wasn't certain what they were. She only knew she didn't wish for Oksana to feel badly.

So she said, "Nothing," once more and grabbed Oksana's hand, tugging her across the yard so they could line up for a footrace.

(21)

Rifka

RIFKA HAD NEVER known hunger before.

She walked along a dusty road, with Nathan at her side. Night had laid itself across the land, so Nathan had said it was safe to come out of the forest. Rifka knew what would happen next: They would walk down the dirt road, as they had done every night for weeks, every step taking them farther away from Kiev and, they hoped, from the approaching German army. When dawn broke, they would forage in the fields, digging bare-handed into the earth, searching for something they could eat. Potatoes. Carrots. Anything.

After they had found some food, they would run into the forest, winding around the trees until they felt safe. Then they would sit and eat. Once their bellies were satisfied—never full, only satisfied enough that the terrible, clawing hunger was held at bay—then they would lie down and sleep.

Now as she walked in the darkness, she couldn't stop thinking about her mother's food. Black bread as soft inside as clouds. Soup thick with vegetables. Pastry drizzled with honey. And milk—icy cold and sweet.

"Nathan," she said, "can't we stop and look for food?"

"No." He didn't take his eyes off the ground. "We have to move as fast as we can at night. You know that."

"I know," she mumbled. But her stomach was a hole. The hole had talons, which scraped her insides as they stretched up, up until they reached her throat. It hurt to talk. It hurt to move. She didn't know how much longer she could walk.

The road was a gray ribbon, stretching on forever. They would never get to the end of it. Never get far enough away.

She stumbled and had to swallow a sob. She missed Mama so much! And Isaac and Saul, and baby Avrum, and Papa.

"Why can't we go home?" she asked for the thousandth time. "We haven't seen any soldiers."

"Not yet." Nathan's tone was grim. "They're coming, Rifka." And then he said, as he had said to her so many times before, "We have to escape to one of the Stans. It doesn't matter which one."

She understood. Kazakhstan. Uzbekistan. Turkmenistan. Tajikistan. She knew little of them except for their names. They were all parts of the Soviet Union to the southeast. All thousands of kilometers away. All, hopefully, would not be conquered by the German army.

"I know," she said again.

They continued walking. Each step hurt. Rifka wore her mother's boots, which were too big. Although she had put on three pairs of woolen socks—all she had brought with her—the boots still rubbed her ankles. The straps of her knapsack bit into her shoulders, but she didn't dare throw out anything inside it. She knew she would need the woolen undershirts and underwear in the winter.

"Have courage, Rifka," Nathan said gently. "We must escape. If not for our sakes, then for our mothers'. They sacrificed so much to send us away."

Tears sprang to Rifka's eyes. She hated thinking of her mother at home, alone except for the boys, who were too little to be any help. "They'll be fine," she said in a shaking voice. "The Germans won't hurt them. They're only women and children—not soldiers."

Nathan hesitated. "Yes. You're right."

In the east, the sky had turned gray. The sun was rising! Rifka felt her heart lifting from her belly up into her rib cage, where it belonged. "It's time to find food!"

Nathan pointed at a cottage in the distance. "There's a farm. Let's . . ."

He went still. "Rifka," he whispered. "Do you hear that?"

Rifka listened with all of her might. The breeze rustled through the fields of wheat. Nathan's and her breathing rasped in her ears. Nothing out of the ordinary.

And then she heard it. A far-off rumble.

Her eyes met Nathan's. "It's a tank," he said. "I bet it's the Germans."

Rifka gasped. "What should we do?"

"Hide. If the Germans see us . . ."

He didn't finish the sentence. He didn't have to. Rifka knew what he would say: the Germans would kill them.

She looked around frantically. The long road, the farm fields, the cottage, and on the horizon, the forest. If they went into the woods, there was no guarantee the soldiers wouldn't see them. They had to be tucked out of sight.

"The farm," she said. Nathan nodded.

Together they raced down the road. Rifka moved so fast she felt as though she were flying. She glanced over her shoulder. Nothing. But the rumble was growing louder.

She and Nathan reached the farm fields at the same time. They ran between rows of planted cabbage, making for the cottage. In the dawn, its white stones looked bluish, as bright as a beacon to Rifka. She flung herself at the front door, hammering on the weathered wood.

Nathan pushed her aside so hard she stumbled backward several steps. "Keep out of sight," he whispered, and she slunk back even more, confused.

The door opened. An elderly man stood in the doorway, dressed only in trousers and an undershirt. An old lady peeked over his shoulder. "Who are you?" he asked Nathan. "What's the meaning of this?"

"I'm a traveler," Nathan said, slipping one hand behind his back and making a staying motion at Rifka. "I was hiking when I heard the German army approaching. Please, if you could hide me until the Germans have passed, I would be so grateful. I can stay in the barn. I won't cause any trouble, I promise you."

The old man grunted. "Fine. Now leave me and my wife in peace."

"Thank you, a thousand thank-yous," Nathan said. He bowed low, remaining half bent over until the door closed.

Then he snatched up Rifka's hand, and together they ran from the cottage to the ramshackle barn with its thatched roof.

Inside, it smelled of hay and horses. Slivers of light filtered through the slatted walls. As Rifka's eyes adjusted to the dark, she saw a horse and a cow in separate stalls, and piles of hay neatly stacked in one corner.

Nathan nodded toward the hay. "Get behind it."

She scurried around the bales of hay, tucking herself into a pocket of space between the straw and the wall. Her breathing crashed in her ears. It was so loud! She pressed a hand over her heart, begging it to slow down.

Nathan came into view. He squeezed his legs between the hay and the wall. Then he tried to sit down. "I can't fit," he whispered.

Together, they pushed the bales of hay forward a precious inch. Then Nathan sank down next to Rifka.

"Why didn't you want the farmers to see me?" she whispered.

"We don't know who we can trust," he whispered back. Then he put his fingers to his lips.

In silence, they waited. Rifka rested her head against the rough wooden wall, listening. Outside, the rumbling had become a roar. The tanks were coming closer.

They grew louder and louder, until the only sound in the world was the roaring of tanks tearing up earth as they rolled toward Kiev. Rifka shut her eyes. Mama and her brothers! What would happen to them?

At last, the roaring lessened. Now Rifka could hear other sounds: the tramp of footsteps and the mutterings of voices. More soldiers. She had to put her hand over her mouth so she didn't cry out in fear. Barely daring to breathe, she listened to the footsteps thundering past. There must be hundreds of men.

They went on without stopping, finally growing fainter. When all Rifka could hear were the animals shifting in their stalls, she turned to Nathan. He smiled at her.

"We're safe," he whispered. "We can keep going south without worrying about running into the Germans."

She smiled back. Just then, the squeal of unoiled hinges came to her ears. A sudden wash of light flooded the barn. Someone had opened the barn door!

She held herself still. Who was there?

A footstep sounded on the packed earthen floor of the barn. "Boy, where are you?" It was the old farmer.

Nathan stood up. "I'm here," he said. "Thank you for sheltering me."

"Get out from that corner," snapped the farmer. "I want a decent look at you."

Rifka sat frozen in place. What did the farmer want with Nathan?

Nathan lifted his chin. He stood tall and straight. Without a word, he edged his way around the hay, then vanished from Rifka's sight. She heard him walking across the barn toward the farmer.

"Call yourself a traveler, do you?" said the farmer. "You look more like a Jew to me. Why else would you hide from the German army?" He must not have expected a response from Nathan because he went on, "Give me all the money you have or I'll tell the Germans I have a Jew in my barn."

Rifka's heart beat faster. Nathan couldn't give the farmer money—they didn't have any! Would the farmer turn them over to the Germans?

"I don't have any money." Nathan's voice shook. "But I'll leave right now. I won't cause any trouble for your family."

"Leave?" The farmer sounded angry. "And why should you leave when all four of my sons are in the army fighting those accursed Germans and leaving me and my wife alone to tend to the farm? You're staying here."

"What do you mean?" Nathan asked.

"You'll do the chores we can't manage," the farmer said. "In return I won't shoot you or turn you over to the Germans. Come."

This was madness! The old man couldn't force Nathan to remain on the farm!

Rifka waited for Nathan to refuse or fight back. But he said nothing.

The barn door creaked. Rifka peeked over the top of the hay pile. Nathan and the farmer were leaving the barn. Sunlight from outside poured through the door's opening, showing Rifka the frightened expression on Nathan's face—and the rifle in the farmer's hand.

Rifka ducked down behind the hay again. No wonder Nathan hadn't fought back! What could they do now? How would they get away from here?

All day she remained in the barn. A few times the farmer and Nathan came in: once to milk the cow, and again to brush the horse. Often Rifka heard voices outside: the farmer ordering Nathan to feed the chickens, his wife telling Nathan to fetch water from the well, and Nathan replying, "Yes," and nothing else.

When night fell, she finally came out from behind the hay.

Her body ached everywhere from staying in one position for so long.

She didn't know what to do. How could she help Nathan escape? Should she sneak into the cottage and find him?

In the darkness, she crept to the cottage.

But she couldn't open the front door more than a hair's breadth. Something big, like a bureau, had been shoved against the door from the inside. Clearly, the farmer didn't want Nathan running away at night. If she or Nathan tried to move the bureau, it would make a racket and wake the farmer.

She turned away from the cottage. There had to be another way!

Her legs were shaking so badly it was hard to walk. She knew she had to eat and drink or she wouldn't be able to help Nathan or herself.

She drew a pail of water from the well and drank deeply. Afterward, she ate whatever she could find—a hard, small potato wrenched from the ground and kernels of chicken feed in the grass by the henhouse. When her stomach was satisfied, she went to the barn and slept inside on the ground.

The next day she had to wait a long time before she heard Nathan again. "Yes, Comrade," he said as he came into the barn.

Rifka counted one set of footsteps. Only Nathan was here! She sat up straighter behind the hay, wondering if she dared call out to him.

Nathan's head appeared over the stack of hay. "You have to get away from here," he whispered.

"Not without you," Rifka whispered back.

His face looked deadly serious. "You must. The farmer will never let me leave. All the time he or his wife watches me. He's outside the barn right this minute, feeding the chickens. I'll find a way to escape from him somehow, but I don't know how long it will take. It might be days or weeks. You could starve to death waiting for me."

"I can't go on without you! I can't—"

"You have to! The sooner you leave, the better your chance of survival. Don't argue," he went on, interrupting her protests. "You have to go on alone."

(22)

Oksana

ONE DAY SLIPPED into the next. In the mornings, Babulya changed the dressings on Oksana's shoulder. The damaged skin faded from red to pink to peach. Soon Oksana could lift her arm over her head without any pain. Babulya pronounced herself quite pleased.

Oksana had begun calling Valentina's grandmother *Babulya* in her head. She didn't think Babulya would mind. Sometimes, she wished Babulya was her real grandmother, for she braided Oksana's hair and cared for her injured shoulder, and when she laughed at Valentina's jokes she always smiled at Oksana, silently inviting her to laugh, too.

Every day, they ate breakfast in the communal kitchen. *Together*, Oksana marveled. And if she knocked over the salt or didn't finish her bowl of kasha, Babulya wasn't angry. Instead, she would tell her to fetch a dishcloth to wipe up the spilled salt or say sometimes she wasn't hungry early in the morning, either. Then she would give Oksana twenty-three kopecks to pay for her school lunch, and leave for work at Lebedev's Market, the grocery shop she managed.

After breakfast, Valentina and Oksana would walk three blocks to school.

They chattered the whole way. Oksana longed to have a sketchbook—a proper sketchbook with thin pages and no lines—and a set of colored pencils. Then she could draw in color for the first time in her life. Valentina said she wanted to construct a robot that could sew and take over Babulya's evening seamstress work.

Valentina also liked to tell Oksana scientific facts she'd learned from a library book she was reading, like how long it took your fingernails to grow from the bed of the nail to the tip (one month) or how many liters of blood your heart pumped every minute (five to seven).

During school, Oksana tried not to let her mind wander. Because then she would start wondering about her mother. Was she going to be all right? If she died, then Oksana would be alone, and there would be no one in the world who loved her.

The thoughts made her feel prickly and hot all over, as though she were about to be sick. She would stare at something in the classroom, imagining what it would look like if she drew it, sketching imaginary lines in her mind until the sick feeling in her stomach had finally gone away.

After school, she didn't worry about her mother because she was so busy. She and Valentina had one hour of free time before they had to help Babulya in the shop. They usually played in the schoolyard or in the park, then would trudge to Lebedev's Market.

The work at the shop was deadly dull. Lebedev's was set up like most of the shops Oksana had visited: First, customers selected an item they wanted, like a block of cheese, and stood in a line to have it weighed so they knew its price. Then they stood in another line to pay a cashier and get a receipt. Finally, they went to a third line to pick up their purchase.

Oksana and Valentina worked at the third counter, where the groceries were wrapped and given to waiting customers. No matter the time of afternoon, the shop was jammed, with lines winding up and down the aisles like snakes.

Oksana's hands moved clumsily as she wrapped food in brown paper and tied the bundles with string. She couldn't make herself move faster, especially since her thoughts were bursting with ideas of what she'd rather be doing, like sketching the customers or playing tag in the park or running alongside the canals lining the river.

"Maria Yakovlena always smacks me for being slow," Valentina whispered one afternoon to Oksana.

Maria Yakovlena was an elderly lady who worked at the shop. Babulya said she had been born without a sense of humor, and therefore they ought to pity her. Valentina refused to pity anyone who smacked her.

Now Oksana shrugged. She didn't understand why Valentina got so upset when Maria Yakovlena hit her. "She's a grown-up," she whispered back. "She's allowed to hit."

"No, she's not." Valentina looked startled.

"I'm still waiting for my bread," a lady complained.

Hastily, Oksana slipped a loaf of black bread into a sleeve of wax paper. She handed it to the lady with a smile.

The lady snatched the loaf. "You two aren't being paid to gossip."

Oksana ducked her head. "I beg your pardon—"

"No, we aren't," Valentina interrupted cheerfully. "Thank you for explaining our job to us."

The customer narrowed her eyes, but Valentina only continued to smile innocently at her. At last, the lady turned away and flounced out of the shop.

"Valentina, you mustn't talk like that!" Oksana whispered.

"Why not?" Grinning, Valentina pushed a bag full of canned vegetables across the counter at the next customer. "She couldn't prove I was being rude. For all she knew, I was agreeing with her."

Shaking her head, Oksana concentrated on wrapping her customer's order. Valentina was too bold!

Valentina poked her in the side. "Do you see the man by the bins of potatoes?" she whispered. "He's come here for the last three days in a row. Always at four o'clock. Watch him."

Oksana glanced at her section of counter. Empty. Maria Yakovlena was still weighing the next person's order.

She craned her neck to see the man at the front of the shop. He was an ordinary-looking fellow, in a shabby blue suit and a black hat. He stood at the bins of potatoes, peering at them as if looking for the perfect one.

"Maybe he likes potatoes," she whispered.

Valentina shook her head no. "He never buys anything. Watch."

Obediently, Oksana looked at the man again. His hand hovered over the potatoes. Finally, he picked up one, inspected it closely, then set it down as if dissatisfied. He left the shop, the bell on the door tinkling after he had gone.

Suddenly, a woman at the end of the line set her cans back on a shelf and hurried outside.

"The same thing happens every time he comes in," Valentina said in a low voice. "He picks up a potato, puts it back, and then a customer follows him out. The potato is a signal, I'm sure of it. He's telling whoever is watching him that it's safe for them to meet. I bet he's a criminal or a spy."

The words tumbled out of Valentina's mouth so fast Oksana could scarcely keep up. A criminal in Babulya's shop! What if the secret police found out—and somehow Babulya got in trouble?

Maria Yakovlena smacked Valentina's hand. "Lazy girls," she grumbled, handing them each a block of cheese. "You should have come to my station ages ago to take these."

Valentina glared at Maria Yakovlena. Without a word, she grabbed the cheese and wrapped it.

Meekly, Oksana took her cheese. She wished she could be stronger like Valentina. Glare at people who dared to hit her. Laugh and smile cheekily at annoyed customers.

But she could only be herself. Weak, cringing Oksana.

The girls worked quietly for the rest of their shift. After the final customer had left and they were sent to sweep the stockroom, Valentina seized Oksana's hand. "We should ask my grandmother if we can take an afternoon's leave from the shop. We can wait in the street and once that man comes outside, we should follow him!"

Oksana shrank back. "We mustn't! What if he *is* a criminal—or worse?"

Valentina laughed. "What could be worse than a criminal?

I'm going to do it," she added, and Oksana groaned because she knew that meant she would do it, too. There was no way she would let Valentina do something dangerous on her own.

Fortunately, when Valentina asked Babulya that night, Babulya said she couldn't spare them from the shop this week, so Oksana was granted a reprieve.

Babulya snapped on the radio. Even though they always listened to state-sponsored radio stations, Babulya said it was safer to listen in their apartment than in the communal parlor. "You don't want to react improperly to news reports when someone might be watching," she told the girls.

Oksana didn't mind. The apartment was cozy. Babulya set up her sewing machine on the table and worked for a few hours, hemming trousers and skirts, sewing pillowcases, and letting out seams on coats. Oksana and Valentina sat on the sofa or their shared bed to do their schoolwork. For a long time, the only sounds were the scratch of their pencils on paper, the whir of Babulya's sewing machine, and the flat voice of the man on the radio.

"Comrade Gorbachev will now address the nation," the announcer said.

Comrade Gorbachev was the general secretary of the Communist Party. He often talked to the nation, either on state television or on the radio, mostly about boring things. Oksana returned to her homework.

Then the words "Chernobyl" and "accident" leapt out at her.

She and Valentina sat up straight. Babulya took her foot off the sewing machine's pedal. Barely breathing, they listened.

Comrade Gorbachev said the area was rapidly being decontaminated and it posed no threat to citizens.

Valentina gasped. "Maybe we can go home soon! Papa will be healed, and we can return to Pripyat!"

Oksana's stomach twisted. She wouldn't go back there. Not ever. There was no reason, with Papa dead. No job waiting for him, no apartment for them. Nothing.

Babulya turned off the radio. "What are you working on, Khusha?" It was the first time she had used Oksana's nickname.

Oksana stared at her homework sheet. The numbers blurred before her eyes. "Geometry."

"Excellent." Babulya sat down on the bed between the girls. "You can teach it to me. I was hopeless in mathematics in school, I'm afraid."

"What about your sewing?" Oksana asked.

"That dress will still be here tomorrow." Babulya tapped Oksana's textbook. "Go on, then. Tell me how to find the angles of that triangle."

Somehow, explaining geometry to Babulya untied the knots in Oksana's stomach. And she almost brought herself to lean against Babulya. She couldn't quite manage it, though, so she settled for giving Babulya a smile instead.

■ ■ ■

Before bed, she locked herself in the bathroom. Then she took the zippered fabric pouch Babulya had made for her to hold her washing things off its shelf. Inside were her comb, toothpaste, toothbrush, and bar of soap.

And something else. Something she hadn't shown anyone, not even Valentina.

Sitting on the floor, she removed two envelopes from the

pouch. They were the letters her mother had written to her. In the first one, her mother had written how glad she was to know where Oksana was staying—Valentina's mother had telephoned the different hospitals in Minsk until she had learned where Oksana's mama was being treated, and she had told them Oksana's new address. *I'm relieved you're safely far away,* Mama had written.

Oksana opened the letter she had gotten last week. Although she had read it so many times that she had it memorized, she read it again.

I've been released from the hospital, it began. *As soon as I find a job and a place to live, I'll send for you. People say that a poisoned wind has swept across Minsk. The May bugs haven't come out, nor the maggots, which I'm told is a sign of radiation. It's a mercy that you didn't go up to the rooftop garden with me that morning! My doctor said my wearing a hat and being up there only a half hour probably saved me. Your father's parents were evacuated to Minsk, too, and stayed here in the hospital for a day before leaving to move in with Papa's brother. I don't want you living with them—we needn't get into why—so you must stay where you are a bit longer.*

That was all. No mention of how much her mother missed her. No questions about how Oksana was managing in Leningrad, or if Babulya was kind to her, or if she had enough to eat. Nothing.

Tears rolled down Oksana's cheeks, so fast and hot she couldn't stop them. Carefully, she carried the letters across the bathroom.

Then she ripped them into pieces and flushed them down the toilet, so she would never have to read them again.

(23)

Valentina

FRIDAY EVENINGS WERE the best part of the week. Babulya permitted them to watch a television program in the communal parlor.

The treat always began in the communal kitchen, which was full of women cooking and men reading newspapers like *Pravda* and *Izvestia*. Valentina and Oksana would unlock Babulya's cupboard and load their plates with bread, then go to the refrigerator and select some fruit and cheese from containers that bore the label GOLDMAN in Babulya's tidy handwriting.

On this final Friday night in May, the parlor was empty. Usually, other residents were there. Then they had to argue about what to watch. There wasn't much to choose from, of course, as only state-approved programs were shown, and so the arguments never lasted long. Most times, everyone would agree on a travel or nature program.

"*Film Travel Club*?" Oksana asked, naming their favorite show.

"Yes, please!"

Oksana snapped on the television. They settled themselves

on the sofa, their plates balanced on their legs, prepared to let *Film Travel Club* take them far away. The past two Fridays, they had gone to Australia's Outback and America's Grand Canyon.

This time, the destination was Brazil's rain forest. Before they even began eating, though, Valentina accidentally knocked over her glass. Water splashed across her skirt.

She sighed. "I'd better go upstairs and change. Tell me everything that happens while I'm gone!"

"I will," Oksana promised, her gaze glued to the screen.

Valentina raced up the stairwell to the sixth floor. She flung open the door to the apartment.

The room was dark except for the flames of two candles burning on the table. Her grandmother sat beside them, a silver cup halfway to her lips.

For an instant, Babulya was frozen in her chair. Then she rushed across the room and grabbed Valentina by the arm, dragging her inside. She shut the door behind them.

Her hand on Valentina's arm was shaking. "My God," she said in a low, urgent voice. "Did anyone see?"

Valentina shook her head. What was wrong? What could be so terrible about lighting candles in the dark?

"Thank goodness." Babulya dropped her arm. Watching her, all Valentina could think of was what her mother had told her years ago: Babulya did dangerous things.

Perhaps this was what Mama had meant, but Valentina had no idea what her grandmother was doing—or why she looked so frightened.

"Sit down, Valya," Babulya said. As Valentina waited, Babulya rinsed the silver cup in the sink, then returned to the table. She began polishing the cup with a cloth, keeping her eyes trained on her hands as she spoke. She didn't look frightened anymore, only calm. "You mustn't tell anyone what you saw me doing in here tonight," she said. "That's very important, Valentina. If anyone found out, I could get into terrible trouble."

"For drinking wine and lighting candles?" Valentina asked. That was ridiculous!

"For worshipping my faith," Babulya said. She set the cup in a box on the table.

Her faith? She must mean Judaism. But . . . that was forbidden. They weren't supposed to pray or attend religious services or celebrate holidays.

Valentina didn't want to hear more. She jumped up. "I should go downstairs. Oksana will be wondering where I am—"

"Sit down," Babulya said again. In the candlelight, she looked tired.

They both sat at the table. Babulya took Valentina's hands in hers.

It was the first time Babulya had touched her, other than to braid her hair, in the four whole weeks they had lived together. Babulya's skin felt warm and soft. Like Mama's.

Tears rose to Valentina's eyes. She mustn't cry. Not in front of Babulya, not in front of anyone. She had to be tough and make her parents proud.

"Before you and Oksana came to me," Babulya said, "on Friday nights I went to Grand Choral. Do you know what that is?"

"No."

"It's a synagogue downtown," Babulya said. "The largest

in the Soviet Union. You probably know that many synagogues and churches and mosques were closed or destroyed after the Communist revolution. Grand Choral still stands. It's fallen into terrible disrepair. Sometimes members of the secret police come to services. Anyone they see there, they might put under surveillance."

Surveillance! Valentina's heart beat fast. Babulya could get arrested! Babulya could disappear, like the people Mama and Papa had warned her about, those who refused to follow the rules or criticized the government. And Valentina could get in trouble, too, for staying with someone who had might have been targeted by the secret police.

"Why do you go?" she asked. "You ought to stay home!"

"That is precisely what I've been doing ever since you and Oksana arrived." Babulya's hands tightened on hers. "I promised your mother I wouldn't put you in danger, not while you're living with me. Every Friday night, instead of going to Grand Choral, I stay here. I let you girls watch television downstairs while I celebrate Shabbat alone."

Valentina hadn't heard the word before. "What's Shabbat?"

Babulya sighed. "So much has been lost in only a few generations," she murmured to herself. To Valentina, she said, "Shabbat is the holiest day of the week. It begins at sundown and is meant to be a day of rest and renewal."

She nodded at the twin flames. "We light candles to usher in the light and warmth of Shabbat. We drink wine and eat bread. We pray and sing and celebrate God." A shadow crossed her face. "At least, we used to."

Sighing, she released Valentina's hands and got to her feet.

She cupped her hands around the candles and blew softly. The flames died, leaving the room dark except for slivers of red sunlight around the edges of the curtains.

Babulya turned on a lamp. In the sudden brightness, Valentina's eyes were dazzled. Blinking, she watched Babulya place the candles and silver candlesticks beside the cup in the box.

"You mustn't tell anyone about what you saw me doing tonight," Babulya said again. "Not even Oksana. She's a kind girl, and I'm sure she's trustworthy, but I don't want to burden her with such a big secret.

"I wouldn't have chosen to burden you with such a big secret, either." Babulya closed the box's lid, then carried it to the wardrobe, where she stowed it on the bottom shelf, behind their shoes. "Now that you know, however, we both must be very careful. You mustn't mention it on the telephone with your mother, or in a letter. You never know who might be listening to your calls or reading your mail."

Valentina shivered. She knew her grandmother was right. Then why was she doing something that she knew could get her arrested? "Why don't you stop celebrating Shabbat?" she asked. "If it's so dangerous, why can't you be like me and Mama and Papa and forget about Judaism?"

Babulya opened the curtains, letting the light from the reddened sky fill the room. At last she looked at Valentina. "As long as I'm not free to worship how I choose, my heart and mind are in chains. And I have lost too many people to hatred already. I can't lose my own soul."

What was she talking about—losing people to hatred? Before Valentina could ask, her grandmother said gently, "That's enough. Your mother wouldn't want you to know more."

But Valentina had to ask: "Is this why we never saw each other until now?"

"Yes." Babulya's voice was quiet. "Your mother was afraid if we remained in contact and I was arrested, it would place all of you in danger. She hoped if we stayed apart, the police would leave the three of you alone. She wanted to keep you safe."

Valentina didn't understand. "Why didn't you stop attending that synagogue? Then we could have known each other."

Babulya looked down. "I offered to stop going. But your mother feared the damage might have already been done. That I might already have a file with the secret police. She said we had to end our relationship. She was right to do so. She had your well-being to consider."

Valentina didn't know what to think. Had Mama been wrong to cut Babulya out of their lives? Or had she done the only thing she could to keep them as safe as possible?

"What about the man in the shop?" she asked. "The one who handles the potatoes."

Her grandmother looked bewildered. "What do you mean, the man with the potatoes?"

So he, at least, had nothing to do with Babulya. "Never mind," Valentina said. "I made a mistake."

"Go on downstairs," Babulya said. "Oksana must be wondering what you're doing."

Valentina took off her damp skirt and hung it on a laundry line to dry. She slipped into a fresh skirt, nodded goodbye to her grandmother, and trudged down the stairs, her thoughts whirling. Why had Babulya chosen to worship in the first place, when she knew how hazardous it was? What had she meant when she'd said she'd lost too many people to hatred?

Oksana was running up the stairs toward her. "Valentina!" She waved a slip of paper. "The program is over, so I went to check our postbox. We forgot to look when we got home. This is for you," she added.

Valentina took the paper and saw it wasn't a paper at all, but an envelope, lined with a black border.

She knew what those ink lines meant.

Someone had died.

"No," she heard herself say. Suddenly her hands were shaking so hard she could barely rip open the envelope and take out the letter. She recognized the handwriting: it was from her mother.

My dearest Valya, she read,

I have terrible news. You must be brave.

Papa died yesterday.

A cry ripped from Valentina's throat.

"What's happened?" Oksana asked breathlessly. "Is it your father?"

But Valentina could only nod her head and keep reading.

I'm so sorry, my love. His poor body gave out on him before he was able to have the bone marrow transplant operation. I spoke to his doctor on the telephone, and I promise you that in the end, your father's death was a mercy. His pain is finally over.

He was buried in a Moscow cemetery with the nuclear workers and firemen who have already died. I wish I could be with you now, and I wish I had the money to telephone you instead of write a letter. The only thing that cheers me is knowing that you are my courageous, clever Valyushka and somehow we will be together again.

Your father was a hero. I want you to remember that always. After the explosion, he pulled pieces of the rubble off his colleagues, helping them to escape. He stayed when it would have been easier to run. He has been awarded Ukraine's Order of Courage in the Third Degree and the Soviet Union's Order of the Badge of Honor. When we are reunited, I will give them to you. In the meantime, stay strong, my Valya, and know that no matter what happens to us, I remain,

Your loving Mama

Valentina heard herself screaming, "No!" over and over, and then she felt herself sinking down onto the cold concrete steps. Papa was dead. *Dead.*

Oksana dropped down beside her. "I'm so sorry about your papa." Oksana hugged her, and Valentina hung on as tightly as she could and let the tears come.

Footsteps rushed down the stairs. "What's happened?" It was Babulya's voice.

Valentina couldn't say anything. Her whole body shook with sobs.

"Valya's father died," Oksana said.

There was a pause. Then Babulya said softly, "Oh, my poor, sweet child."

She sat down with Valentina and Oksana. Her arms came around them. Valentina rested her head in the curve of her grandmother's neck and stretched out her hand until she found Oksana's. Together the three of them sat on the stairs, touching without speaking. They stayed like that for a long time.

(24)

Rifka

RIFKA CROUCHED ON the outskirts of the woods and wondered if she dared to move. Overhead, warplanes flashed silver in the nighttime sky. German airplanes, she was sure of it. She had learned to recognize the deep drone of their engines.

In the week since she had left Nathan behind at the farm, she had learned many things. How to steal food from a farmer's fields on her own. How to walk all night until she thought her feet would fall off, without anyone there to encourage or help her. How to hide herself under bushes or a pile of leaves so she could sleep without fear of discovery.

But tonight . . . tonight was different.

Before, she'd always heard German airplanes in the distance. Now they were so close, the whine of their engines filling the air so completely that she could near nothing else. What were they doing up there? This was the countryside, not a big city, and it couldn't possibly be a target.

A high-pitched whistling sounded. Then another. And another, and then so many that she couldn't count them all. She looked up in time to see the sky was flooded with silver dots.

The dots were moving—they were hurtling down—

The ground exploded in front of her, sending up a shower of dirt and grass. She felt herself scream and fall backward, but she couldn't hear herself.

The fields beyond the woods came apart. More silver dots were racing down from the sky and shooting into the earth, throwing dirt and crops and grass into the air.

Bombs, Rifka thought. She had to move!

Somehow her arms managed to work, and she pushed herself off the ground. Her legs shook so badly, they almost folded underneath her. She grabbed a tree branch to steady herself.

The thin, pale whistling sounded again. More bombs.

She plunged into the woods. She moved so fast, the trees were a black blur. Deeper, she had to go deeper, someplace where the trees clustered thickly together and would take the brunt of the bombs.

All around her, the world was exploding. The earth heaved as if it were the surface of the sea, and somewhere, in a corner of her mind, she knew the force of the bombs was rippling through the ground and she was about to die.

She tripped over a tree root and went flying. She landed so hard she couldn't catch her breath. Quickly, she scrambled to her feet. A part of her brain registered a sharp, stinging sensation in her hands, but she took no notice of it and rushed forward. Deeper—she had to go deeper.

Through the web of interlocking tree branches, she glimpsed a glimmer of water.

Water! Was it the Dnieper River? She might be safe there. Surely the Germans wouldn't shoot at water, for they had nothing to gain, did they?

She dashed between the trees. A little farther and she would reach the edge of the woods, and then the water's edge.

She burst out of the woods. The ground was soft and marshy, and her boots sank a little. She tugged herself free from the muck and kept moving. Ahead, the water stretched out, as flat as a mirror. Dark shapes crossed its surface. She recognized their hulking outlines—the river was crowded with naval vessels.

These ships were the Germans' target. She had run directly to the most dangerous spot.

She stumbled backward, colliding hard with something. She cried out in fear.

A hand gripped hers, pulling her forward. No! She mustn't go toward the ships!

She tried to yank herself free, but the hand wouldn't let go. Still running, she looked at the person who was forcing her toward the water. It was a middle-aged man in the patched clothing of a peasant.

"Let go of me!" she screamed.

He paid no attention to her, only continuing to drag her closer to the water's edge. And then she realized shadows raced all around them: men and women and children, running toward the water with bundles in their arms.

She barely had time to wonder where everyone was going when the man pulled her onto a wooden dock that extended out over the water. She tightened her hold on his hand. She wouldn't fight him any longer. If the others were headed toward the water, they must have a plan to reach safety. She must do everything she could to stay with them.

Alongside the man, she dashed across the wooden boards.

The end of the dock was approaching. She saw no rowboats waiting for them on the water. The man must want them to jump.

Together they leapt into the darkness.

She hit the water, and the man's hand was wrenched from hers. The water was icy cold. At once, her skirts pulled her down, and she had to kick hard to keep her head above the surface.

People jumped off the dock, so many of them she couldn't begin to count them all. Beneath the whistling of the bombs, she heard children crying and screaming. But she couldn't see them clearly, nor the men and women swimming or sinking around her, for the night was dark except for the silver dots falling from the sky.

Her legs churned to keep herself afloat. Already her breath came in gasps. She couldn't tread water much longer. Her knapsack was so heavy her back ached, but she mustn't take it off. It held everything she owned in the world.

Across the water, the navy ships glided, swathed in darkness. None had turned on their lanterns or searchlights, she supposed so the warplanes couldn't see them. The Germans must be trying to destroy the Soviet navy, in hopes of defeating her country.

The man grabbed her shoulder. The sudden weight pushed her under. She sucked in a mouthful of water. Her legs kicked once, twice, then her head broke the surface. She spit out water, sputtering.

"Come!" the man shouted in her ear.

She couldn't have said why she trusted him, but she nodded. He began to swim toward the center of the river.

To her right, a bomb hit the water. Dimly, she heard people screaming, and then she felt underwater reverberations as the bomb burst. The force pushed her far to the left.

Gasping, she wiped water from her face so she could see. Where was the man? Before the bomb hit, he had been right in front of her . . .

There! Closer to the middle of the river now, and swimming steadily. She took a deep breath and followed.

Each stroke hurt. Her lungs burned. But she kept kicking and gliding, letting the current carry her. Behind her, she sensed other people were swimming.

The man had reached a vessel of some sort. It was low to the surface, not like the giant navy ships. As she swam after him, she saw him lift himself up, dripping, over its side and drop down inside it.

She was almost there. Her lungs felt as though they would explode. With a final burst of strength, she kicked hard. The tips of her fingers brushed the low ship's gunwale.

Hands hooked under her armpits and pulled her up, out of the water. She was dropped onto the ship's deck.

Coughing, she looked around. The deck was long and broad. Water lapped over the gunwales, splashing into the bottom of the boat. Crates had been stacked in some spots on the deck, with people sitting huddled around them.

It was a barge, she realized. A shipping barge. Back home, she had sometimes seen them floating down the river.

Would the Germans assume the barge was filled with civilians and try to avoid bombing it? But how could they deliberately miss the barge when it was surrounded by targets?

On her hands and knees, she crawled to the barge's side.

She should jump. She was safer in the river than up here.

She hesitated. Dozens of people were swimming toward the barge. They couldn't possibly all fit. Why did they want to come on here? What did they know that she didn't?

She crawled to a corner of the barge and curled herself up tight, hugging her knees to her chest, trying to make herself as small as possible. Cool night air scraped over her, making her soaked clothes feel even colder. She couldn't stop shivering.

Someone on all fours came over to her. It was the man. He had lost his cap, and water ran down his face and beard. "Are you all right?" he shouted.

She nodded. "Why did you help me?"

"You're a child, and you're alone," he shouted. "No child should be alone in a time of war."

A lump rose in her throat. This man, who didn't know her, had gotten her onto this barge simply because she had been alone. There were good people left in the world, people who cared for no reason other than they were decent.

Before she could thank him, he had crawled away to check on other passengers. She huddled in the corner, tears gathering in her eyes, praying she would survive the night and watching bombs fall out of the sky like stars.

(25)

Oksana

THE MORNING AFTER she learned her father had died, Valentina refused to get out of bed. Babulya let her miss school, for it was a Saturday and they only had classes in the morning. But the next morning, Valentina didn't want to get up, either. Nor the next day, or the day after.

"This isn't good for you," Babulya said, sitting on the edge of the girls' bed. "You must go on living, Valyushka. Your father would want you to."

Oksana said nothing as she changed into her school uniform. Staying home for four days in a row! She could scarcely believe Babulya was letting Valentina get away with that. Her papa would have whipped her for being so naughty. But Babulya hadn't done a thing except kiss Valentina's cheek.

"I can't go to school." Valentina's voice was clogged with tears. "Please don't make me."

Oksana tied her shoes with short, angry jerks. Valentina got away with everything! She lay in bed and cried and cried, as if she were the only person in the world whose father was dead. And Babulya kissed and coddled her, and let her do as she wished, while Oksana had to act perfect all the time so Babulya wouldn't throw her out. She was sick of it!

She turned around. Valentina was sitting up in bed, and Babulya had her arms around her. Of course. Because Valentina was safe and loved, and Oksana was not.

Where had that thought come from? Papa had loved her, hadn't he? She didn't understand what she was thinking or why tears were burning her eyes.

"You're spoiled!" Oksana burst out. "All you do is lie around in bed crying while the rest of us have to carry on!"

"What are you talking about?" Valentina looked surprised.

Head down, Oksana rushed to the door. She grabbed her satchel, which hung on a hook next to the mirror. Babulya had covered the mirror in black cloth, saying they needn't concern themselves with their appearances while they were in mourning. But Babulya hadn't done that for Oksana's father. No one had let her lie in bed and cry. Instead, her mother had gone into her bedroom and left Oksana alone in the parlor. All night.

Hot tears filled her eyes. She flung the door open and hurried along the corridor. Behind her, Babulya shouted, "Wait!" but she ignored her. She clattered down the stairs and across the front hall, ignoring the kitchen. She wouldn't have breakfast today. She'd rather go hungry than stay in this building for another minute.

Outside, the street was filled with grown-ups going to work and children walking to school. Quickly, Oksana fell in step behind a group of little boys and girls. Her heart beat fast. She was bad. And stupid and slow and weak.

Heat rushed into her face. She felt as though she were going to be sick.

The little kids in front of her turned into the schoolyard. For a moment, she looked at the two school buildings, the primary and the middle schools, joined by a shared playground. Children from her class were already playing in the yard, racing about in a game of tag or rolling marbles or standing about talking. She saw two of her friends, Yulia and Lyudmila. Her stomach roiled. She couldn't do it. She couldn't go in there and pretend she was fine.

She hurried away, following the streets wherever they took her. Finally, she stopped in front of a park. It was little more than a scrubby patch of grass and a few birch trees, but she could hide here for the day.

She settled herself under a tree. She had to figure out what to do next. Surely Babulya would throw her out, now that she'd been rude. She'd have to go to Minsk. Mama would be so happy to see her. With Papa gone, everything would be different. She and Mama would bake cakes together and cuddle on the sofa, telling each other about their day, and in the morning, her mother would braid her hair for school and say how proud she was of Oksana's excellent marks.

Oksana wiped at her eyes with the backs of her hands. She mustn't cry like this. She had to be perfect.

Intending to read through today's lesson, she slid her history textbook out of the satchel. But her hand lingered on her notebook. Did she dare to draw?

Mama would never see it, she told herself. That made her decision, and she tore a sheet out of the notebook. Then she began to sketch the trees in front of her. She had to get their shapes just right, and the roughness of the bark, and the way the leaves caught the light . . .

She frowned at her pencil. If only she had a set of paints! Or colored pencils. This would have to do. A true artist would use whatever was at hand.

For a long time, she was lost in her drawing. When she finally stopped, she realized she was stiff and hungry. She wished she had some pocket money, but she'd left this morning before Babulya had had a chance to give her twenty-three kopeks for her school lunch.

A man passed the park. He wore a shabby black suit and hat. It was the man from Babulya's shop, the one who handled the potatoes!

Oksana jumped to her feet. Valentina had said the man might be a criminal, but later she had said he could run a black-market business. What if Valentina was right and he was a black-market worker? Could he get Oksana a train ticket to Minsk?

She threw her things into her satchel, then rushed after the man. He had reached the corner and was looking around, as if searching for someone. Oksana's steps slowed. Maybe she should follow him and see what he was up to before she approached him.

A woman went up to the man. They talked for a moment, then the man slipped his hand into his coat pocket and gave her something.

Oksana squinted. It was a small box containing canisters of film for a camera. But the words printed on it weren't in Russian. She wasn't sure what language it was. The film was a foreign product. Valentina had been right—the man did sell things on the black market!

The woman tucked the box into her purse. Then she said something to the man and strode away. He walked off in the opposite direction.

Oksana had to do something. The man might be able to help her get a train ticket.

She rushed after him. When she caught up to him, she stepped in front of him, barring his way. He looked at her with hard eyes.

"What do you want?" he snapped.

"A train ticket to Minsk."

"Where do you think we are, a train station?" He laughed. "Little girl, go to school and stop wasting my time."

She raised her chin. "You work on the black market. I know you can help me."

Suddenly, he grabbed her arm. "Who are you?" he demanded. "What do you want?"

"A tr-train ticket to Minsk," she stuttered. His grip was like iron. She'd never be able to shake him off and run away. What had she done?

He stared down at her, then let go of her arm. "Even the secret police don't resort to using children," he muttered. Louder, he said, "I can't help you."

"Yes, you can." An idea came to her. "I could work for you and earn the money for a train ticket."

He laughed again. "Little girl, get out of here."

"No, I could do it," she insisted. "I've seen you at Lebedev's Market, and I followed you today from the park. But I bet you never saw me. Nobody notices children. I could deliver goods to your customers, and no one would pay attention to me."

Looking annoyed, he turned and began walking away. Her heart sank. He wouldn't help her. She would remain stuck here in Leningrad, without her mother.

"Please, don't go!" She raced after him, darting in front of him and forcing him to stop. He stared down at her with stony eyes. "My father died in the nuclear accident in Pripyat," she said in a rush, afraid he would walk away again. "My mother got radiation poisoning and had to go to a hospital in Minsk, and I didn't have anywhere else to go except here. I want to be with my mother."

Suddenly, she wanted her mother so badly she could barely breathe. Tears filled her eyes.

The man sighed. "You remind me of my niece." His voice was gentle. "She would never take no for an answer, either. She died several years ago."

Oksana swiped at her tears. "What happened to her?"

"Cancer. It's a hard death, and one no child deserves." He crouched down so they were eye to eye. "My work is dangerous," he said quietly. "It might seem easy, but it isn't. The lady you just saw with me is an office worker during the day and a photographer at night. She's a freelancer. You know what that is?"

Oksana nodded. Everybody knew about freelancers. Their work was frowned upon by the government, but lots of people did it anyway. Many citizens' paychecks only covered their basic needs, and to say "Let him live on his salary" was like putting a curse on someone. Therefore, many people freelanced to earn extra money. Even Babulya freelanced by sewing during the evening. Sometimes freelancing was the only way to afford everything you needed.

"My customer needed color film," the man continued. "Our Russian color film is terrible, so I got her some from East Germany. It sounds simple, but it isn't. I never know whom I can trust or if the police are after me. Do you truly want to do something dangerous?"

"I need to get to my mother," she said to the man. "I'll do whatever you need in exchange for a train ticket. I'll do a good job."

The man gave her a measuring glance. "You don't frighten easily. My niece didn't, either. What's your name?"

"Oksana Ilyinichna Savchenko."

"You may call me Comrade Orlov." He shook her hand, looking serious. "Meet me here tonight. Seven o'clock. I'll have a delivery for you to make."

"Yes, Comrade." Her heart thumped hard in her chest. She had done it. She was one step closer to seeing her mother!

He lit a cigarette. "Don't be late," he said, and walked away.

■ ■ ■

She spent the rest of the day in the park. She didn't go to the market after school, or to the apartment after the market, but by the time the streets were filled with grown-ups walking home she was so hungry she couldn't stand it anymore. She walked back to the apartment, wondering if Babulya would give her supper before throwing her out. She'd have to find a place to stay while earning a train ticket. But where?

Slowly, she climbed the stairs to the apartment. Outside the door, she took a deep breath. She could hear Babulya's and Valentina's voices within, but she couldn't make out what they were saying. They didn't sound angry.

She went inside. Babulya and Valentina were sitting at the table, their heads bent together. Babulya's sewing machine was still tucked away on a shelf, and Valentina's textbooks weren't strewn about, as they usually were at this time of day.

They saw her and froze. Then Babulya rushed across the room.

Oksana cringed, waiting for the smack that was surely coming.

Babulya hugged her. For an instant, Oksana held herself as stiff as a board. This couldn't be happening. She was dreaming.

But Babulya felt real, and warm and soft. It *was* happening. Oksana let herself melt against Babulya.

"My dear Khusha," Babulya said. "We've been so worried about you! I was about to call the police. Are you all right? Where have you been?"

"In the park. I'm sorry, I didn't mean to worry you." Oksana couldn't understand Babulya's reaction. "Why were you worried? I thought you'd be glad to be rid of me."

"Oh, my poor child," Babulya said, releasing Oksana. Holding her hand, she guided her onto the sofa. "How cruelly your parents must have treated you to make you feel so alone."

Oksana didn't understand what Babulya meant. She glanced at Valentina, who nodded solemnly. Oksana felt herself flush. "I'm fine," she muttered.

"You are better than fine," Babulya said, putting her arm across Oksana's shoulders. "You are wonderful and kind and creative and clever. You seem to think you're bad, and I have no doubt it was your father who made you think so. But you are *good*, Khusha."

Oksana didn't know what to think. She *was* bad. And weak and stupid. Papa had told her so, when he hit her. Afterward, he had always been sorry and said she was his angel. But she had known he was lying. The truth came out when he was angry, didn't it? When his tongue was unguarded and he said what he really thought?

But . . . he had been wrong about Jews. Babulya and Valentina were nothing like he had said. They were kind and smart and funny.

He had been wrong about them. Which meant he could have been wrong about other things.

Like her.

She let out a sob. Babulya cupped Oksana's face in her hands, forcing her to look up. She smiled at Oksana. "You are lovable," she said.

"Then you won't throw me out?" Oksana asked.

"Throw you out?" Babulya looked astonished. "My stars, what made you think such a thing? I adore having you and Valentina live with me. You girls have brought me so much happiness that sometimes I don't think I can fit all of it in my heart."

Oksana didn't know what to say. Inside, she felt soft and golden. Babulya cared for *her*. Babulya thought she was good.

The soft, golden feelings were too much. She didn't know what to do with them. She shrugged and looked away.

But Babulya seemed to understand, for she kissed the top of Oksana's head and said, "Why don't you girls do your schoolwork while I make supper? Valentina can show you what you missed in class today."

"I went because I wanted to see you," Valentina said.

Oksana smiled a litte. She would have to work quickly. In one hour, she had to sneak out and meet Comrade Orlov. But Babulya wasn't going to throw her out. She cared about her; she wanted her here.

And Mama loved her, too. Surely the only reason she hadn't sent for Oksana yet was because she couldn't afford a train ticket. She would be overjoyed when Oksana arrived in Minsk.

Yes, she was doing the right thing by working for Comrade Orlov, Oksana decided as she and Valentina opened their knapsacks and got out their textbooks. She was clever, despite what Papa had said.

Papa. Suddenly she couldn't breathe. He had said she was stupid, and she was smart. He had said she was weak, and she was strong. He had said she was bad, and she was good.

She hated him.

There was a ball deep in her belly, burning. It was so hot she still couldn't take a breath, and she heard herself let out a sharp cry. She felt Babulya's arms come around her, and heard Babulya's voice in her ear, saying, "You're safe, Khusha. You're with me."

"I hate him!" she cried.

"Yes," Babulya said, holding tightly to her. "You have every reason in the world to be angry."

She was. For what felt like the first time, she was. And the ball in her belly burned so hot all she could do was hold on to Babulya's arms and let out sobs that had screams in them.

|26|

Valentina

VALENTINA DIDN'T KNOW what to do. She had never seen anyone act like Oksana was—crying as though her heart had broken and clinging to Babulya as though she was afraid to let go.

"You are safe," Babulya said over and over. "You are good."

"I hate him," Oksana sobbed.

"Of course you do," Babulya said. "But someday you must let him go. Even in death, he is controlling you. Telling you what to think and how to feel. But *you* should be in charge of yourself. Nobody else. You form your own opinions. You think for yourself. Not him. Do you hear me, Khusha?"

Oksana lifted a tearstained face. "Yes," she whispered.

Valentina reached out and touched Oksana's hand. "You *are* good," she said fiercely, and she meant it.

Oksana smiled a little. She wriggled out of Babulya's arms and muttered something about washing her face and going for a walk. She slipped from the room.

"Let her go," Babulya said when Valentina tried to follow

her. "She has just made some big discoveries. She needs to be alone."

"All right," Valentina said, although she didn't want Oksana to be on her own.

Later, after Oksana had returned and they had gone to bed and Babulya's soft breathing told her she was asleep, she squeezed Oksana's hand. She had no idea what to say. She wished she had the perfect words to explain to Oksana that she was wonderful and her father had been a bully.

Since she didn't, she continued squeezing Oksana's hand. Oksana squeezed back. They fell asleep holding hands.

■ ■ ■

Days passed, and sometimes Valentina forgot her father was dead. When she woke in the morning and the final dregs of sleep hadn't yet fled; when she was lost in her schoolwork; or when she, Oksana, and the other girls chased one another during recess, she felt as light as the birds flying overhead. Then something would remind her—she would receive a five on an exam or hear a joke and think, *I must tell Papa*—and she would remember she couldn't tell him anything.

Then she couldn't breathe. She would have to look at the sky or the ceiling and count to ten, concentrating on filling her lungs and letting the air out. At first, she thought no one noticed, but one day she caught Oksana looking at her in the classroom when she was doing her breathing trick. Oksana smiled at her, and somehow Valentina was certain she understood, even though they never spoke of it.

She had so many memories of him she couldn't count

them all. Papa had been clever and merry and interested in how everything worked. When they had lived in the secret city in Siberia, they had ridden many times in a reindeer-pulled sleigh across the snow. Bundled in furs, she had leaned against her father and listened as he pointed out the constellations in the sky.

In Pripyat, they had gone hiking in the forests and filled their bags with cherries or wild roses. They had spent hours taking apart the toaster and putting it back together. During the past year, before he had left for his night shift, he had read Boris Zakhoder's stories to her; their favorite had been "The Hermit and the Rose," and he had read it to her again and again without tiring of it.

And now he was gone, and there would be no more hikes in the Pripyat forests, or bedtime stories, or experiments on household appliances. There was only her mother, and the letters she sent to Valentina from Kiev. Finally she had gotten a job. The pay wasn't much, she wrote to Valentina, and the position was a hospital orderly, hardly the teaching work she preferred. Even so, she had taken it. Eventually, she hoped to be assigned an apartment, so Valentina could come to Kiev and live with her. *Besides*, she wrote, *it's best if I begin working again soon. You understand why.*

Valentina did. Once a grown-up had spent more than three months without a job, the government would classify her as a parasite. Not elderly people, of course, or mothers with young children, although most of them worked. But if you were a healthy adult without a job, sooner or later the government would believe you were someone who lived off others' work.

They might begin a file on you. And the last thing you wanted, her parents had taught her, was to attract the government's attention.

Her mother's letters were full of strange news about Kiev. Its streets were nearly empty of children. Parks stood deserted, and only handfuls of students played in schoolyards. *It is like living among ghosts, to live in a city with so few children*, her mother wrote.

One weekend the lady with whom her mother stayed had gone to the countryside. There the chickens had black cockscombs, not red ones. *Because of the weather*, Valentina's mother had written, and Valentina knew what she meant. The weather—her mother always wrote that, instead of radiation, no doubt afraid the secret police might read her mail. Her mother was saying that radiation had turned the chickens' cockscombs from red to black. And her friend said farmers could no longer make cheese, and when milk spoiled it didn't go sour but instead curdled into white powder.

Valentina desperately hoped her mother would change her mind and move to Leningrad. She didn't want to live in Kiev, where the air was poisoned and where few children remained.

Plus, Kiev didn't have Babulya. Or Oksana.

And nowhere, anymore, had Papa.

■ ■ ■

The last day of school came. Babulya woke the girls early so she could curl their hair. She had pressed their uniforms the night before. Yesterday, they had bought bouquets of flowers for their teacher. It was customary to give teachers flowers on the first and last days of school. Much to Valentina's disappointment, Babulya had told the girls to use their pocket money to purchase the flowers.

"But Yekaterina Federovna has been our teacher for only a few weeks," she had protested. "Can't we draw her a picture instead?"

Babulya had been horrified. "Certainly not! She's your teacher, no matter for how long, and therefore she should get flowers."

Now Babulya fussed with their hair bows. "You girls look beautiful. Oksana, be sure to curtsy and speak clearly when you present your teacher with the flowers. You have such a lovely voice, it's a shame you tend to speak softly."

"Yes, Tetya Rita." Oksana smoothed her skirt over her knees. "Your stitches are always even. How did you learn to sew so well?"

"My mother taught me. She was a seamstress." Babulya handed each of the girls a bouquet. "Carry these carefully, girls. You'd better be off. It wouldn't do to be late on your last day."

They rushed out of the apartment. As usual, the lobby was filled with children leaving for school and grown-ups hurrying to work. Valentina and Oksana fell in with a group of younger kids. At the schoolyard, their friends Yulia and Lyudmila waved them over.

"Isn't it marvelous?" Yulia was bubbling with excitement. "Sixth grade at last!"

"And the summer holidays!" Lyudmila added. "My family's going to Latvia next month."

"I went to Latvia when I was little," Valentina said. "It was wonderful. There's a big beach and lots of theaters."

Lyudmila beamed. "What are you two doing this summer? Are you going home?"

Valentina and Oksana glanced at each other, then away. "I—I don't know," Valentina faltered. She and Oksana didn't talk about the future. It was too frightening to think about. Someday, when the poison had finally leached from the air, Oksana would be sent away to Minsk and Valentina to Kiev. But would that be the end of the nuclear accident's consequences? Or was the radiation still inside their bodies, eating them up from the inside? Would they die as their fathers had?

Valentina felt as though she were about to be sick. She let her mind go blank and the other girls' voices surround her. After a moment, she felt better.

"I hope you stay here forever," Yulia said.

"Me, too," Valentina said, and was surprised to realize she meant it. Maybe there was a way to convince Mama and Oksana's mother to move to Leningrad. Babulya might be able to find them jobs.

She told Oksana her idea when they lined up to go inside.

"I won't be allowed to stay," Oksana whispered as they filed into the school. "My mother won't want to move here just so I can stay friends with a . . ."

She broke off, a flush creeping across her face. Valentina knew what she had been about to say: . . . *so I can stay friends with a Jew.*

Deep down, she knew Oksana was right. Her plan wouldn't work. When it was time for them to leave Leningrad, they would have to stop being friends.

Fortunately, the summer holidays were too busy for

Valentina to fret for long. Every morning, she and Oksana played in the park or ran alongside the sun-dappled canals. In the afternoons, they helped Babulya in the market. Sometimes, in the evenings, Oksana went for a walk and Valentina worked at her new "job."

She had become a freelancer, like Babulya. One night in the communal kitchen, she had fixed one of the dials on the stove. The other residents had been impressed with her handiwork, and she had begun fixing their broken appliances for a small fee, which she gave to Babulya to help with household expenses. Old toasters, electric coffeepots, lamps—Valentina fixed anything. Last week she had even rewired one of the switches in the hallway.

On Friday nights, Babulya continued to send them to the communal parlor to watch television. Valentina wondered what precisely her grandmother did alone in the dark while they watched travel programs. She lit candles and drank wine, Valentina knew that much. But what else? And why did she risk her safety to do these things?

"Because my soul needs it," Babulya said when Valentina lingered in the room one Friday night after Oksana had gone downstairs. Valentina had told Oksana her belly ached and to go on without her.

She'd been feeling sad ever since she'd helped Babulya put tomatoes into the produce baskets at the market that afternoon. Babulya had said tomatoes were one of Leningrad's specialties, along with cucumbers in June, and blueberries and mushrooms in August. Tomatoes had been one of Valentina's father's favorite foods. Whenever she saw them, she thought of him—and thinking of him hurt.

"Run along," Babulya said. "You'll miss the start of your program."

Valentina played with the fringe on the blanket hanging over the end of the sofa. The last thing she wanted to do now was go downstairs and have to smile and act ordinary in front of whoever happened to be watching television. If only she could stay here, where she didn't have to put on a smile for anyone.

"Why do you celebrate Shabbat anyway?" She frowned at the fringe.

There was a pause. Then Babulya said, "Worshipping makes me feel close to my relatives who have died."

Valentina thought again of her father. Could going through the Shabbat rituals with Babulya help her feel nearer to him? "May I stay with you?" She saw the refusal in her grandmother's expression and hastened to add, "It might make me feel like Papa is here."

Babulya's face softened. "I can hardly refuse such a reason. Very well. You may join me tonight."

She took the box out of the wardrobe. Valentina watched as she removed the silver candlesticks and cup, setting them lovingly on the table.

Babulya lit the candles. In the glow of the flames, her face looked younger. She covered her eyes, then made circling motions with her hands. She said some words in a language that Valentina didn't know.

Then she lowered her hands. "Repeat after me," she said, and Valentina echoed the unfamiliar words, beginning with *Baruch atah Adonai.*

When she was done, Babulya smiled at her. "You have just welcomed the start of Shabbat."

Valentina smiled back.

They blessed and drank from the cup of wine ("Only a sip," Babulya said) and blessed a loaf of bread. Babulya ripped off a piece and tossed it into the courtyard ("Because we must always give something to God," she told Valentina). Then they pulled pieces from the loaf for themselves to eat.

Babulya taught Valentina the words to one of the prayers. "It's called *Shema Yisrael*. It's the centerpiece of our morning and evening prayer services," she explained. "It means that the Lord is our God and there is one God. My parents taught me to say it every night before I went to sleep. Many times when I feel sad or lonely or weak, I say the words to myself and I feel stronger."

Valentina decided to try it for herself. Once the rituals were done, she hurried downstairs to join Oksana in the parlor. Later, while they were watching a nature program with the Kozlov boys from down the hall, she thought of her father.

As always, she felt as though she were drowning. She said the first few words of the *Shema Yisrael* in her mind. She couldn't remember the rest.

The words soothed her. She wasn't sure if it was because they made her think of Babulya or because they reminded her that Papa's soul was out there, somewhere.

From that night on, Valentina joined her grandmother every Friday evening to welcome Shabbat. Oksana fixed plates of food in the communal kitchen while Valentina and Babulya lit candles in secret. Valentina loved saying the prayers with her grandmother. For the first time, she thought being Jewish wasn't terrible. She even found the courage to say so to Babulya.

"Terrible?" Babulya had stroked Valentina's hair, looking thoughtful. "I'm not surprised you used to feel that way. But I'm so glad our religion doesn't make you ashamed anymore."

"I'm not embarrassed." Valentina traced the carvings on one of the candlesticks. "Not exactly. But I hate the way some of my teachers and classmates treat me. They think I'm not good enough for them to teach me or play with me."

For a moment, Babulya didn't say anything. She continued stroking Valentina's hair, her touch soft. "I wish I could take this pain away from you," she said at last. "I wish I could tell you that someday when you become a grown-up, other people's opinions magically stop mattering to you. But I can't. What I can tell you is that none of this is your fault."

Valentina leaned against her grandmother. "I know," she said, as she had said to her parents many times in the past when they'd had the same talks. This time, though, she actually meant it.

■ ■ ■

Oksana knew what they did: Valentina had told her after the first time. She knew she could trust Oksana, who had only smiled and said, "It sounds nice."

When she confessed to Babulya that she had told Oksana, Babulya gathered the girls in their room. "We mustn't ever speak of it in public," she warned them, and they promised they wouldn't.

The month of June melted into July, bringing with it long nights of sunshine. Once when the sun still blazed at two in the morning, Babulya woke the girls and took them to Nikolaevsky Bridge, where they stood with a crowd who had gathered to watch the many bridges of the city open and close, all of them at different times. It was like watching Leningrad come apart and knit itself back together again and again. From then on, Oksana wanted to walk the bridges every night, but Babulya said it had been a special occasion and they needed their rest more than they needed to traipse around the city.

Valentina found it strange to sleep when the sun was shining. It didn't set until two or three in the morning, appearing again only a couple of hours later. The sky darkened to gray, never black. It was as though the whole city was so happy it didn't want to fall asleep, for fear of missing a single moment.

Oksana loved the long days, too. Babulya said she had never looked better. One night in August, she asked the same doctor who had treated Oksana's burned shoulder to come to their apartment. Many doctors made house calls, but not the kind who worked in hospitals, so Valentina had expected him to refuse. To her surprise, though, he stopped by one evening before his shift, when they were washing up from supper. He examined Oksana.

"Wonderful," he told Babulya. "You'd hardly know it's the same child. The burn's healed nicely. And if the scale in your bathroom is accurate, then she's gained nearly five kilograms in three months. She's at a healthy weight now. Has pink in her cheeks, too." Smiling, he ruffled Oksana's hair. "I wish all of my patients could recover as well as you have. I suppose your grandmother has told you the three things you must do to grow up to be a healthy adult?"

Valentina expected Oksana to say that Babulya wasn't her

grandmother, but Oksana only shook her head no.

"Eat, sleep, and play," the doctor said. "I suspect you weren't getting enough of any of those before, especially the third. No need to get up. I'll see myself out," he said to Babulya, who had started to rise from the sofa.

After he was gone, Babulya put away her sewing for the night and read to them from one of the books they had checked out from the public library. It was about a green-eyed girl who lived in the Ural Mountains and guarded vast underground riches. As Valentina curled under the blanket beside Oksana and the late-night sunshine slanted through the open window, she wished she could hold on to this moment forever. Everything felt so cozy, her and Oksana and Babulya together.

If only their mothers could join them.

(27)

Oksana

BY THE LAST week of August, Oksana felt that she had to tell Valentina about her black-market work or burst. One night after supper, she asked Valentina if she wanted to go on a walk.

"You can go, but be home by half past eight," Babulya said.

"Thank you!" they chorused, and hurried outside, into a street turned red and gold by the evening sunlight. Children played tag, dodging the occasional automobile, and grown-ups walked hand in hand, chatting as they headed home or to restaurants. A couple of cats slunk out of an alley, no doubt hoping for a handout. Down the street, a man had set up an ice cream cart, and little kids were flocking to him.

"Where do you want to go?" Valentina asked.

"Just follow me." Oksana was so excited she bounced with each step. Valentina would be so impressed when she told her about working for Comrade Orlov. And wait until she saw the money Oksana had hidden in her winter galoshes at the back of the wardrobe. Fifty rubles—enough for a fancy dress but not for a train ticket. Soon, though.

"Okay." Valentina fell in step beside her. "If you were a color, which one would you be?"

"I'd like to be green," Oksana decided. "Green like grass or the leaves on a tree."

"That's a perfect color for you," Valentina said. "It's pretty and calm and you can see lots and lots of it in nature and never tire of it."

Oksana's face warmed. That was the nicest thing anyone had ever said about her—that you couldn't tire of her company. "What about you?" she asked.

"Blue," Valentina said immediately. "Blue like the sky or the sea, so I could be many different shades and go on forever."

"We're both colors from nature," Oksana said.

Valentina grabbed her hand, swinging it lightly as they walked. "That's because we're so alike."

"Now it's my turn," Oksana said. "If you could pick your own name, what would it be?"

As they turned the corner, Valentina leaned closer to Oksana. "I'd be Rifka," she whispered. "That's what my mother wanted to name me. She couldn't, because it's a Jewish name. But if I could truly have any name I chose, then I'd want the one my mother wanted to give me. What about you?"

Oksana blinked. She had expected Valentina would pick something glamorous or mysterious-sounding, like Natalya. "I'd be Klavdiya," she said, feeling that her choice was inadequate compared to Valentina's. "Because it's pretty."

"It suits you." Valentina smiled. "Let's race to the corner."

"No." Oksana gripped Valentina's hand, holding her back. She had to do it now. "I have to tell you a secret." She took a deep breath. "I work for a black-market supplier."

Valentina's eyes went wide. She didn't say anything.

"I deliver goods to his clients," Oksana said. Was Valentina upset or excited? She couldn't tell by Valentina's shocked expression. More words tumbled out of Oksana's mouth, so fast she couldn't stop them. "He's the man from the market, the one who touches the potatoes. I've been working for him ever since that day I played truant and missed school. He's paid me fifty rubles so far. It isn't much, but I'm saving up for a ticket to Minsk. I don't really go for walks after supper. I make deliveries instead. Why won't you say anything?" she burst out as Valentina continued to stare at her. "I thought you'd want to join me."

"You're working for a *criminal*," Valentina said. "What you're doing is illegal. And . . ." Her expression clouded. "Why do you want a ticket to Minsk? Aren't you happy here?"

This wasn't going at all the way Oksana had expected. She looked around to see if any of the passersby were paying attention to them. Nobody spared them a glance. Good.

"I'm very happy here," Oksana said. "But I miss my mother. Do you want to come with me and make a delivery?"

"I—I don't know," Valentina faltered.

"Fine. I'll go by myself." Oksana swallowed her disappointment and hurried down the street.

Up ahead, Comrade Orlov lounged against a shop front, smoking a cigarette and looking bored. The bulge in his suit coat pocket must be the package he had for her.

For the first couple of weeks she had worked for him, they would transfer the package from his pocket to hers when she pretended to bump into him. Slowly, though, that had changed. First, he had begun by talking to her for a few minutes, saying it was a beautiful night or asking if she had seen the swans in the Summer Garden yet, for every newcomer to Leningrad ought to. Their conversations had grown, and she had found herself telling him about her drawings. He had told her that she shouldn't ever stop drawing, for she had been given a gift, and gifts ought to be treated with respect.

Now he smiled at her, as he always did, and ruffled her hair. "Have you been to the Peter and Paul Fortress yet?" he asked by way of greeting.

She shook her head no. She wanted to visit the citadel, but it was far off, in another part of the city, and she didn't want to spend her pocket money on a Metro ticket. Not when she was saving up to go to Minsk. "Babulya says it's beautiful."

"It is. I'll show you a photograph of it sometime, so you can sketch it." With one hand, he patted her cheek, and with the other he slipped a package into the pocket of her skirt. "The park," he said in a quieter voice. "Under the birch trees. And be careful."

She nodded and walked away. Along this street, then down another, zigzagging in case anyone was watching. She didn't look behind her, but she heard the footsteps of many people. Slow, unhurried footsteps—not the sound of someone following her.

When she reached the park, she walked toward the patch of birch trees. In the bright sunshine, she could see a man standing there, hands in his pockets. He must be the client.

Suddenly, a car screeched to a stop in the street behind her. Four men rushed past her. The client standing in the birch trees turned and ran.

"Stop him!" the men shouted at one another.

Oksana jerked to a halt. Her heart pounded. Those men might belong to the KGB—the secret police.

The client raced across the grass, but he was no match for the men following him. One of them threw himself at the client, knocking him to his knees. Then all of the men were on him, scuffling and swearing. Finally, they hauled him to his feet.

Footsteps whispered in the grass behind Oksana. She whirled around. It was Valentina. Her face was pale, and she was breathing hard.

"Quick," she said. "Pick some wildflowers."

Oksana stared at her.

"Pick wildflowers," Valentina insisted. "Then the police will think we're just two ordinary girls playing in the park and picking flowers."

Of course! Valentina was so clever.

Oksana knelt in the grass. Her hands shook as she plucked a red flower. She kept her head down as the men marched past, but she couldn't resist one peek once they had gone by. The men had surrounded the client and were quick-stepping him to the street. They pushed him inside the car, got in themselves, and roared off.

Oksana and Valentina looked at each other. Oksana let out an unsteady breath. "Thank you," she said. A thought occurred to her. "Did you follow me all the way here?"

Valentina nodded. "I couldn't let you do something dangerous by yourself."

Suddenly, Oksana wanted to cry. "Thanks," she said. She wished she had the proper words to let Valentina know how much she appreciated her kindness.

"Should we see what's in the package?" Valentina asked.

Oksana glanced around the park. A couple of teenagers stood together, talking and laughing, and an old couple walked hand in hand. She and Valentina were safe.

She slipped the package from her skirt pocket. It was the shape of a rectangle and wrapped in brown paper. She ripped the paper. Inside lay a passport. A foreign passport, it had to be, for she'd never seen anything like it. This one had a blue cover and letters stamped in gold.

Quickly, she flipped the booklet open. A photograph stared up at her, of a man with dark hair and brown eyes. It was the man the police had just arrested.

Valentina gasped. "Look at the words—they're in English. I think one of them says *America*."

America! Oksana's heart raced. She closed the booklet and looked at Valentina. There was only one reason she could think of for a black-market supplier to deliver an American passport to a client. But it couldn't be . . .

"Maybe the man really is an American citizen," she said.

"Then why would he need to get a passport from your boss?" Valentina's voice sounded shaky. "He must be a Soviet." Deep down, Oksana knew Valentina had to be right. "A defector," she whispered.

Oksana had heard the word many times, but she had never spoken it aloud before. To be a defector was to be a traitor, because it meant you were pledging your loyalty to another country. You had escaped the Soviet Union and planned to live somewhere else forever. Comrade Orlov's client must have ordered an American passport because he wanted to become an American. Somehow, the police had found out.

Hastily, Oksana wrapped the brown paper around the passport again. Together, she and Valentina left the park.

"You can't work for your boss anymore," Valentina said when they reached the street. "It's too dangerous."

Oksana took a deep breath. Valentina was right: the work was dangerous. Supplying clients with foreign products was a minor crime; helping people defect to other countries was treason. But . . . she needed to be with Mama again. So that they could be a real family.

"I can't stop," she said.

"You could get arrested!" Valentina said in a horrified whisper.

"I won't," Oksana promised. "The police didn't even look at us. I'm too young for them to suspect me. And now I know how to act if a client gets picked up."

"You're being stupid!" Valentina rushed into their apartment building, leaving Oksana behind on the pavement.

Oksana hesitated. Was she being stupid? Reckless, probably. But being reunited with Mama was worth the risk, wasn't it?

Sometimes, in her dreams, she showed up unannounced at Mama's apartment. And Mama would hug her and exclaim, "My darling Khusha! How I've longed to see you again!" It would be just the two of them in a new apartment. No Papa to hit her. No Papa to become angry or disappointed. Nobody to hide from. Only her and Mama, and at last Mama would treat her the way she had always hoped for, because Papa wasn't there anymore.

The risk *had* to be worth it. Slowly, she sat down on the

building's front steps. She ignored the children playing on the pavement, and the classical music pouring through someone's open window, and the smell of linden trees and river water.

She let herself remember the last time she had seen her father. It was the night of the explosion, before he had left for his shift. They had eaten supper together.

"We're running a safety drill tonight," Papa said.

"Who will be there?" Mama ladled lentil stew into bowls while Oksana set out the silverware.

"Comrade Dyatlov is in charge." Papa took his bowl, but he didn't begin eating. He leaned back in his chair, taking a long drag on his cigarette. "The rest are men from my shift, including that Jew Kaplan. He got the promotion that should have been mine," he said for the hundredth time.

Oksana was listening with only half of her brain. She was wondering how artists could paint waves so that the water looked as though it was moving.

"His daughter's in your class," Papa said to Oksana, waving his cigarette for emphasis. "I bet she's as dirty and sneaky as he is."

It was like a sort of magic, to capture movement on a piece of paper, Oksana thought. "Oh, she's not so bad," she said absently.

The room hushed. Instantly, Oksana realized her mistake. Her father stared at her. "I can't believe a daughter of mine would say such a thing!"

"I'm sorry! I didn't mean it!" Oksana looked to her mother for help, but Mama sat stiff and silent, her eyes trained on the kitchen table.

Oksana turned to her father. "Papa, I'm sorry! Valentina's awful! She's a cheat like her father!"

Papa's face had turned dark. She knew that look—he was going to belt her.

She closed her eyes and hugged her arms to her chest, waiting. She didn't move. She knew from experience that trying to run away only made him angrier.

She listened for the whisper of his leather belt easing out of his trouser loops. He always did this part slowly.

But she only heard the creak of his chair as he stood up. Suddenly, he yanked down the sleeve of her school blouse, exposing the bare skin of her shoulder.

Something pressed into her skin—red-hot, burning—and she started screaming, even though she knew he hated for her to react. Her eyes flew open. The back of her shoulder was on fire. She could smell singed flesh. Frantically, she pushed his hands away.

He threw his cigarette onto the linoleum and ground it out with the heel of his shoe. "That'll teach you to talk back," he said calmly.

She fell to the floor, clutching her shoulder and sobbing. Her skin felt hot and bumpy. "Please, please," she said, but she didn't know what she was asking for.

He sat down at the table. Oksana's mother hadn't moved from her chair. Her eyes were shiny with tears. She didn't say anything.

Oksana pressed her forehead to the floor. She gritted her teeth, but she couldn't stop whimpering. Her shoulder had turned to flame.

From across the room, she heard the clink of silverware. Her father was eating his soup.

She lay on the floor, crying, hoping her mother would come to her. *Please*, she begged silently, wishing her mama could magically hear her words.

But her mother stayed at the table, talking quietly with Papa. As Oksana lay there, she thought of Valentina. It was all her fault. If it wasn't for Valentina, Papa wouldn't have hurt her. She'd do something at school tomorrow to get back at Valentina. She'd challenge her to a footrace. And then she'd win, and she'd tell Papa and he'd be happy with her.

Now Oksana pulled her mind back to the present. She was shaking.

She wrapped her arms around her knees, hugging them to her chest. She was in Leningrad, thousands of kilometers from where her father lay buried in the nuclear reactor. He was gone, and she was alive, and he couldn't hurt her anymore.

She had a best friend, a true best friend who asked her the most wonderful questions and did dangerous things with her so she wouldn't be alone. She had an almost-grandmother who loved her. And she was smart and brave. It didn't matter if her father hadn't thought so. She *knew* she was.

The knots in her stomach loosened. She let out a deep breath and went inside.

In the apartment, Valentina was messing about with some junk she'd found in the rubbish bins in the courtyard behind their building. So far she'd assembled a ceramic teapot missing a handle, a coil of wire, several bootlaces, two cracked glass jars, and a leather glove. They lay on the floor, and she stood over them, frowning. "I can't possibly make a robot with this," she was saying to Babulya when Oksana came in.

Babulya had set aside her sewing and was reading a letter. "All inventors probably say 'I can't' at the start of their work," she said. She looked up and smiled at Oksana. "Did you find something to sketch? Valyushka said you'd stayed outside to look for inspiration," she explained when Oksana didn't say anything.

"Oh. Yes. I did." Oksana moved over to Valentina. Was Valya mad about her decision to keep working for Comrade Orlov?

To her relief, Valentina flashed her a smile. "Pitiful, isn't it?" she asked, nodding at the odds and ends on the floor. "I don't know how I'll ever be able to test my ideas without the proper supplies. And I'll never be able to afford what I need."

"You do earn pocket money by working at the shop," Babulya reminded her.

"I know." Valentina collapsed dramatically on the sofa. "But I need *riches* to fund my inventions. I need to find a wealthy investor."

"While you're doing that, you may pick up your things," Babulya said as she read her letter. "And please put them on the balcony. That glove smells like garbage."

"Well, that *is* where I found it," Valentina said cheerfully.

"Who's the letter from?" Oksana asked. In the four months she had lived with Babulya, she had never known her to receive a letter before.

"A very dear, very old friend." Smiling, Babulya tucked the envelope into her apron pocket—but not before Oksana glimpsed it. The sender had drawn a bird in black ink on it, and it was postmarked Uzbekistan.

Together, the girls moved Valentina's junk onto the balcony. In the courtyard below, a couple of cats yowled.

"I didn't know your grandmother has friends in Uzbekistan," Oksana said to Valentina.

Valentina shrugged. "I guess she does. I wonder what the drawing of the bird meant."

After Valentina had gone inside, Oksana rested her cheek on the balcony railing. It had to be nearly nine o'clock, but the sky was still blue and flooded with clouds.

It had hurt to think of her father, but there had been good times with him, too. On summer holidays, they had gone to the village where her parents had grown up, and drunk juice from birch and maple trees and picked mushrooms and sorrel. Papa taught her to gather stinging nettle and goosefoot. They always celebrated Ivan Kupala, the night of the summer solstice. They searched for ferns, for it was said that ferns grew in places where the earth's treasure was buried. Her father had leapt over a bonfire with her in his arms, when she had been too frightened to jump on her own.

She didn't understand how he could have been both wonderful and terrible. Why couldn't he have been one or the other? Then she would have been able to love or hate him.

Instead, she felt stuck.

|28|

Rifka

ALL NIGHT THE barge floated down the river. Rifka huddled beside some crates, shivering in her wet clothes. Eventually, the bombs stopped falling. The sky became black again. Maybe the warplanes had run low on fuel and had to fly back to Germany. Or maybe they had set up an airfield in her own country. She didn't know.

Some passengers talked in whispers. The only other sound came from the splash of water against the sides of the barge. Rifka looked back. She couldn't see the shadows of the navy ships anymore. Had they been sunk? Or had they stopped, for some reason?

She should have stayed in the woods. Then she would have been able to walk home to Kiev. She wanted her mother so badly her chest ached. She didn't care what would happen to her if she went home; she could survive anything, as long as she was with her family. But now, alone, and not even knowing where she was . . . She pressed her fingers to her eyes, forcing the tears away. She'd go home. As soon as the barge docked. She'd find a way back.

"Only if you wish to die," said the man who'd pulled her into the water, when she told him her plans. "The Germans have surrounded Kiev. They may have already captured it. That's why we were running." He waved a hand to indicate the other people sitting on the barge.

"Why do you want to escape the Germans?" Rifka asked. The man had blond hair and blue eyes—surely he was a Ukrainian, not a Jew, and had nothing to fear from the German army.

The man sighed. "When they reached my village, they burned many of the farms. They shot some of my neighbors. Those of us who were left ran to the woods to hide from them. One of us had heard there might be a barge coming down the river, and so we ran to the water, hoping to board the barge and get away from here."

Rifka looked around. Even in the darkness, she could tell there couldn't be more than fifty people sitting on the deck. "What about the people who were left behind?"

"I don't know," he said softly. "Some probably drowned. Others may have been killed by a bomb. I hope many made it back to shore."

She shuddered. All those people, women and babies and children and men, dying in the dark. "I hope they all swam to shore, too," she said fervently.

The man fell silent. After a while, Rifka decided to try to sleep. She curled herself into a ball, holding her satchel tightly. If she could find a way to return to Kiev, should she go?

Then she thought of the last time she'd seen her mother. Mama had said she was sending her away because she loved her so much.

Because she wanted to give Rifka a chance to survive.

The thought tightened Rifka's chest. Did that mean her mother and brothers might die after the Germans conquered their city? Surely the Germans wouldn't kill a woman and her babies.

She stared up at the night sky. It looked like a pool of black ink. It was the same sky Mama and her brothers saw from their apartment; the same sky Papa saw from the battlefield.

She could still feel close to them, even if she was far away. And she would say the prayers her father used to say to her every night, when he tucked her into bed. She would pray, and she wouldn't forget who she was, and she would escape, for her family's sake.

Closing her eyes, she felt tears seeping out from under closed lids. She didn't think she'd fall asleep, but eventually she felt her body relaxing and her mind drifting off.

The next thing she knew, someone was jostling her shoulder and saying, "Wake up, child."

Her eyes flew open. An old woman was leaning over her. "Come," the old woman said. "The barge has docked. It won't be traveling any farther."

Hastily, Rifka scrambled to her feet. While she had slept, her clothes had dried, but her woolen coat and layers of heavy skirts felt stiff and smelled of river water. Her trousers, which she wore under the skirts, itched her legs.

But she was alive. And the sky, which was wide and gray, was filled with clouds, not airplanes, and the air smelled of hay and grass, not smoke or burning wood. She didn't know where she was, but it hardly mattered—the Germans weren't here.

"Come along," the old woman said. "We must move quickly."

We? Rifka saw some of the barge's passengers stood on the grassy bank, waiting for her and the old woman. She had thought she would have to go on alone.

The man who had helped her last night beckoned to her. "Hurry!" he called. "We want to find a route well before nightfall."

And that was how Rifka found herself part of a group of Ukrainians—Ukrainians, who she had always thought hated Jews!—and how she and her new friends began to make their way southeast, away from the Germans. Even though the Ukrainians were kind to her, when they asked her name, she said Yelena, and she prayed only in her mind, so no one would hear the Hebrew words.

Sometimes Rifka and her companions hitched rides on hay carts, from farmers who were traveling to market. Most days, though, they walked. The dirt roads took them farther and farther away from Ukraine, and Rifka saw the land change from the flat steppes she knew so well to hardened, dusty plains. No trains were running. They had all been bombed or recommissioned by the Germans, Rifka was told.

There were days when she was so hungry she could think of nothing but food. Other days, she was so tired each step was agony. Her face was chapped from the wind, and her skin itched everywhere from wearing the same dirty clothes all the time. Her blisters burst and filled her boots with blood. Eventually, her boots fell apart, and she had to rip pieces of fabric from the hems of her skirts, to wind around her feet and pray they kept her safe from frostbite.

So far, it had not snowed. The sky had turned the color of pewter, and the temperature had dropped to about forty degrees, but nothing had fallen from the clouds except rain. Surely, though, the first snowfall was coming, for they had been on the road for weeks. Then what would they do? How would they survive?

"You mustn't ask yourself those questions," said the old woman when Rifka asked her. "You're only borrowing trouble."

"All right." Rifka shivered in the cold. It was night, and the group was preparing to lie down in a field and sleep. Some of the grown-ups were draping their coats over their children, while others were resting their heads on their satchels, which they used as pillows.

She lay on the ground, cushioning her head on her knapsack. It was time for her to say her nightly prayers in her head. First, she asked God to keep her like Sarah, Rachel, Rifka, and Leah, the mothers of her religion. Her chest felt warm when she reached her namesake, Rifka. This was the prayer her father used to say at bedtime. He would place his hand on her head and say the words in his deep voice. She used to feel so special.

Slowly, she felt herself drifting off. The next thing she knew, hands had seized her shoulders and she was being yanked to her feet.

"She's speaking Hebrew!" shouted a man's voice. "She's a Jew!"

Oh God, what was happening? Eyes blinked at her in the darkness. The others were waking up—they would hear the man!

Panic swamped her chest. "I'm not a Jew! I wasn't speaking in Hebrew; I was asleep."

"She was talking in her sleep," said the man to the others.

"Muttering about wanting Adonai to protect her. Adonai is the name of the Jewish God. She's a Jew!"

One of the women—Rifka couldn't see who it was in the darkness—stood up. "You never told us why you were alone in the woods, when we found you," she said slowly. "Or why you had to leave Kiev. Those were mostly Jews escaping Kiev, that's what I heard."

"Leave us," said a man. "You're on your own now."

"No! Please!" Rifka gasped. "I'll die out here if I'm by myself."

"Go," said the man gripping her shoulders, and he pushed her forward so hard she nearly fell. He marched her toward the road as she tried to appeal to the others.

"You've known me for three months," she cried. "We've become friends! Don't turn me out, please!"

They looked away from her. She called out to Anatoly, the man who had helped her onto the barge, but he only hung his head, not meeting her eyes.

"Please!" she shouted, even though she already knew it was useless. "I'll die out there!"

The man holding her dragged her onto the dirt road. Then he released her. Another man shoved her satchel into her arms. "Go now, and count yourself lucky this is all we're doing to you."

She understood what he meant: she was lucky they hadn't beaten or killed her.

Clutching the satchel, she began to run. She didn't know which direction she went, east or west, only that it was away. She ran until the strips of fabric around her feet came loose. Her breath hitched in her chest. She looked around. There was nothing in sight except a dirt road and fields. No buildings, no people.

She would die out here on her own once the snows came.

Her religion had destroyed her life. It had convinced her mother to send her from Kiev. It had been the reason the Ukrainian farmer had taken Nathan. And now it was the reason she was alone.

She began walking. She would never worship again. God had left her in the wilderness to die—why should she praise Him?

She walked until she could walk no longer, and then she slept until the sun was high in the sky. The thermos in her satchel was half-full of water, and she had a piece of bread, but those would run out soon. Then what would she do?

Trying to conserve her supplies, she ate only a mouthful of bread and drank a sip of water. Her head felt so light, as though it might fly away.

She got to her feet and kept walking. She didn't know why she was trying to live. She ought to lie down and give up.

Something inside her, though, wouldn't let her. She plodded along. The way the sun moved across the sky told her that she was heading southeast, away from the fighting.

For three days, she survived on the water and bread. When she had nothing left, she walked for another day. Sometimes, she saw cottages in the distance. She didn't dare go to them and ask for help. The people here probably hated Jews, too. And it wouldn't matter that she didn't worship anymore. They would say her Jewishness was in her blood and bones.

On the fourth afternoon, snow began to fall. The ground turned white, and her feet grew wet and cold. She had to clamp her jaw to keep her teeth from chattering. Every part of her cried out for her mother.

She didn't want to live anymore. She couldn't go on like this. Life was too hard. And lonely.

She sank to her knees. The snow was so cold. Gritting her teeth, she lay down. She closed her eyes. Snowflakes fell on her face.

Oh God, oh God, she thought over and over. She didn't know why she was calling out to God now, but she couldn't help it.

Gradually, she became warm. The snow was a blanket, cocooning her. She felt herself floating up into the sky.

Dimly, she heard the tramp of footsteps in snow. Someone touched her arm. She wanted to open her eyes and look at the person, but her lids felt too heavy.

"Ona, she's alive!" called a girl's voice in Russian.

"Quickly, help me carry her inside." It was a woman's voice.

Hands hooked under Rifka's armpits and legs. She felt herself being lifted into the air. She couldn't bear it. She had to see what was happening to her.

With her little remaining strength, she opened her eyes.

A girl was holding her legs and struggling forward in the snow. Someone else was holding Rifka's armpits—she couldn't tilt her head back to see who it was.

The girl looked worried. "Good, you're awake," she said. "We're almost home."

Rifka had never seen anyone before who looked like this girl. Her black hair was gathered into dozens of tiny braids that rained down her back. She wore a tight-fitting cap that was embroidered with colorful designs. Her skin was tawny beige.

"Don't fall asleep," the girl said urgently. "Or you might not wake up."

Rifka's eyelids shut. It hurt too much to keep them open.

"Don't fall asleep!" the girl shouted.

"I won't," Rifka tried to say. The words, though, stuck in her throat, and she sank into a welcome blackness.

1291

Valentina

SEPTEMBER FIRST WAS the start of sixth grade. Before the bell rang, Valentina and Oksana waited in the yard with their friends Lyudmila and Yulia. Valentina could scarcely wait to go inside: this year they were supposed to begin algebra.

"Sixth grade at last!" Yulia exclaimed. "Next year we'll finally be the oldest in the middle school."

"Yes, and the boys will be as hopeless as ever." Lyudmila sighed.

"Ugh. Who cares about them?" Valentina rolled her eyes.

"They aren't so bad," Yulia said.

The girls stared at her. Yulia blushed. "Why are you all looking at me?" she asked, and Valentina and Lyudmila burst into laughter. Oksana looked away.

Later, when they were lining up to go inside, Valentina whispered to Oksana, "Are you all right? You looked upset when we were talking about boys."

A flush crept up Oksana's neck. "I don't like being around boys. They're so rough on the playground."

Now that Valentina thought about it, she'd never seen

Oksana playing with boys. She cringed when boys raced past on the play yard or in the communal kitchen. She shrank, too, when she and Valentina bumped into one of the men from their apartment building in the stairwell. Valentina had thought Oksana was shy, but she didn't act that way with girls. Valentina thought of how Oksana's burned shoulder had looked, and she squeezed Oksana's hand. "I won't play with any boys if you don't want to."

One of the boys in their class turned around. He pretended to pick his nose and flicked the imaginary snot at them.

Valentina made a gagging sound. "Besides, why would I want to?"

This time, Oksana laughed.

Their new teacher picked up right where their fifth-grade teacher had left off. They were expected to study the periodic table in chemistry, memorize portions of Pushkin's poems in literature, and learn about the Great Patriotic War in history.

The best part, though, was listening to the teacher talk about the statue of Peter the Great, which was called the Bronze Horseman. Valentina remembered seeing it with Oksana in Decembrists' Square on May Day, when Babulya had let them wander the city.

"The statue," the teacher said, "is now on top of a granite boulder known as Thunder Stone. The story behind this boulder is fascinating. Many years after Peter died, Catherine the Great decided to have a statue erected in his honor. For the pedestal, she wanted to use a boulder from Lakhta. This was located over two hundred kilometers away, off the Gulf of Finland. According to legend, the boulder had been hit by lightning. In order to use it, however, engineers had to transport it to the city. Your task is to write an essay explaining how you would have sent the boulder to Leningrad. Remember, no cheating and finding out how the engineers truly did it!"

That night, Valentina and Oksana spent hours drawing diagrams, trying to figure out how it could have been done. Valentina came up with a complicated pulley-and-lever system, while Oksana decided the stone should be rolled to the sea, then set on a ship's deck and sailed to Leningrad.

The next day at school they found out what had truly happened: a road was cut through the forest to the stone, which was then lifted with levers onto a log platform. It took about five months to pull the stone nine kilometers to the sea, where it was placed on a raft and towed to the place that would eventually become Decembrists' Square.

"Brilliant," Valentina told Oksana. They spent that evening drawing the platform and the raft, debating how many levers had been used and how wide the raft had been.

On their way to recess the following day, their teacher drew them aside. She held their assignments in her hand. "Valentina, have you considered becoming an engineer?" she asked.

Valentina nodded. "Yes, or an inventor. I've always wanted to build things."

"And how about you, Oksana?" the teacher asked. "Your drawings are very good."

Oksana turned red. "I want to be an artist," she said softly.

"You're both talented," their teacher said. "Everyone else turned in essays. You were the only ones who gave me diagrams and schematics. I'm afraid I had to give you threes because the assignment was to write an essay and you didn't follow the directions. But don't be discouraged. I've never seen such clever responses to this assignment in my twenty years of teaching. Well done."

She patted their shoulders before sending them out to the schoolyard, where Valentina said to Oksana, "I didn't know you want to be an artist."

Oksana looked down. "It isn't a proper career," she said softly. "My drawings are stupid anyway."

"Drawings can't be stupid," Valentina objected. "And if yours are half as good as your drawings of Thunder Stone, they must be marvelous. Will you show them to me? Please?"

Oksana smiled a little. "Okay." That night, Oksana spread her drawings across the floor of their apartment. They were pencil sketches of people or familiar sights from Leningrad: the massive Palace Bridge; the spire of the Peter and Paul Fortress; the statues in the Summer Garden.

Valentina couldn't stop looking at them. "I love them," she said. "They're wonderful."

Babulya looked at them, too, and pronounced them excellent. Oksana was as red as a strawberry by now, and Babulya tugged her braids, saying she'd have to grow accustomed to compliments, if she was going to be a famous artist. She hung Oksana's drawings on the laundry lines and said they were the prettiest decorations she'd ever had.

From then on, Oksana sketched every night when she didn't go on a "walk"—which was what she told Babulya she was doing while she delivered packages for Comrade Orlov. She had met him the night after the client had been arrested and given him the passport back. She'd worried he would be angry with her for failing, but he'd said he was grateful she was safe and that she should stay away for a few days, until they could be certain the client hadn't told the police about him.

She had told Valentina everything after she had returned home that night. Valentina had begged her to stop working for Comrade Orlov, but she had said no, she had to go on. And when she met him a few nights later, he had smiled at her and handed her a package, she had delivered it, and everything felt normal. She was safe, she assured Valentina later that night, after they had brushed their teeth and were alone in the bathroom, the one place where they could speak freely. Valentina wasn't sure if Oksana was right, but she knew how badly Oksana wanted the money. So she didn't say anything.

■ ■ ■

In the second week of October, Babulya sent Oksana upstairs to get an early start on her schoolwork while she and Valentina stayed in the communal kitchen to fix supper.

"I needed time alone with you," Babulya told Valentina as she unlocked their cupboard. "Oksana will be twelve next week."

Valentina put a pot on their designated burner. "I know. I've been making her a pencil holder." On nights when Oksana sketched or went for a "walk," Valentina locked herself in the bathroom to work on Oksana's gift, much to the annoyance of the Kozlov boys, who knocked on the door in vain and finally had to go downstairs to use another toilet.

Valentina didn't care: Oksana's present would be marvelous. When Valentina had taken out the garbage to the rubbish bins in the courtyard, she'd scavenged them until she'd found a broken teacup. Then she'd gone to the far side of the court-yard, to look through the rubbish bins there. The building on the street behind them shared their courtyard, so she had double the amount of trash to go through. She found a hand-ful of bolts and screws. She'd glued the pieces of the teacup back together, and then she'd soldered screws onto the cup's surface. An old gentleman from one floor down had lent her his soldering gun. She'd taught herself to use it and had only burned herself twice.

"We need to plan her birthday celebration." Babulya set out the ingredients for vegetable soup. Around the room, sev-eral women stirred pots or washed dishes. A couple of toddlers sat in a corner, playing with blocks. At the table, the man with the spectacles lit a cigarette. His name was Comrade Popov, Valentina had learned, and ever since she and Oksana had arrived he watched them with narrowed eyes. That was how he looked at everyone, though, so Valentina didn't think much of it.

"It isn't every day a girl turns twelve," Babulya went on, handing Valentina a handful of carrots. "What shall we do?"

"A birthday tea!" Valentina chopped the carrots. "We ought to have it on a Saturday afternoon, after school lets out. And we should have lots of sweets. Sugared donuts and fruit dumplings and cake and ice cream—"

Chuckling, Babulya held up a hand. "As much as I'd like to shower Oksana in gifts and sweets, I'm afraid I can only afford a small, simple party. What's her favorite dessert?"

"*Sirok.*" Just saying the word made Valentina hungry. Sirok was a cheesecake covered in chocolate.

Babulya laughed again. "It would have to be the most

expensive and decadent dessert, wouldn't it? We'll have it," she said quickly when Valentina opened her mouth to beg. "Oksana should have her favorite dessert on her birthday. And we'll have biscuits and jam and pots of tea."

"No boys."

"Naturally." Babulya dropped the chopped carrots into a pot. "I can't think of any twelve-year-old girl who would willingly invite boys to a birthday tea. Next year, however, may be a different matter."

Valentina wrinkled her nose. "Maybe."

"You'd be surprised at how these things change. So no boys. I assume girls are acceptable?"

Valentina wasn't sure why her grandmother and the other ladies in the kitchen were laughing. "Of course *girls* are fine. Lyudmila and Yulia should come."

"I'll speak to their mothers. We'll have to come up with a plan to keep Oksana out of the apartment until the tea is ready, so Oksana can be surprised. And I want you girls to fuss over her. She's had little enough love in her life, poor thing, and everyone ought to feel cherished on her birthday."

"How did you celebrate your birthday when you were my age?" Valentina watched her grandmother season the soup.

"My mother fixed a lovely tea," Babulya said. "Everybody gave me presents. That was a rule in my family: we all had to give a gift. My brothers drew me pictures, as they were too little to do much else. My parents gave me a book or a dress. When I turned twelve, they bought me a flute."

Babulya had played the flute! Valentina thought of her mother's piano playing. Both Mama and Babulya were musicians. She hadn't realized they had anything in common.

"Do you still play?" she asked.

"Gracious, no! I haven't taken my flute out in ages."

"That's too bad," Valentina said. "Mama plays the piano whenever she can. She tells me it makes her feel as though her soul is flying."

Babulya stirred the soup harder.

But later, after they had eaten and washed up, and Valentina and Oksana were trying to memorize the beginning of Pushkin's poem "Ruslan and Lyudmila," Babulya opened a box she kept stowed in the wardrobe. She took out three pieces of a flute. They were tarnished, and she wiped them clean with a rag. Then she fitted them together and blew across the mouthpiece.

The first notes were squawks. As Babulya continued to play, however, the notes strengthened and sweetened, until they were so beautiful that Valentina and Oksana put down their textbooks and listened. The music sounded like silver.

At last, Babulya stopped. She had tears in her eyes. "It does feel as though my soul is flying," she said, and packed the flute into the box. She didn't put it back in the wardrobe, though, but left it in a place of honor on a shelf, where they could see it every day.

(30)

Oksana

FOUR DAYS BEFORE Oksana's birthday, she went to Comrade Orlov's shop after school. He owned a photography store on the outskirts of Avtovo, on the ground floor of a shabby, five-story building of stained concrete.

It was the most wonderful place she had ever seen. Glass cabinets filled with cameras and lenses and film lined the walls. Between them hung framed black-and-white photographs of Leningrad. In one of them, Oksana recognized the silhouette of the Bronze Horseman, her favorite sight in the city.

Today, Comrade Orlov stood behind the counter, helping a customer select a camera lens. Oksana waited patiently. For the past few weeks, she had stopped by Comrade Orlov's store on Thursday afternoons. Comrade Orlov had said that because she had been such a responsible employee, she had proven her trustworthiness and she could now know where he worked. Oksana wished Valentina would visit the shop, too, but Valentina always refused when she asked. "Black-market workers are too dangerous to be around," she would say. "I wish you wouldn't go, either, Khusha."

But Oksana couldn't stop. Not when she was close to earning enough money to go to her mother.

So she waited while the customer paid for his purchase and left the store. Then she went to the counter, expecting Comrade Orlov to give her a package and an address.

He handed her a paint set. Under its glass top, Oksana saw seven paints—all the colors of the rainbow—and a brush with bristles that looked impossibly soft and fine. It was so beautiful that Oksana had to catch her breath. What she wouldn't do for paints like these! And a proper brush, not the fountain pens or pencils she had from school that she had to make do with. She could create *real* pictures with these paints.

But they weren't hers. "Where do I take this?" she asked.

"The location is in this shop," Comrade Orlov.

Oksana looked up quickly from the paints. What did he mean?

He smiled at her. "Happy birthday, Oksana."

Then . . . these paints *were* for her? She couldn't believe it. She stared at him until he began to laugh.

"It's your birthday present," he said. "Last week, you told me you were about to turn twelve. And it's time you nurtured your gift properly."

Oksana touched the paint set's glass top. "This is mine? Truly?"

Comrade Orlov laughed again. "Truly. The paints are from France," he added, taking them from her and opening the hinged glass cover. "They're watercolors. See how pale they are? And once you begin working with them, you'll see the colors bleed together a bit on the page. The effect is a picture that looks soft, almost like a dream."

Watercolors! Oksana had heard of them, but had never used them in school. She was accustomed to oil paint, bright and bold, not these delicate colors. They did look like they came from a dream. She couldn't wait to go home and try them out.

She was smiling so wide her face hurt. "Thank you, Comrade Orlov. Thank you, thank you so much!"

He waved away her thanks. "Go along," he said, handing the paints back to her. "I haven't any deliveries today, but I'll expect to see you tomorrow."

"Yes, Comrade Orlov."

She put the paints in her school satchel, which she hugged to her chest the whole walk home.

Later, after they had washed up from supper and Babulya sat on the balcony, playing her flute, Oksana showed Valentina her paints, and Valentina said grudgingly that she supposed even black-market men weren't so bad—sometimes.

■ ■ ■

Two days later was a Saturday. Once the noon dismissal bell rang, Yulia and Lyudmila fell in step alongside Valentina and Oksana.

"Let's go to the park," Valentina said. She sounded excited.

"Yes, let's!" Yulia said.

Oksana's stomach grumbled. "Let's go after lunch."

Valentina sent a strange look to Yulia and Lyudmila. "You can't possibly be hungry," she said. "We just ate breakfast."

"That was hours ago," Oksana said. "And Babulya says I'm growing and should eat a lot." At some point, she had begun calling Valentina's grandmother Babulya instead of Tetya Rita. The first time, she hadn't meant to, but when Babulya and Valentina hadn't objected or even seemed to notice, she had continued doing it. The name Babulya felt right.

The girls rounded the corner. Oksana and Valentina's apartment building stood halfway down the street. Thank goodness! Oksana was starving. She could scarcely wait to eat her ham-and-butter sandwich.

Valentina darted in front of her. "You can't go home!"

"Why not?" Was something wrong? Oksana tried to look at the apartment building, but Lyudmila and Yulia blocked her way.

"Because . . . because . . ." Valentina stuttered, her eyes wide. Then she tapped Oksana on the shoulder. "Because you have to catch me first!" She sprinted away.

Oksana grinned and tore down the street after Valentina. The sheer joy of running swept through her, and she laughed. She glanced over her shoulder: Lyudmila and Yulia were on her heels.

Down another street, two right turns, skirting babushkas in black clothes and stray cats and other children delighted to be free from school. Oksana shot around another corner and saw the gleaming waters of a canal in front of her.

Babulya said no two canal bridges in Leningrad were alike. During the summer, when Oksana and Valentina had been free to roam the city, they had climbed onto the parapets of the arched granite bridge over the Fontanka River. They had crossed the Palace Bridge, from which they could see the green-and-white splendor of the Winter Palace, and they had rubbed the Blue Bridge's obelisk for luck.

This bridge was made of plain metal. Here in Avtovo there were no fancy bridges. Valentina was up ahead, standing at the edge of the canal. Oksana hurried toward her. Autumn sunshine shone like burnished gold on the surface of the river, and the sound of the water lapping the sides of the canal was as gentle as a lullaby. There was beauty everywhere, Oksana realized. It felt like a grown-up thought.

She reached Valentina and smiled. "You've always been faster than me."

Valentina's face turned red. "Let's not talk about that."

Oksana felt heat creeping into her cheeks. She knew what Valentina meant: the last time they had raced each other in Pripyat, on the morning of the explosion, where smoke had drifted across the sky and the air in the schoolyard had tasted of metal. And she had called Valentina a cheating Jew.

Her face was on fire. "I—I'm sorry," she stammered.

"There you are!" Yulia exclaimed behind them. "You're both too fast."

Neither girl responded to her. They looked at each other. Oksana hoped Valentina knew how sorry she was.

Then Valentina's grin flashed out. She grabbed Oksana's hand and squeezed. "Let's go home. Babulya would say we've worked up a good appetite from all that running."

Something welled up in Oksana's chest, something so warm and gentle that she couldn't contain it. She squeezed Valentina's hand back. Valentina forgave her. She still wanted to be friends!

"I'm starved," Lyudmila chimed in. "I could eat a cow!"

"Why do people say that?" Yulia asked. "Wouldn't the hooves hurt, going down?"

Oksana and Valentina laughed. They linked arms with the other girls and walked back. Oksana's heart swelled until she thought it would burst. What lovely friends she had, friends who forgave her for the bad things she had done, friends who didn't care if she was perfect or got low marks or wanted to be an artist instead of an engineer. They liked her exactly the way she was.

When they reached their building, Valentina invited Yulia and Lyudmila to come upstairs with them.

"What are you doing?" Oksana whispered. "You know they can't stay for lunch." Babulya never had friends over to share a meal. She didn't have the money to feed extra mouths.

"They won't stay long," Valentina whispered back. "I want to show them the blueprints for my telephone invention."

Oksana couldn't imagine Lyudmila and Yulia had any interest in telephones, but she didn't want to hurt Valentina's feelings. Together, the four of them trooped up the stairs. As they walked along the corridor to their room, Valentina shouted, "You'll love my blueprints!"

"Why are you yelling?" Oksana asked.

"I'm not yelling!" Valentina yelled, and opened the door to their room.

Oksana stepped inside and froze.

The apartment had been transformed. Babulya had taken down the washing and had strung ribbons of all colors on the laundry lines. The table had been covered with Babulya's only tablecloth. There were baskets of biscuits and plates of sandwiches and a platter with chocolate *sirok*. Cups had been set at each of the four place settings.

Babulya stood next to the table. "Happy birthday, dearest Oksana," she said.

This was her birthday party. A party just for her.

Suddenly, she couldn't speak. All she could do was smile at Babulya.

Babulya must have understood, for she took Oksana's hand and led her to the table. "I know your birthday isn't until Monday," she said, "but we wanted to have the whole afternoon to celebrate." She looked over her shoulder at the other girls. "Let's have a feast."

Everyone cheered. As Yulia and Lyudmila sat down, Oksana hugged Valentina. "Thank you," she managed to say around the lump in her throat. "Nobody's ever done anything like this for me before."

Valentina hugged her back, hard. "Happy birthday."

"This is the best birthday of my life," Oksana said.

"It hasn't started yet," Valentina objected.

"It's already the best," Oksana said. She went over to Babulya. Then she did something she had never done before: she took Babulya's hands in hers and kissed them. "Thank you, Babulya. For everything."

"You're very welcome." Babulya reached for a tea cup. "It's my honor to deliver Oksana's birthday toast. Oksana, you are a smart, strong, and creative young lady." She lifted the cup higher. "To Oksana!"

The girls raised their cups. "To Oksana!"

They all drank. Then Babulya passed around the plates

of biscuits, and ham-and-butter sandwiches. After they had stuffed themselves, it was time for presents. From Lyudmila, Oksana received an entire bar of chocolate ("That cost me three weeks of pocket money," Lyudmila said while Babulya smothered a laugh), and from Yulia she got a string of colored beads ("The blue beads match your eyes," Yulia said).

Valentina fetched her present from the back of the wardrobe. She had covered the gift in sheets of *Pravda* newspaper, and Oksana guessed it was because they couldn't afford wrapping paper. Somehow that made the gift even better, and she took her time unwinding the twine and pulling back the newspaper.

Inside lay the strangest-looking object she had ever seen. It was a teacup covered all over with little metal screws. Was she supposed to drink from it?

"It's a pencil holder," Valentina said. "You can keep your paintbrushes in it."

Oksana couldn't stop smiling. Valentina had made this for her! It must have taken her ages. That must have been what she was doing when she disappeared into the bathroom for a long time at night. "It's beautiful," she said. "I'll keep it always."

After that, they ate *sirok* and drank cups of hot jam tea. At last, it was time for Lyudmila and Yulia to leave. Oksana and Valentina walked them to the lobby.

"Thank you again." Oksana hugged each of them in turn. "See you in school on Monday."

"See you on your real birthday," Yulia said. "Shall we tell the teacher and ask her to make you stand in front of the class and give a speech?"

"Or maybe we should ask her to sing to you," Lyudmila said.

"Please don't!" Oksana said.

The girls laughed. "We won't. Goodbye!"

"Goodbye," Oksana and Valentina echoed.

Upstairs, they started to clear the table.

"Not yet," Babulya said, going to the wardrobe. "Oksana hasn't received her present from me."

"You don't have to give me anything," Oksana said.

"I want to." Babulya handed her a small packet wrapped in newspaper.

Inside lay a sketchbook. Oksana flipped through it. The pages were so thin they were almost translucent.

"To go with your new paints," Babulya said. "You must have hoarded your pocket money for months to buy those. I thought you ought to have proper art paper, too."

It was too much. All of it—too much kindness, too much thoughtfulness, too much togetherness. For a moment, Oksana wanted to push the sketchbook back into Babulya's hands. She wanted to yell, *Don't you know I'm a bad person and I don't deserve parties and presents?*

But she didn't. She looked at Babulya's and Valentina's happy faces, and the leftover chocolate *sirok*, and the presents sitting beside the bed. Valentina, Babulya, Yulia, Lyudmila, and Comrade Orlov hadn't given her gifts because they had to.

They'd *wanted* to.

Cautiously, she stepped close to Babulya. Then she hugged her.

"I love you," she said to Babulya's shirt. Saying it this

way was easier than looking up into Babulya's face.

Babulya's arms came around her. "I love you, too, my dear Oksana," she whispered into Oksana's hair.

"I beg your pardon," said a woman's voice from behind them.

Oksana turned around. The door gaped wide—she and Valentina must have forgotten to latch it.

Standing on the threshold was her mother.

(31)

Valentina

EVERYTHING IN VALENTINA turned to stone. She could only watch as Oksana flew across the room into her mother's arms and think, *Please, don't leave.*

"Mama!" Oksana sobbed. "I missed you so much."

"I missed you, too." Eleonora Ivanovna had a soft voice. She hugged Oksana back.

Valentina couldn't stop staring at Eleonora Ivanovna. She wore a dark coat and fur cap. Her blond hair reached the tops of her shoulders. Oksana looked so much like her.

But Oksana was nothing like her. Oksana's mother had stood by while her husband beat their daughter. She hadn't stopped Oksana's father from burning Oksana with a cigarette. She hadn't protected Oksana. And Valentina hated her so much she was shaking.

Babulya laid a hand on Valentina's shoulder. "Shhh," she murmured. "Remember Oksana loves her mother."

Valentina looked, and she saw Babulya was right: Oksana's face had lit up. Valentina turned away, pressing her cheek into her grandmother's hand.

"The government has finally assigned me an apartment," Eleonora Ivanovna said to Babulya. "At last I can take Oksana home. I am in your debt for minding her for me."

"Caring for Oksana has been my pleasure," Babulya said.

Tears pricked Valentina's eyes. She wanted to beg Eleonora Ivanovna not to take Oksana away, to tell her that Oksana was happier with them. But Babulya's hand tightened on her shoulder, and she didn't say anything.

Eleonora Ivanovna let go of Oksana and gently nudged her away. "Gather your things. We have a train to catch."

Smiling, Oksana nodded and hurried to the wardrobe.

"You're leaving already?" Valentina exclaimed.

Shivering, Eleonora Ivanovna drew her coat more tightly about her. "Mercy, this city is freezing! Yes, we have to get on this train. If we miss it, we won't be able to leave until morning, and I need to be at work on Tuesday."

Valentina couldn't believe it: They were leaving. Now. She and Oksana would probably never see each other again.

Valentina rushed to Oksana. "Don't leave," she whispered. "You're happy here with us. I know you are . . ."

Oksana looked up from the suitcase she was packing. "I *am* happy with you and Babulya," she whispered back. "But it'll be different this time with my mother, now that my father isn't here anymore. I know it."

"But we won't see each other again." Valentina struggled to keep from crying. "We probably can't even write letters to each other. Your mother wouldn't like it."

"I'll find a way to write to you." Tears welled up in Oksana's eyes.

"What are you two whispering about?" Eleonora Ivanovna

asked. "Khusha, we simply must make that train."

Swallowing hard, Valentina picked up Oksana's bag. "I'll carry this downstairs for you."

Eleonora Ivanovna's hands fluttered nervously at her sides. "That isn't necessary, Valentina." It was the first time Valentina could remember Oksana's mother addressing her by name.

"Thank you again," Eleonora Ivanovna said to Babulya, then turned to Oksana. "Come along. Say farewell to Valentina and we can be on our way."

The girls hugged each other tightly. Valentina tried to think of what Babulya would want her to say.

"Have a good journey," she said at last.

"You're my best friend always," Oksana whispered, then stepped back. Her face was now blank. Valentina understood why: their friendship had to be kept a secret from Oksana's mother.

So she didn't say anything as her grandmother kissed Oksana, once on each cheek, and then once on the forehead for extra luck. She didn't say anything when Babulya and Eleonora Ivanovna shook hands, or when Eleonora Ivanovna scurried to the door, Oksana trailing in her wake.

At the threshold, Oksana looked back to where Valentina and Babulya stood and gave them a tremulous smile. "Goodbye."

"Goodbye and safe travels." Babulya pinched Valentina's arm, a sure sign she was supposed to say farewell, but Valentina couldn't get her voice to work. She waved instead.

Oksana vanished into the gloom of the corridor. Motionless, Valentina listened to her footsteps grow fainter and fainter. A creak sounded, the door to the stairwell—the building manager was forever saying he would oil the hinges, and he never did—and then the footfalls died away.

Oksana was gone.

With a sigh, Babulya closed the door. "I'm glad we had the chance to give her a birthday tea." She wrapped an arm around Valentina's shoulders. "And I'm glad you gave her the pencil holder. Every time she uses it, she'll think of you."

Tears filled Valentina's eyes. "I don't have anything to remember her by."

"You have memories. That can be enough."

Suddenly, it was more than Valentina could bear. She pushed away from her grandmother. "Memories aren't enough! All they do is hurt. I don't have Papa or Mama, and now I don't have Oksana, either. Everybody's gone!"

Babulya shoved a pillow at her. "Punch that."

Valentina blinked. "What do you mean?"

"I imagine you want to hit something, and quite hard, too," her grandmother said mildly. "You may punch this pillow. I've punched a number of pillows in my day, and I promise you, it's every bit as satisfying as breaking something, without any pesky cleanup."

Valentina took the pillow her grandmother offered. She tossed it onto the bed and then hit it with all of her strength. Then again and again until her arm hurt and her breath was coming in short gasps and she couldn't do it anymore. She slid down to the floor. Everywhere she looked, she saw evidence of Oksana.

The table was still cluttered with the remnants of the birthday tea: plates dusted with crumbs, a half-eaten piece of chocolate *sirok*, a pot of long-cold tea. Overhead, the brightly colored ribbons shone in the lamplight. Along the wall, several pen-and-ink drawings had been pinned. Valentina's favorite was the picture of the Bronze Horseman. Oksana had worked so hard on it. And she hadn't even thought to show it to her mother...

The room blurred. Valentina blinked, wishing she could order the tears to go away. "Will Oksana be all right?" she asked her grandmother. "What if her mother is mean to her?"

"Then we will do everything in our power to help Oksana." Babulya settled down on the floor beside Valentina, tucking her skirt primly under her legs.

Valentina gave her a long look. "How'd you know to do that? Hit the pillow?"

"Because I've lost many people I love, too." Babulya's voice was gentle.

"Your husband—my grandfather," Valentina guessed.

"Yes, my husband." Babulya took a deep breath. "And many others." She stroked Valentina's hair. "The people we love are never lost to us. Your father will never leave you, not truly. His actions will echo in your life and in the lives of your children and in the lives of your children's children. And you and Oksana will never forget each other. Of that I'm certain."

Valentina wasn't sure. "Truly?"

"Truly." Babulya kissed the top of her head.

"How can you be so sure?" Valentina asked.

"Perhaps it's time I told you a story."

As they sat on the floor, listening to the wind hurl itself against the windowpane, Valentina heard her grandmother's story about herself as a young girl, living in Kiev with her parents and little brothers until war broke out. She listened as Babulya told her about leaving the city in the dark with her cousin Nathan. They had foraged in fields for food and slept in forests. They had sought refuge in a barn, and her grandmother had cried when she'd had to leave Nathan behind.

Valentina listened as Babulya told her about hiking through the countryside on her own and the night when German bombs rained from the sky. She listened as Babulya told her about finding a group of friendly Ukrainians and about traveling with them until they found out she was a Jew. She barely breathed as her grandmother told her about walking alone down dirt roads and about the day the first winter snow fell.

"How did you survive that?" she asked when Babulya paused.

Babulya smiled. "I met my best friend."

| 32 |

Rifka

THE WOMAN CALLED Ona and the girl with the black braids carried Rifka into the house. They set her on the floor and pulled off her wet clothes. Rifka didn't protest. She felt as though she had come apart from her body and was floating near the ceiling, looking down on everyone.

The room she was in was small and warm. A fire crackled in the fireplace, and it sent out licks of heat that touched her face and her bare arms and legs. A prickling sensation spread across her skin, and then it turned into needles, stabbing her with red-hot points. She cried out from the pain.

"Shhh, my dove," said the woman called Ona. She and the girl with the black braids bustled about Rifka, rubbing her fingers and toes and wrapping her in blankets. "Your body is waking up from the cold," the woman told Rifka. Her face was kind, and her brown eyes so dark they might have been black. "You'll be well soon."

Rifka licked her dry lips. "I don't want to be well. I want to die."

"I imagine you do," the woman said quietly. She turned

to the girl with the black braids. "I must see to the little ones. Give her hot tea, plenty of it."

The girl nodded, and the woman hurried away. Rifka rested her back against the wall, trying not to moan as the needles in her skin grew hotter and sharper. The girl went to the stove, where a kettle was whistling. She poured boiling water into a cup and carried it to Rifka.

"Tea," she said, giving the cup to Rifka, who folded her hands around it and almost whimpered at the warmth. "Why do you want to die?" the girl asked as she sat down.

Rifka stared into her tea. There was nothing she could say that anyone else would understand. She didn't reply.

"Well, you mustn't die," the girl said.

Rifka swallowed some tea. It was so hot, it hurt going down. "Why not?"

"Because we saved you, my mother and I," the girl replied. "My grandmother always says if you save someone's life, you are beholden to her forever."

"I think you said that backward." Rifka sipped more tea. It still hurt, but the needles in her skin were softening. "Don't you mean the person you save owes you for the rest of her life?"

"No, not at all!" The girl leaned forward. "By saving someone, you are doing holy work. So you owe the person you save a debt because they are the reason you did a sacred deed."

The thoughts in Rifka's head were swirling like the snow outside. She was so tired. "I don't understand," she mumbled, her eyes closing. "Who are you, anyway?"

"Feruza Chorieva," the girl said. They were the last words Rifka heard before she drifted away into the darkness again.

■ ■ ■

She didn't want to live, but when she woke she put on the dress, sweater, and woolen leggings Ona gave her. She didn't want to live, but she sat at the table in the warm kitchen with Feruza's seven little brothers and sisters. She didn't want to live, but she ate the dumplings and pilaf she was served, and she couldn't help smiling when the smallest girl climbed onto her lap. She didn't want to live, but she washed in the wooden bathtub in the kitchen, and when she was clean, she dressed in a white nightgown. She didn't want to live, but she slept in a big bed with Feruza and three of her sisters, and when she woke, she helped Feruza and Ona make porridge for breakfast.

After everyone had eaten, Ona—which Rifka had learned was Uzbek for *Mama*—asked her if she had anywhere to go.

Rifka swallowed hard. "No." For some reason, it felt like the hardest word she had ever said. "I'm from Ukraine. I've come all the way from Kiev to escape the Germans."

"Well, then you must stay here," Ona said, as if that settled everything.

"But I can't pay you." Rifka's face burned with shame. "I don't have any money. I don't have anything."

"You have a clever mind," Ona said briskly. "You must, or you wouldn't have survived on your own for as long as you did. And I imagine you aren't afraid of hard work, seeing as you traveled from Kiev to Tashkent. You will help around the farm and go to school, and that will be payment enough. My husband is away, fighting in the war, and I can use every spare pair of hands I can get."

Rifka didn't want to cry, but she couldn't help it. She

couldn't remember the last time someone had been so kind to her.

"Thank you," she said, and then Feruza took her hand and led her to the barn to milk the cow. When Rifka touched the cow's cold teats, she squealed with surprise and startled the cow so much that it kicked over the pail. She and Feruza laughed so hard she nearly cried again.

After that, Rifka's days soon fell into a new rhythm. In the morning, she helped Feruza feed the chickens and milk the cow. During the day, she, Feruza, and Feruza's brothers and sisters went to school. In her borrowed shift dress, she sat at the desk she shared with Feruza and listened as their teacher talked and wrote on the chalkboard. After school, she and Feruza raced each other up and down the long, dusty roads. In the evening, they did their schoolwork by lamplight, and at night they slept in the big bed with Feruza's sisters, waiting until the little girls had fallen asleep before they began whispering and giggling. And at no time—not in the morning, or the evening, or at night when the bedroom was dark and quiet—did Rifka pray. She had decided to ignore God, as He had ignored her.

Nobody asked her to leave. Nobody asked her why she had no one else to care for her. They acted as though they wanted her there. Ona said she was a dear girl and such a help, especially when she played with the smallest children so Ona could weave more blankets on her loom and earn much-needed money for the household. Feruza laughed when they raced, and her little sisters begged Rifka to tell them more folktales about the witch Baba Yaga. They liked her. But would they still care for her if they knew she was Jewish? Rifka didn't dare tell them.

The first snows had melted ("Snow never lasts long on the ground around here," Feruza had explained) and the days were racing toward January when Rifka couldn't stand it anymore. She was lying on her back in the big bed with the other girls, staring into the darkness and wondering if the Chorieva family would still be kind to her if they knew who she was.

She rolled onto her side and poked Feruza. "Are you awake?"

"I am now," Feruza said crossly. "What is it?"

Quickly, before she could lose her nerve, Rifka said, "I'm a Jew."

She waited. Surely now Feruza would demand that she leave.

"Oh," Feruza said sleepily. "Is that all? Good night."

Rifka waited longer. There had to be more.

A light snore sounded. Feruza was asleep again.

Something that had been tied tightly in Rifka's chest loosened the smallest bit. She smiled up into the dark.

December slipped into January, and then January into February, and still she heard nothing of Nathan or her family, although she asked every Ukrainian refugee she could find who passed through Tashkent. February became March, and she turned thirteen, and March stretched into the summer months. She played with Feruza and her siblings and helped Ona with the farm.

Sometimes she surprised herself by thanking God for a beautiful day or for Ona or for Feruza most of all. And on her fourteenth birthday, she prayed the *Shema Yisrael*. Her father had told her it was the first thing she should say in the morning and the last in the evening. It felt good to say the words again.

And life was good. She had learned Uzbek, from hearing Feruza and her family use it so often, and she had grown stronger by eating three meals every day and racing Feruza from their home on the outskirts of Tashkent to school. She liked her classmates, all girls with dark braids like Feruza, and she liked hearing the muezzins of the Muslim temples in the distance. Most of all, she liked Feruza.

They played tricks on some of the fellows from the boys' school, and they sang songs when they fed the chickens. They climbed trees and helped Ona make *dimlama*, a meat-and-vegetable stew. They hid in the barn to talk, and sometimes Feruza cried because she was frightened her father would die in battle and sometimes Rifka cried because she was scared she would never see her family again.

But they made each other laugh, too. After school, they wrote funny skits and performed them in front of Feruza's adoring brothers and sisters. They survived their mathematics classes by making faces at each other when the teacher's back was turned, and at night, after the others had fallen asleep, they whispered secrets to each other. In the dark, if Rifka was the only one left awake, she could admit to herself that if it weren't for Feruza, she would still wish she were dead. She thought having a best friend was like being given a new set of lungs when you had been gasping for air.

If it weren't for the refugees from other parts of the Soviet Union trickling into Tashkent, Rifka could have convinced herself there wasn't a war at all. She saw no Germans, heard no warplanes, felt no bombs. The fighting was far away, in places like Leningrad and Stalingrad. She didn't hear much of what was happening in the rest of the country; the Chorieva family didn't have a radio, and she wasn't sure if she could trust the rumors she heard at school and in the marketplace.

Every day she wondered what was happening to her family. The Germans had conquered Kiev—she knew that much. Probably, Mama and the boys were struggling with food shortages. She hoped they were getting enough to eat. She hated to think of them going hungry.

She turned fifteen, and then sixteen. She was beginning to think of a profession for herself—for she couldn't remain in school much longer, no matter how much she wanted to—and she was considering teaching music when word spread across Tashkent like wildfire: the war in Europe was over. There was still fighting in the Pacific Ocean, but here, in the Soviet Union, the guns had silenced at last.

"Don't go back," Feruza begged Rifka. "You don't know how bad the fighting may have been in Kiev. It could be dangerous."

"I have to go." Rifka folded her spare dress and placed it in her old satchel. "My family's there. At least, I hope they are. If they're not, I'll find them."

Feruza sank onto the edge of the bed. "I know you have to do this," she said in a low voice. "Please don't forget us. I'll never forget you. You're the sister of my heart."

Tears rose in Rifka's throat. "You're mine."

"You've heard my mother's story about the blackbird, haven't you?"

Nodding, Rifka closed the satchel. Over the years, she had heard Ona's story many times. Blackbirds are almost magical, she would say, for they can walk on land like humans and swim in the sea like fish, but they can also fly into the sky. They are a link between heaven and earth, between sky and land.

"They're a symbol for eternity," Feruza said. "And I think . . . like them, our friendship could last forever. If you want it to," she added, looking quickly at Rifka.

"Our friendship will last for all of our lives," Rifka promised, and hugged Feruza. Later, as she walked away from the farm, she had to blink very hard so she didn't cry.

Most trains weren't running yet, so she had arranged to ride to the border in the back of a hay cart. From there, she traveled any way she could. Sometimes it was in a wagon; sometimes on foot; and once she caught a train that went all of thirty kilometers before it reached a section of track that had been bombed out by the Germans and came to a stop.

The farther north and west she went, the worse the sights were. Villages had been razed to the ground. Forests had been burned. Farm fields had been pillaged, leaving them fallow. And everywhere she looked, she saw desperate people: hungry children and mothers in rags, exhausted fathers in tattered uniforms returning home, gray-faced old men and women weeping over their ruined homes. A sick feeling grew and grew in Rifka's stomach.

By the time she finally reached Kiev, it was nearly the end of summer.

The city was a wreck of broken stone and shattered brick. Some buildings that still stood looked like shells, with only a couple of walls intact and the insides reduced to rubble. Others were completely gone, leaving behind gaping holes. Silently, Rifka walked the streets. Was her family still here? Would she find anyone she knew?

At last she came to Dorohozhytska Street. Parts of it, too, had been bombed out. But her apartment building was still standing. Mama and the boys must still live there, for they wouldn't have left unless it had been bombed. She raced toward it, weaving among sad-faced people she didn't know.

Inside, the stairwell was just as she remembered: a rickety wooden structure whose third step creaked when she stepped on it. She climbed the stairs as fast as she could. Mama, and Papa, and the boys—she was almost to them!

The apartment door was unlocked. She stepped inside. "Mama, it's me, Rifka! I've come home!"

The kitchen was empty. Mostly, it looked the same: an old black stove, a table and chairs, some wooden shelves nailed to the wall. The dishcloths, hanging over the lip of the sink, were the blue ones she remembered. But the shelves, where her parents had kept their books, now held a stack of white plates.

"Mama?" she called again just as a middle-aged woman came into the kitchen from the direction of the bedrooms.

The woman's eyes widened. "Who are you? Get out of my house!"

"But . . . this is my family's house," Rifka faltered. "The Friedmans."

"They don't live here now," the woman snapped. "This apartment belongs to me and my husband. Now leave before I call for help."

The sick feeling that had been in Rifka's stomach for months was now twisting up her insides. "Where's my family?" she heard herself ask. "Where did they go?"

"They aren't my concern," the woman said. "Get out of here!"

Rifka looked around the kitchen again. "Those are my mother's dishcloths. And that pot on the stove—I recognize it! These are my family's possessions! Why do *you* have them?"

The woman pushed her. "Stop asking questions!"

A thought occurred to Rifka. She shoved the woman aside and rushed into the kitchen. As the woman raced to the window, Rifka ran her hands over the floorboards. It had to be here . . .

The woman flung open the window and yelled, "Help me!"

Rifka ignored her. There it was, the floorboard missing a couple of nails. Carefully, she lifted it up. In the hole below, flecked with dirt, lay her mother's Shabbat candlesticks and a wooden box.

Everything within Rifka went cold. Mama wouldn't have left their home without their most precious possessions—not unless something terrible had occurred. What had happened to her? And to Saul and Isaac and Avrum?

"Help me!" the woman shouted again.

Rifka grabbed the candlesticks and the box containing her flute.

"Thief!" the woman shrieked.

Clutching her family's treasures, Rifka raced out of the apartment. She didn't stop running until she reached Melnykova Street and someone caught her by the arm.

"Let go of me!" She pulled her arm free.

The man who had grabbed her held up his hands, as if to show he meant no harm. He was an old man dressed in black. Something about his wizened face looked familiar.

"Eliezer Leontyevich?" she gasped. He was a cobbler who had lived down the street from her family.

"Rifka Friedman?" he asked. When she nodded, he sighed. "I thought it was you. My poor child."

"Do you know where my family is?" she asked. "I went to our apartment and . . ."

She broke off as sorrow crossed his face.

"My dear girl," he said gently. "They're dead."

Rifka jerked back. "You're lying!"

"No," he said. "I'm not. When the city fell to the Germans, they ordered all the Jews of Kiev to appear right here—at the corner of Melnykova and Dorohozhytska Streets—at eight in the morning. Everyone assumed we would be sent to labor camps.

"Thousands of our city's Jews showed up at the gathering place. We were told to bring money, warm clothing, and identity papers. I didn't go. I hid in a friend's apartment.

"But our friends and families went, Rifka. They were marched through the streets and the cemetery, then into fields outside the city. Finally, the soldiers stopped them at the Babi Yar ravine. They ordered everyone to take off their clothes."

"No," Rifka cried. "No, please."

He continued talking as if he hadn't heard her. "And then," he said quietly, "the Germans shot them all."

Rifka left Kiev that night. All she wanted was to get away, as fast as she could. She couldn't stay in the city where her family had been murdered.

She hitched a ride with a group who was heading north and had bundled their meager possessions into a horse-drawn cart. She sat in the back, on top of a suitcase, and pressed the heels of her hands to her eyes, trying to push back the tears.

Mama, dead. And Isaac and Saul and Avrum. Murdered

only weeks after she had last seen them. Papa was gone, killed in battle. The old man, Eliezer Leontyevich, had told her that, too. And Nathan had never returned to Kiev and was either in the ground or had escaped elsewhere. Her aunts and uncles, her cousins and grandparents, all murdered at Babi Yar.

There was no one left. No one and nothing, except for a flute and a set of candlesticks. She was alone.

She stared up at the stars until she thought her heart would break. She would never hear Mama's voice again or feel her embrace. Never laugh with Papa at one of his silly jokes or feel his hand on her head as he prayed over her. Saul, Isaac, and Avrum would never grow up. She would never know the men they could have become.

She sat in the hay cart, crying silently, tears running down her cheeks until the stars blurred and the sky turned into a mix of silver and black. She wished for the oblivion of sleep, but it would not come. All she could do was cry until she felt empty.

The people she was traveling with ignored her. They had sorrows of their own, she imagined. And she didn't want to talk to anyone. She didn't want to talk ever again.

Morning dawned blue and warm. As the cart rumbled over the rutted dirt road, one of the old women travelers asked Rifka where she was going.

"I don't know," Rifka said. She thought of Feruza. Maybe she ought to return to Uzbekistan. There, she had people who loved her and whom she loved.

"I'm heading to Leningrad," said the old woman. "Oh, I know what you're thinking," she said, although Rifka hadn't been thinking anything at all. "I've heard the stories, too. It was under siege for almost three years, and there are bodies in the streets. I don't care. Leningrad has the biggest synagogue in our country. I want to find other people like me, who survived."

Now Rifka was listening. "You're a Jew?" she whispered, fearful someone might be listening. It was always a dangerous time to be Jewish.

The old woman smiled at her. "Yes, and I can tell by the look on your face you must be, too. Come to Leningrad. We can meet others."

"Yes," Rifka heard herself saying. "I'll come."

■ ■ ■

Leningrad was a husk of a city. Entire blocks had been bombed out, and many of the buildings that were still standing were pockmarked with bullet holes. Rubble cascaded across the roads, and broken windows glittered in the summer sunshine.

It should have looked like a dead place. But the water in the canals shone. The air smelled of soot and grass. People swept up crushed stone and brick and dust. The city was still alive, Rifka realized.

The old woman from the hay cart found her a place to live with her third cousin's husband's family, a one-room apartment crammed with ten people. Rats came out in the dark, even though there was little food to be had, and the smallest children screamed from night terrors, ripping Rifka from sleep again and again.

She had to get out of this place. She knew no one else in the city, though, and had nowhere else to go.

Her first Friday night in Leningrad, she felt her mother's presence around her like an embrace, and she knew she should go to Shabbat service at the Grand Choral Synagogue. She needed to say the Mourner's Kaddish for her family.

Before the war, she hadn't gone to temple. Her parents had said it was too dangerous. Instead, they worshipped at home, with the curtains drawn so no one could see. For Passover, they bought matzah from their synagogue and ate it in secret in their apartment.

So she didn't know exactly what to do during the service. She bowed at the wrong parts. She said the words in the wrong rhythm. And when she began to say the Mourner's Kaddish, she burned with anger.

There was no mention of the dead in the Kaddish. The prayer contained two parts—an affirmation of life and gratitude for God. How could she proclaim the goodness of life when her life had been destroyed and her entire family wiped out? How could she be grateful to God, who had let all of this happen?

She heard her mother's voice in her head. *God gave us free will.* Those were the words her mother had said to her when she was little and upset because someone had spit on her in the street or called her family dirty Jew rats. *That means,* her mother had said many times, *that we have the power to do terrible evil or great good.*

Tears flooded her eyes. God hadn't murdered her family. The German soldiers had. People had killed. Not God. She didn't have to hate God. She could love Him again.

Continuing to recite the familiar Hebrew words, she felt her heart filling until she thought it would burst with love and grief for her family. And somehow she didn't feel alone anymore. She wiped away her tears, and by the time she got to the final word, she was smiling a little.

During the service, the women and men sat separately, but afterward the young people mingled together on the front steps. A young man—a boy, really—with a thatch of dark hair beneath his kippah approached her. "I haven't seen you here before," he said. "Are you new? I can show you around." He flashed her a grin. "My name's Yuri Goldman."

She wanted to tell him to leave her alone. There was something so beautiful about his smile, though, that she relented. "I'm Rifka Friedman."

"Rifka," he said, shaking her hand, "may I take you around the city sometime?"

"Maybe," she said, determined not to say another word and encourage him. She had no use for boys, even boys with beautiful smiles.

Yuri, she soon discovered, was determined, too. She had gotten a job in a seamstress's shop, and one day as she was leaving work she bumped into him on the street, coming home from his factory job. Somehow, she found herself walking around the Field of Mars with him and laughing at his jokes despite herself.

They were married three months later. They were young and poor and happy. They moved out of his parents' apartment into a one-room place. On Friday nights, they went to services or Rifka lit the Shabbat candles at home. She always used her mother's candlesticks. On Sundays, their days off, they walked hand in hand in the Summer Garden. In the evenings, Rifka played her flute and Yuri read books. Once a month, she wrote a letter to Feruza. And every day, she missed her parents and brothers.

Five years after Rifka and Yuri's wedding, she gave birth to their daughter. Rifka lay in bed, cradling their baby. "She's the most beautiful baby in the world," she told Yuri, who grinned down at her.

"That's because she looks like you," he said, running one gentle finger down the baby's cheek. "What shall we name her?"

Rifka looked at the baby in her arms. Everything about her was perfect: her soft skin, her rosebud of a mouth, her wrinkled fingers and toes. Rifka couldn't help thinking of the day her brother Avrum had been born. The old, familiar sadness tugged at her heart. But there was something else, too: gratitude that she had at least seen him before he had been killed.

"Galina," she said suddenly.

"Galina?" Yuri looked surprised. "I thought you had your heart set on Annushka."

"Galina means 'light,'" she told him. "And I want no more darkness."

Smiling, he leaned down to kiss her forehead. "Then Galina it is. Galina Yurievna Goldman."

Rifka leaned back against the pillows, holding her daughter close. She didn't want to let her go. Until the midwife had placed Galina in her arms, she hadn't known it was possible to love so deeply. But one look at her daughter had made her fall in love forever.

| 33 |

Oksana

OKSANA LOVED THE train ride to Minsk. Her mother had brought a deck of cards and they played *p'yanitsa* and Svoyi Koziri. When Oksana won two rounds of *p'yanitsa* in a row, her mother laughed and said Oksana had always been good at games. When Oksana got hungry, her mother didn't fuss about the expense but bought her rolls from a tea cart. When Oksana realized that in her rush to pack her things she had forgotten the black-market money, it didn't matter because she was with her mother at last and she hadn't needed the money after all. And when Oksana finally felt brave enough to show her mother some of her drawings, her mother didn't scold her and say she ought to think about a sensible career. She said the drawings were pretty.

By the time they reached Minsk, the bubble of hope in Oksana's chest was so big that she thought she might burst. She had been right—things would be different without Papa.

Her mother had an apartment on Volodarkovo Street. The street was lined with crumbling apartment towers and shops, and the air stank of metal and smoke from the nearby factories. Oksana didn't care. She knew the apartment would be wonderful because it belonged just to her and Mama.

The apartment consisted of two rooms—a bedroom for her mother and a common space, which had a kitchen and a sofa for Oksana to sleep on. The common room felt empty. There was a table with four chairs in the middle of the kitchen, a sofa and two wooden chairs in the sitting area, but that was all. No pictures, no rugs, no decorations. Oksana understood why: they had had to leave everything behind in Pripyat. It didn't matter—they could start over here in Minsk. Here they would hang up her drawings. Here she and Mama would laugh over supper, and she would tell Mama about her friendship with Valentina, and Mama would understand and say she and Valentina could write letters to each other. Here she wouldn't have to be scared.

"Put your things by the sofa," Oksana's mother said. An excited note hung in her voice.

Mama was excited because Oksana was home. Oksana's heart filled until she thought her chest couldn't contain it.

She put her suitcase beside the sofa, then joined her mother in the kitchen area. Mama was rummaging through the refrigerator. "We'll have a light supper," she said. "Sandwiches and salad. I'll go to the market after work tomorrow."

"I can help," Oksana said. "I can make the sandwiches."

"Good." Her mother turned on the radio, and they hummed as they got to work. Oksana found a loaf in the bread box and a chunk of ham in the refrigerator. After she had made the sandwiches, her mother told her the plates were kept in the cabinet under the sink.

Oksana opened the cabinet doors. Inside was a stack of

plates and several empty glass bottles. She recognized the bottles' labels. She knew what had been inside them.

Vodka.

Her stomach twisted. When her father had drunk vodka, he had gotten mean. On those nights, she had tried to sit on a corner of the sofa, huddled up to make herself as small as possible. She hadn't said a word. She had stared at the floor, hoping he wouldn't notice her.

But he was gone. She was fine, she was safe, she was with her mother, and everything had changed. Bottles of vodka shouldn't frighten her anymore.

Her hands, though, still shook when she reached for the plates.

Just then, she heard a key scraping in a lock. As she watched, the front door opened to reveal a middle-aged man. He wore a fur hat and a dark coat. He carried a bouquet of flowers.

"Boris!" her mother exclaimed, hurrying over to him.

Who was this man? And why did he have a key to their apartment? Oksana stood frozen by the sink.

"It's so good to see you," the man said, kissing her mother's cheek. Then he came into the kitchen and held out the flowers to Oksana. "I'm delighted to meet you at last," he said. "Your mother has told me so much about you."

She didn't know what to say. "Thank you," she mumbled, burying her nose in the flowers so she didn't have to look at him.

"Oh, Boris, how kind!" her mother said. "They must have been frightfully expensive."

Oksana looked up. The man was waving away her mother's

thanks. Mama helped him out of his coat and hung it on a hook. He took off his cap. Oksana saw he had thick brown hair. He smiled at her.

She didn't want to smile back. She wanted to be alone with her mother, eating and giggling at the table while snow softly fell outside. She wanted this stranger to leave.

She had to smile, though. She knew that. She mustn't make anyone angry.

"Thank you," she said again. "For the flowers. They're very pretty."

Her mother hurried back into the kitchen. "Oksana, this is Boris Maksimovich. My boss."

He frowned at her. "You didn't tell your daughter about me?"

Her mother's hands twisted together. "I wanted you to be a surprise."

His face relaxed. "That's all right, then." He glanced at Oksana. "You may call me Dyadya Boris."

He wanted her to call him *uncle*. There was a stone in Oksana's stomach now, pulling down and down. She bobbed in an awkward curtsy, murmuring, "Yes, Dyadya Boris."

"What's for supper?" he asked.

He was going to stay and eat with them? Oksana looked at her mother, hoping she would say she and Oksana hadn't seen each other in months and needed time together, just the two of them.

Her mother, though, looked apologetic. "I only have sand-wiches and salad. I haven't had time to go to the market yet."

He sat down at the table, stretching out his long legs. "I like sandwiches."

Oksana's mother grabbed the plates and set them on the table. "Oksana, fix a sandwich for yourself."

Because this man was going to eat *her* sandwich.

Silently, she made another sandwich and carried it to the table. Her mother and Dyadya Boris had already begun eating. They were talking about a film they had seen last week. Every time they laughed, Dyadya Boris touched her mother's hand.

Mama's cheeks were flushed. She looked so happy. Oksana had never made her look like that.

The sandwich tasted like dust. She had to choke it down.

Throughout supper, she barely spoke. She watched her mother and Dyadya Boris talk and laugh, and the stone in her stomach was so heavy she felt as though she would be sick.

After they had finished eating, Oksana washed up while her mother and Dyadya Boris sat on the sofa—*her* bed— with their heads close together, murmuring to each other. Sometimes her mother would laugh.

Oksana wiped the counter over and over. She didn't want to be near Dyadya Boris. She didn't want to hear her mother laugh or see her flushed cheeks.

At last, Dyadya Boris stood up and came toward her. He was smiling. "I think the counter is clean by now."

"Oh." Oksana didn't know what to do. "I—I like to clean."

"An admirable quality." He ruffled her hair. "Eleonora, see me out."

"Of course." Her mother scurried over to the door, where she held out his coat and cap for him.

Oksana looked away. Her mother and Dyadya Boris whispered to each other. Then there was a pause. Oksana knew what they were doing. They were kissing. She didn't have to look.

Kissing. Her mother was kissing and laughing with this man, this stranger, who had a key to the apartment and who made her mother's cheeks flush.

Her mother hadn't missed her. She hadn't been alone in Minsk, pining for her daughter. She had been busy finding a new man.

Tears rose to Oksana's eyes. Hastily, she wiped them away. She mustn't cry. She mustn't make anyone upset with her.

The door opened and closed; Dyadya Boris was gone. Oksana's mother came into the kitchen, smiling and rosy-cheeked.

"Isn't he marvelous?" She touched the bouquet of flowers lying on the counter. Humming, she took a pitcher out of a cupboard and filled it with water.

Oksana watched her arrange the flowers in the pitcher. She had to say something. She had to or she couldn't bear it. "I . . . I thought it was going to be just the two of us," she said at last.

Her mother looked up. "Boris is a wonderful person." Her voice was pleading. "You'll see. I'm his secretary at the law firm." She smiled, her eyes going soft. "He's such a gentleman. And clever and kind and handsome. You should see how he treats me! Like a queen. And he'll treat you the same. You'll come to care for him, too."

Maybe her mother was right. Maybe things could still be different, even with Dyadya Boris in their lives. She forced herself to smile. "Okay," she said.

"Good girl." Her mother kissed her on the cheek. "Now, into pajamas and then to bed. It's been a long day, and you have school in the morning."

But after her mother had gone into her bedroom and closed the door, Oksana went to the sofa, where she had left her things. She took a notebook out of her school satchel and wrote a letter to Valentina. She told Valentina how much she missed her and Babulya and how her mother had already found a new—what was he, anyway? A companion? A suitor? She didn't know what to call him. *A new man*, she decided on. She told Valentina how badly she had wanted for it to be just her and her mother. When she was done, she felt a little better.

In the morning, she asked her mother if she could mail a letter to Valentina. "I want her to know that we arrived safely and to thank them for hosting me," she said quickly, hoping her mother wouldn't look closely at her. Maybe someday she could tell Mama that she and Valentina were friends. But not yet.

"Fine." Her mother sounded distracted. She was pouring buckwheat cereal into a bowl with one hand and combing her hair with the other. "There are envelopes in that drawer. I'll post it during my lunch break. Finish your breakfast. I have to register you at school, and I promised Boris I wouldn't be late."

"Thank you." Oksana slid the paper into an envelope, sealing it carefully. She wondered how long it would take the letter to reach Leningrad. Maybe two or three days. Then Valentina would write back to her. She'd check their mailbox in the front hall downstairs every day; she'd get home from school before her mother left work, so she would intercept any letters from Valentina. Maybe she and Valentina could write secretly to each other.

"Oksana!" Her mother snapped her fingers in front of Oksana's face. "Stop dreaming!"

"Sorry." Oksana rinsed out her bowl in the sink, then rushed to the bathroom to finish getting ready.

■ ■ ■

Oksana thought she would like her new school. Several of her classmates smiled when she entered the room, and the teacher lent her a fountain pen because she hadn't brought one. She discovered they were learning mostly the same topics as she had in Leningrad, so she wasn't behind, except in history. Then again, she was always behind in history, so she supposed she ought to grow accustomed to it.

At lunch, the girl who sat in front of her in class set her tray down beside hers and said, "Hello, I'm Dominika," with a grin. That was when Oksana knew school would be all right. She grinned back.

After dismissal, she milled about in the play yard with some of the girls. They told her which teachers were the worst (the music teacher smelled of cabbage and couldn't carry a tune) and which were the best (the red-haired cafeteria lady sometimes sneaked them extra helpings, if the head cook wasn't looking). They told her which boys were annoying teases and which were handsome and therefore unattainable. They told her about the sweet shop they went to whenever they had pocket money, and later, as she walked home, she felt full and warm, even though the October wind blew through her coat.

By the time her mother came home from work, she had done most of her schoolwork.

"Hello!" Oksana called from the table, where she was finishing her mathematics assignment.

"Hello." Her mother's voice was quiet.

It was probably time to make supper. Oksana started to stand up just as Dyadya Boris strode into the kitchen. He must have come in with her mother. His face was dark.

"What's the meaning of this?" he shouted. He slammed a piece of paper onto the table, on top of Oksana's mathematics sheet.

It was her letter to Valentina.

"Nothing," she said quickly. "It's nothing. Only a letter to a friend."

"You wish I weren't around?" he demanded, taking a step toward her. She backed up, bumping into the cupboards. There was nowhere to go. "You wish it was just you and your mother?"

"I didn't mean it!" Oksana cried. "I'm sorry! I was wrong."

Behind Dyadya Boris, Oksana saw her mother come into the kitchen and stand by the doorway on the opposite side of the room. Her face was anxious.

"Mama, please, believe me!" Oksana cried. "I didn't mean it. I shouldn't have written those things. I'm glad Dyadya Boris is here. Truly, I promise I am!"

Her mother looked down.

"Your mother is as disappointed in you as I am," Dyadya Boris snapped. "You ungrateful child!"

He slapped her face.

Oksana gasped. Her hand flew up to touch her burning cheek. "I'm sorry. I won't do it again."

He crumpled up the letter. "No, you won't."

He turned on his heel and left the room. Standing still, her hand on her cheek, Oksana watched him leave. He didn't say anything to her mother as he passed her. The door banged shut behind him.

Oksana's mother jumped, as if she'd been startled awake. She scurried across the room.

"How bad is it?" she asked, taking Oksana's hand away from her face and inspecting her closely. "Not bad at all. A wet washcloth should make you feel better."

"You didn't stop him," Oksana said.

Her mother didn't reply. She fetched a washcloth from the bathroom, ran it under the faucet, and pressed it to Oksana's cheek. "There, that's nice and cool, isn't it?"

"You didn't stop him," Oksana said again.

"He didn't mean to hurt you." Her mother didn't look at Oksana. "You mustn't make him angry. He can't help himself when he's upset. He's always sorry afterward."

Oksana realized what her mother wasn't saying. "He's hit you."

"It isn't his fault!" Her mother sounded impatient. "You know how it is with men. They can't stop themselves. They don't have self-control, like we do. That's why it's up to you and me to prevent this sort of thing from happening again."

"What do you mean?" Oksana took the washcloth from her mother's hands and held it to her throbbing cheek.

"Oh, you know very well!" Her mother looked annoyed.

"We know better than to make them angry, or to talk back to them, or to laugh at them, or hurt their feelings. We know what not to do, and when we do the wrong thing, we have no one to blame but ourselves."

Oksana couldn't believe her ears. "You mean it's my fault that Dyadya Boris hit me?"

"Well, you wrote nasty things about him. Mean, unwelcoming things. He had every right to be angry with you."

"So when Papa hit me, when he burned me with the cigarette . . ." She couldn't finish the sentence.

"You were to blame," her mother said calmly, then clucked her tongue. "Come now, Oksana, don't look so upset! Men have tempers, and we women must do everything we can to soothe them and make them happy."

Oksana staggered to her feet. She had to get away from her mother. Now.

"What is it?" Her mother stood up. "Is your cheek getting worse? I'll get some ice."

"No," Oksana managed to say. "No ice."

Then she rushed across the room into the bathroom, where she shut the door, then shoved the clothing hamper against it.

Her mother thought all of this was her fault. Every time Papa had hit her, every time he had yelled and cursed. She was to blame.

"Oksana," her mother called through the door, "do you want an aspirin?"

"Go away!" she shouted. "Don't talk to me!"

There was a pause. Then her mother's footsteps retreated. Tears flooded Oksana's eyes. Babulya had said hurting someone else was unacceptable, no matter the reason.

And Babulya had said Oksana was good. Valentina had said she was a talented artist. They had lived together for six months and they had never hit her.

Because they loved her.

She burst into tears. Babulya and Valentina loved her. They thought she was good and clever and strong and lovable.

And she was. She knew it with her whole heart.

(34)

Valentina

AFTER BABULYA FINISHED telling Valentina about her childhood, they didn't talk for a long time. Valentina leaned against Babulya, watching Oksana's birthday candles burn themselves out. She felt unbearably sad. Her grandmother had lost nearly everyone she cared about—even her own daughter, Galina, Valentina's mother.

Valentina nestled closer to her grandmother. "I love you, Babulya. I promise I won't ever leave you."

"That's a silly promise," Babulya said. "Someday you ought to leave me. You should go to university, find a job, fall in love." There was a smile in her voice.

"But my mother did those things, and she stopped seeing you! I don't want to do that."

Babulya sighed. "Your mother wanted to keep you safe. If it hadn't been for the accident at your papa's nuclear plant, I doubt we would have met."

"It isn't right," Valentina argued. "You loved her so much from the moment she was born. Mama says she felt the same way about me, and . . ."

A thought struck her. She sat bolt upright. "Babulya, in your story everyone called you Rifka!"

"Of course they did," Babulya said. "That's my name."

"But you're Rita Grigorievna."

Babulya looked surprised. "Nowadays, many of us older Jews take on proper Soviet names. I couldn't have gotten my job at the market if I went by a Jewish name like Rifka. Anyway, it hardly matters."

Valentina's heart beat with a steady sharpness. "Yes, it does. It proves you're wrong about Mama. She loves you. She always has."

Babulya stilled. "What do you mean?"

"My name was supposed to be Rifka," Valentina said. "Mama said she wanted to call me that, but she didn't dare. Don't you understand?" she burst out when Babulya merely looked at her. "Mama wanted to name me after *you*."

"That can't be right. Jews don't name our children after living relatives."

"Maybe Mama didn't know. Did you teach her about Judaism when she was growing up?"

Babulya's mouth opened and closed twice. "No," she said at last. "I worshipped on my own. I didn't want to put her in danger. Maybe you're right. Maybe she didn't know. Which means she did want to name her daughter after me." She brought her hands to her cheeks. "Oh my stars," she said, and smiled.

■ ■ ■

November was gray and cold. The moon put on his furs again. The waters of the Neva River no longer held the light of the sun and turned black. When Valentina walked to school, she had to bend double to keep the wind's harsh fingers from clawing her face.

Three whole weeks had passed since Oksana had left, and she still hadn't written Valentina a letter.

"She's probably been very busy," Babulya said. "Think of all she's had to cope with—new home, new school, new teacher, new friends. I'm sure once she's settled, she'll write."

But worry creased her brow as she walked beside Valentina down the ice-slicked street toward their apartment. The sky was black as tar, and the lighted windows in the buildings glowed.

"She would find time to write to me," Valentina insisted. "I know it. Something's wrong."

"She's busy," Babulya said again. "I wish I'd asked her mother for their new address, though. Then you could write to her."

Up ahead stood a figure on the front steps of their building. A woman—Valentina could tell that much. The figure turned, light from the first-story windows spilling across her face.

It was Valentina's mother.

"Mama!" Valentina shouted.

Suddenly, she was running and slipping down the icy street, laughing and crying at the same time. She threw herself into her mother's arms.

"Oh, my love," her mother said. "My wonderful love, let me see you."

She held Valentina at arm's length. "You look so much older! And taller. It won't be long before you're taller than me."

"I grew a lot," Valentina said. "Babulya is always having to let out the hems on my skirts."

Mentioning Babulya's name reminded Valentina that her grandmother was here, too. Babulya stood several feet away, watching them intently. Her face was so hopeful.

"Galina?" she said uncertainly.

"Mama," Valentina's mother said in a choked voice, and held out her arms. "I've decided to come home."

■ ■ ■

"It was Valentina's most recent letter that convinced me to leave Kiev," Valentina's mother said later, after she and Babulya had finished hugging and crying and they had gone upstairs to the apartment.

Now all three of them sat around the table, sipping tea. Even though the wind blew outside, Valentina felt warm.

"In your letter," her mother said, "you mentioned that you had realized I wanted to name you after your grandmother." She smiled at Babulya. "If I could have named her Rifka after you, I would have."

"I understand," Babulya said. "Giving her a Jewish name would have been like painting a target on her back."

Valentina's mother nodded. "After I read Valentina's letter, I thought about how unpredictable life is. We never could have guessed that there would be an accident at the power plant and that Nicolai would die so young. And when Valentina, Oksana, and I had nowhere to go in Kiev, I thought immediately of you, Mama. I knew you would love and care for Valentina and Oksana as I would. And I knew it was foolishness to stay in Kiev and eventually send for Valya. Life is too short and precious to live without our families. I've come back to you, Mama, and I don't care if the secret police have a file on you or not—I've come here to live with you and Valya. That is, if you'll have me."

"Oh, Galina," Babulya said, and took Valentina's mother's hands in hers.

Then there were more tears, and laughter, and hugs until Valentina finally had to remind them it was half past eight and they still hadn't eaten and she might die of hunger soon. Then there was more laughter, but her grandmother and mother went downstairs to make supper.

For the next several nights, Babulya told them stories as she sewed. Valentina's mother had never learned about Babulya's childhood, and she listened in silence, her eyes glistening with tears, as Babulya talked about the wartime years.

Babulya told other stories, too. They laughed over the antics of Babulya's little brothers, who had forever been getting into scrapes. They smiled over the courtship of Babulya's parents, who had met when her mother strode into her father's shop and demanded he fix her father's trousers, which he had hemmed too short. They sighed over the uncles Babulya hadn't met, for they had been dragged away by the Cossacks before she had been born, forced to serve in the tsar's army and never seen again. They shivered over the great-grandfather who had been a rabbi and who Babulya's parents wouldn't speak of in public, for fear that his occupation would have made their family targets.

"Targets for what?" Valentina asked.

"Reprisals." Babulya put away her sewing. "Some customers would have stopped coming to my father's tailor shop. Other people would have teased us—or worse."

Valentina looked at the wardrobe's closed door. Inside lay

the box where Babulya kept her Shabbat candlesticks. Today was Friday; they ought to light them. But Babulya had made no move toward the wardrobe. Valentina could guess why; it was because her mother was here and she would disapprove.

She went to the wardrobe. Her mother looked up from the handkerchief she was embroidering for one of Babulya's customers. "Is it already time to go to bed?"

"No." Valentina got out the box and set it on the table, in front of her mother.

"Valya, I don't think we should—" Babulya began.

"Yes, we should." Valentina placed the candlesticks on the table. She glanced at the curtains to make sure they were closed. Then she struck a match and lit the two candles. Covering her eyes, she began, *"Baruch atah Adonai, Elohainu melech ha-olom, asher kid-shanu—"*

"What's the meaning of this?" her mother interrupted. "Valentina, stop at once!"

"It's Friday night." Valentina's hands dropped from her eyes. "I'm lighting the candles to begin Shabbat."

Her mother stared at Babulya. "You taught her this. How could you?"

Babulya met her gaze. "Valya wanted to know. She said worshipping makes her feel closer to her father."

"She's a child!" Valentina's mother said. "She didn't understand what she was asking. She could get in trouble for this."

"We worship in secret," Valentina said quickly. "With the curtains closed. We whisper the blessings. We don't go to a synagogue. Nobody knows."

"It's still dangerous," her mother insisted.

Slowly, Babulya stood up. "My mother and brothers died because of our religion. Most of our family was wiped out. And today we still aren't free to worship. When does it end? I will be cautious, but I refuse to live in a cage."

Valentina turned to her mother. "I understand how dangerous this is. But I feel closer to Papa when we light the candles."

For a moment, her mother didn't say anything. She stood with her head bowed. At last, she looked up.

"You're certain no one has any idea what you do in here?"

"Yes," Valentina said.

"Then say the blessings." Her mother sat down again, her back ramrod straight.

Valentina took a deep breath and began. Babulya joined in. They praised God, who had commanded them to light the candles, and who had brought forth bread from the earth and fruit from the vines.

As they spoke, Valentina thought of all her ancestors who had said the same words. The great-great-great-grandfather who had been a rabbi. The great-great-uncles who had been taken by the Cossacks. The great-grandfather who had died in battle, and the great-grandmother and great-uncles who had been murdered at Babi Yar. And all the others she hadn't known and never would, the nameless children and women and men who had come before her.

She was a knot in a rope that stretched back for centuries. At that moment, she felt so close to Papa, as if he were standing behind her. If she could see him, she knew, he would be smiling at her. And she would smile back at him.

(35)

Oksana

OKSANA DIDN'T KNOW how much longer she could be perfect. For the past three weeks, she had done everything she
could think of to make Dyadya Boris approve of her. She had
gotten all four-pluses at school. She set the table for supper
and washed the dishes and swept the floor. When he spoke to
her, she kept her eyes down and spoke softly.

He hadn't gotten angry with her, not since the time he'd
found her letter. She had learned her lesson, she promised her
mother. She wouldn't speak badly of him again.

But he didn't control her mind. No one did but her, she
knew now. In her thoughts, she hated him. When he entered
the apartment, she cursed him silently, and when she carried his supper plate to the sink, she wished he had choked
on his food.

He leaned back in his chair, fishing in his suit coat pocket.
"I still can't believe you let Oksana live with Jews," he said to
Oksana's mother. He took out a cigarette and rolled it between
his fingers.

Oksana's mother jumped up and got a book of matches

out of a drawer. "I hardly had a choice, Boris. My husband was dead, my family lived in a village near the site of the accident, and I'd never send Oksana to my husband's relatives."

"Why not?" Dyadya Boris asked. He took the matchbook without thanking Oksana's mother.

"His father is a horrible man." Oksana's mother shuddered. "Drunk most of the time. When Ilya was a boy, his father used to whip him black and blue. There was no way I'd send Oksana to him."

Dyadya Boris tossed down the matchbook without lighting his cigarette. "Still, I don't think an old Jewess was a better option. Suppose some of her habits rubbed off on Oksana? Why, she could have taught Oksana to be a cheat!"

Oksana's hands tightened on the lip of the sink. Babulya a cheat! She was the kindest person Oksana had ever known.

"Yes, it was a terrible risk to take," Oksana's mother agreed.

"It certainly was." Dyadya Boris continued rolling the cigarette between his fingers. "We all know what the Jews are like. And old Jewesses are the worst of all. Probably gave Oksana kitchen scraps to eat and threadbare clothes to wear while she swanned around in furs."

Oksana couldn't bear it anymore. "Babulya is wonderful! She took good care of me."

"Did you hear that?" Dyadya Boris demanded, turning to Oksana's mother. "She calls that old Jewess her grandmother! And defends her! Why, the girl sounds like a Jew herself!"

"Please, Oksana," her mother said, her hands twisting together in her skirt. "You made a mistake. Tell Boris you didn't mean what you said."

"I did mean it." Oksana was shaking all over. She knew

she was making Dyadya Boris angry, but she didn't care. She wouldn't lie about Babulya. "She is my grandmother, and I love her."

Dyadya Boris stood up. His face had grown hard. "Over there." He pointed to the middle of the room. "Now."

Oksana stared at him. "No."

"You'll do as I say!" He grabbed her arm, yanking her forward. "You're a stupid little girl who needs to be taught a lesson." He released her arm and unbuckled his belt.

Oksana looked at her mother, who was standing by the window, her hands twisting in her skirt. Mama was weak, Oksana thought with a surge of anger. But Oksana wasn't. She wouldn't stand there meekly and let Dyadya Boris do whatever he wanted to her.

She would fight back.

She grabbed the nearest thing at hand, her school satchel. She'd swing it at Dyadya Boris's head. She'd show him—

"Take this," Dyadya Boris said to Oksana's mother, holding out his leather belt. "You're going to teach your daughter a lesson."

Oksana almost smiled. Not once in her life had her mother raised a hand to her. She hadn't protected Oksana, but she hadn't hurt her, either. Mama would refuse to take the belt from Dyadya Boris. And Oksana would tell him to get out.

Her mother took the belt.

Oksana froze. No. This wasn't happening. Not her mother.

"I'm sorry, Oksana," her mother said quietly. "I have to do it. But you brought this on yourself. I warned you not to make Dyadya Boris angry."

Oksana dropped the satchel. All she could do was watch

her mother come closer, the belt gripped in her hand.

"I'm sorry," her mother said again, and Dyadya Boris spun Oksana around. He held her in place, his fingers digging into her shoulders.

"Please," she started to scream, but the belt cracked through the air and white-hot pain lanced her back. It felt like a line of fire, carved into her skin. She let out a sharp cry.

Before she could catch her breath, the belt struck her again in the same place, tearing into the wounded skin. The pain made her gasp.

The belt hit her a third time. She bit down so hard she tasted blood.

"I can't do more." Her mother sounded breathless.

"That's enough," Dyadya Boris said. "Oksana, I don't ever want to hear you refer to that Jewess as your grandmother. It's an embarrassment to me. Do you understand?"

She swallowed the blood. "Yes, Dyadya Boris."

"Good. Now clean yourself up. You're a mess."

She moved stiffly across the room. Each step hurt. She could feel lines of fire burning into her back, through the skin and muscle, into the bone. She wanted to scream.

No. She wouldn't let them know how badly they had hurt her.

She staggered into the bathroom. She closed the door. Then she locked it. Alone. She was alone. She was safe.

Tears gathered in her eyes. No, she wasn't. She wasn't safe at all. Not even with her mother.

She took off her sweater and blouse, wincing as the fabric peeled away from her bloodied skin. She had to stand on the edge of the tub to see her back in the mirror.

Two red lines crisscrossed her lower back. The skin had split apart, leaving behind bloodied grooves. Soon the bruises would darken to black and purple, she knew. Those weren't dangerous. But she'd have to put salve and bandages over the cuts, or they could become infected.

She couldn't do it herself, although she tried several times. She'd have to ask her mother for help.

The tears in her eyes began to fall. Mama was just as bad as Papa and Dyadya Boris. She'd do whatever a man told her, no matter what it was. No matter who it hurt.

Because she cared more about a man than about Oksana.

Oksana burst into tears. She was good, she told herself. She was smart and strong, and she didn't deserve to be beaten.

She deserved to be loved.

A knock sounded on the bathroom door. "Let me in," her mother said. "I want to see your back."

"Don't pretend you care," Oksana choked out between her sobs. "You don't care about me. You never have."

"Oksana!" Her mother was crying, too. "I do care about you! If you'd only listened to me and not made Boris angry, none of this would have happened."

"It's not my fault," Oksana said. She felt the truth of the words in her bones. "It's not my fault," she repeated. "It's Papa's and Dyadya Boris's and yours."

"Let me in," her mother said again. "I want to fix your injuries."

A wave of anger hit Oksana. It would never change. Her mother would stand by while a man hurt her—or she would do the actual hurting herself. And then she would pretend everything was fine, and she'd tend Oksana's wounds, and she'd act as though what they were doing were normal.

But it *wasn't*. It was horrible, and it was a circle, spinning endlessly in the same track.

Unless she stopped it.

She opened the door.

Her mother slipped into the room. Her face was very pale, her eyes rimmed with red. "Lie down on your stomach," she said softly. "I'll put salve on your cuts."

Oksana lay down on the cold tile floor. She didn't say a word while her mother rubbed salve on her back, or while her mother covered her wounds with bandages. She didn't speak while her mother eased a fresh blouse over her head. Then she stood up.

She hated her mother so much she was shaking all over. "Leave me alone." Her voice was so cold she didn't recognize it.

Her mother's eyes widened. "Khusha?" she said uncertainly. "I thought we could have a cup of tea together. Dyadya Boris left," she added. "He's gone home for the night. I thought we could have tea and talk, just the two of us."

Only minutes ago, there was nothing in the world she would have wanted more. Now she didn't want to see her mother ever again.

"No," she said. "Go away."

Her mother's mouth opened and closed. "All right," she said at last, and slipped from the room. Oksana listened to her footsteps cross the common room. A door shut. Her mother must have gone into her bedroom.

Outside, the sky was black and snowflakes hissed against

the windowpane. Oksana wondered if it was snowing in Leningrad. Maybe Valentina and Babulya were listening to snowflakes whisper against glass, as she was. Maybe they were missing her as badly as she was missing them.

"I love you," she whispered into the silence.

They were her family. Not Papa or Mama or Dyadya Boris. Valentina and Babulya were the ones she ought to be with.

And then she knew what she had to do.

Moving gingerly, she went into the common room to get her satchel. Back in the bathroom, she locked the door and sat on the floor. Her back was on fire. She had to bite the insides of her cheeks so she didn't cry out from the pain.

She set her pen to paper and began to write:

> *Dear Valentina and Babulya:*
>
> *I need help. My mama has a suitor, and he's just like my father. He hits me, and she does nothing. Today, for the first time, she belted me—because he told her to.*
>
> *Now I know she doesn't love me. Or if she does love me, it isn't enough.*
>
> *Could you please take me back? You could keep me a secret. I'd never come out of the apartment. No one would have to know I was there.*
>
> *I left money in a pair of winter galoshes in the wardrobe. Valentina, you can tell Babulya what I did to earn the money. I don't want to lie about anything ever again.*
>
> *If you could please send me the money, then I can take a train back to Leningrad. Or if you can't take me back, please send the money anyway. I really need it.*

Thank you. You are my family, always.

Oksana

When she finished, she hid the letter in her chemise and slept with it close to her heart. She thought about adding a postscript to the letter, explaining what she would do with the money if she couldn't use it for a train ticket to Leningrad.

She would run away. She would go somewhere they would never think of looking for her. She'd come up with a new name. She'd go to an orphanage. She'd heard they were awful places, little better than prisons, but at least the workers wouldn't beat her. She'd live there, going to school, getting good marks so she could go to a university someday. She'd become an artist. She would become herself.

It was too hard to explain. She would have to tell them someday, when she was older and could find the proper words.

In the morning, she went up to the other sixth-grade girls in the play yard before school. She held up the letter. "Whoever mails this for me gets all my pocket money," she said, "and I'll pay you back for the stamp, too." As the girls clamored around her, she could finally take a deep breath. She would escape. Valentina and Babulya wouldn't let her down.

|36|

Valentina

VALENTINA RAN AS fast as she could. She had to get to her grandmother. Babulya would make everything right.

She banged through the market's front doors. The shop was crowded, with three lines snaking up and down the aisles. She weaved her way around the customers until she reached the counter. Babulya, who was weighing a block of cheese, glanced at her.

Wordlessly, Valentina held up Oksana's letter. Babulya must have seen the fear in her face, for she asked one of the other workers to take over for her. She waved for Valentina to come around the counter. Together they went into Babulya's office, where Valentina handed her the letter and waited in silence while Babulya read it.

When she was done, Babulya sat down at her desk. "Well," was all she said.

"We have to help her!" Valentina burst out. "She can't stay there."

"No, she can't," Babulya agreed quietly. "But if Oksana comes to live with us—even if she does so secretly, vanishing one day without a word of explanation to her mother—then her mother will go to the police and ask them to find her daughter. And where do you think is the first place they'll look? Where Oksana lived for almost six months," she answered her own question.

"She could hide in our apartment! No one would know she was there!"

"The police would look. And what sort of life is that for Oksana, living in one small room, never able to go outside or attend school or make new friends?" Babulya pinched the bridge of her nose, as if the thoughts pained her. "I don't see what we can do to help her."

"We could all run away together. Then we wouldn't have to worry about the police looking for Oksana in our apartment."

"Sit." Babulya pointed at the chair in front of her desk. Reluctantly, Valentina sat down. "My dear Valyushka," Babulya went on, "we can't disappear. We don't have the money to buy false identity papers. Besides, if we and Oksana vanished, the police would suspect we took Oksana, because Oksana recently lived with us. Then the police would hunt down all of us."

They had to rescue Oksana somehow. Or else she would be alone, with no one to help, nowhere to hide. And Eleonora Ivanovna and her suitor would keep hurting her.

Babulya reached across the desk to take Valentina's hand. "Look at me," she said. Her face was serious. "The best way for Oksana to remain safe is for her to vanish on her own. Go someplace where no one would look for her. Live with a stranger, someone the police couldn't trace her to. And I can think of only one person who might be able to take her in."

For a moment, they looked at each other. Then Valentina understood. "Your blackbird girl," she breathed, and joy flooded her heart because they would be able to help Oksana after all.

Except her mother didn't agree with her and Babulya. "You haven't even asked Feruza," she pointed out to Babulya. "What if she says no? And won't it look suspicious if Oksana joins her household—a blond Ukrainian girl with a family of dark-haired Uzbeks? Besides, Oksana will need money for travel and false identity papers."

"What is this money Oksana mentions in her letter?" Babulya asked Valentina. "Did she earn pin money fixing things for the neighbors like you do?"

Valentina opened her mouth to tell them about Oksana's black-market work, but her mother kept on talking. "Who could make identity papers for Oksana anyway? We don't know any forgers!"

"Couldn't we ask around to find one?" Valentina asked.

Her mother sighed as she took off her hat. She'd barely come in the door from work before Valentina and Babulya had told her about Oksana's letter. It was her first week at her new job. She'd gotten a position as a music teacher at a primary school that was on the opposite side of Leningrad, so she had to take the train home and didn't get back until early evening. "Ask around for a forger?" she repeated. "Valyushka, that's hardly something we can mention to our neighbors! Someone would probably report us to the police, and then your grandmother and I would be arrested and you sent to an orphanage."

Valentina sagged. Her mother was right. Without false identity papers, Oksana couldn't start a new life with Feruza in Uzbekistan. And even with new papers, Oksana's sudden appearance in a family of Uzbeks would look strange.

There was nothing she could do to help. Oksana would have to stay with those awful people.

Valentina kicked the wall. If only there were something she could do!

"Valya," her mother said in a warning voice.

"Let her be," Babulya said. "The child needs time for her sadness and anger."

Valentina couldn't bear to be in the room anymore. She went down the hall to the communal bathroom so she could be alone. She braced her hands on the sink and thought. When Babulya was a child, she hadn't given up. She had kept on living, even when she didn't want to.

Well, Valentina wouldn't give up, either. She'd help Oksana. No matter what she had to do. She could take the money out of Oksana's galoshes and travel to Minsk herself and then—what? The two of them run away together? The police would find them. Besides, she'd never leave Mama and Babulya.

She thought again of the black-market money in the galoshes. All that money, and there was nothing they could do with it—

She remembered the foreign passport she and Oksana had unwrapped. There *was* someone she knew who could make false identity papers: Comrade Orlov.

And she knew where to find him! Oksana had told her about his photography shop. Valentina would go there straightaway after school tomorrow. Should she tell Mama and Babulya? They'd be sure to object, saying it was too dangerous and they'd go themselves. But if they went in her place, what if Comrade Orlov didn't trust them? Then he wouldn't help Oksana.

But he might be more willing to believe her. A child was less likely than an adult to lie, he might think. Plus, she was Oksana's best friend. Perhaps Oksana had told the man about her.

No, she wouldn't say a word to Mama or Babulya. She would do this all on her own.

■ ■ ■

The next day after school she went to the photography shop. She had hidden Oksana's black-market money in her satchel, while her mother and grandmother had been fixing breakfast in the communal kitchen. Taking a deep breath, she went inside.

The shop was one small room, with glass cases containing cameras and photography equipment. A man in a brown suit stood behind the counter, writing in a big book that looked like the account ledger Babulya used at her shop.

The man looked up. "May I help you?"

Valentina took the money out of her satchel and set it on the counter. The man's eyebrows rose. "Aren't you a bit young to be carrying around so much money?" He sounded amused.

"My friend Oksana used to work for you," she said. "This is the money she earned—"

The man grabbed her wrist. He pulled her after him, through a curtained doorway into a small back room. Then he let go of her. His face was furious.

"Don't you know better than to talk about such matters

out in the open?" he snapped. "So you come to me from Oksana, who was one of my best couriers and who left me without a word of explanation? I ought to run you out of my shop, simply for being friends with that unreliable girl."

"She isn't unreliable," Valentina said quickly. "Her mother showed up one day and took her home. Oksana barely had time to pack. That's why I'm here." The words tumbled out so fast, she was breathless. "Oksana needs false identity papers. I'll pay you for them. If I don't have enough, I'll work for you to pay off the debt."

Muttering something under his breath, the man left the room. Unsure if she was supposed to follow him, Valentina waited. He came back in, holding the stack of money.

"Identity papers are expensive." He tossed the money onto a desk. "If you're foolish enough to go to the police to tattle on me, I'll say you're a liar." He bent down to look her in the eye. "And who do you think they'll believe, little girl?"

"You." Her heart beat very fast. "Please help us. Oksana is in terrible trouble. Her mother and her suitor beat Oksana. We have to get Oksana away from them. She needs new identity papers so they can never find her."

The man's eyes searched her face. "How can I know you're telling me the truth? Prove you truly are Oksana's friend."

She had no idea what to say. "You gave Oksana a set of paints for her birthday," she began, wondering what else she could come up with. "Oksana worked for you because she wanted to earn money for a train ticket to Minsk. And . . . and . . ." She faltered as the man stared at her without expression. "And she's my best friend! She's in danger. See for yourself."

She set her satchel on the floor and fished through it until she found Oksana's letter. Comrade Orlov took it from her. As he read, his face hardened.

"Oksana told me about you." His voice was gruff. "She said you and your grandmother were kind. The way she said it . . . she sounded as though it was a miracle that you would be good to her."

He looked Valentina squarely in the eye. "I'll get the fake papers. It will take some time. A week or two, at best." He handed the money back to her. "There's no charge," he said, and now his voice was gentle. "Not for Oksana and those who would help her."

(37)

Oksana

THEY WEREN'T COMING. Oksana knew it in her bones. Neither Valentina nor Babulya had replied to her letter, and it had been two weeks since she'd sent it. She trudged behind her mother and Dyadya Boris. Even at seven p.m., Volodarkovo Street was still crowded with people hurrying home from work or school. In the descending darkness, passersby looked like black blurs.

Dyadya Boris was annoyed. He was talking to her mother in the low, tight voice that Oksana had learned to dread, for it meant he was going to smack one of them once they were home and no one else could see.

Tonight he had taken them to a restaurant for supper. It was supposed to be a grand treat. Oksana hadn't been to a restaurant in ages, and she had tried to enjoy her sorrel-and-kidney soup and gravy-drenched duck. But her stomach rolled so badly when she was with Dyadya Boris that she had only been able to choke down a few bites.

He and her mother walked a few paces ahead of her down the street. Oksana followed them, her head down and her arms wrapped around herself, trying to keep warm.

"Ungrateful child," Dyadya Boris said to Oksana's mother. "She wouldn't even try the fried cheese cakes."

"Oksana has a delicate appetite," her mother said.

"You're always making excuses for her," he muttered.

No, she wasn't, Oksana thought with a burst of anger. Her mother didn't sit quietly by anymore. When Dyadya Boris demanded that Mama punish Oksana, Mama obeyed. Whatever Dyadya Boris wanted, Mama did. She had slapped Oksana in the face. She had pushed her into a wall.

Afterward, Mama was always sorry. She'd apologize and cry and bring Oksana ice and ointment and bandages. She'd beg Oksana not to make Dyadya Boris angry.

And the whole time, Oksana's hatred of her mother burned so hot she felt as though she would burst into flame.

If Babulya and Valentina didn't send her the black-market money soon, she would have to run away with empty pockets. She'd get away, as far as she could, and she'd come up with a new name. She'd walk into an orphanage and tell them she had nowhere else to go. They'd take her in, she knew. It wouldn't be a home, but an institution, with strict rules. But it would be safe. No one would hurt her.

"I want a drink," Dyadya Boris said.

"I don't have any vodka at home." Oksana's mother scurried to keep up with him.

Oksana gritted her teeth. She knew the routine by now. Dyadya Boris would stop at a store and pick up a bottle of vodka. He'd sit at the kitchen table and drink and get meaner. Oksana would wish she had a room to hide in, but of course the common area was her bedroom and she'd sit on the sofa, huddled as small as could be, hoping he wouldn't take notice of her.

But tonight he would. Because he was already furious.

Somebody grabbed her hand for an instant, then let go. What had just happened? Oksana turned around, scanning the crowd of people streaming along the pavement. Who had touched her? She didn't recognize anyone—

And then she saw Valentina. She stood a few feet away, watching Oksana. Behind Valentina, wearing a cap pulled low over her face, was Babulya.

They had come!

She made a movement toward them. Valentina shook her head and pointed across the street at an alley between two apartment towers. She must want to meet there. Of course. Oksana's mother and Dyadya Boris mustn't see them. They wouldn't approve of Oksana seeing her Jewish friends.

Nodding and holding up a hand, signaling that she would come soon, Oksana hurried after her mother and Dyadya Boris. Her family—her true family—had come! She felt as though fireworks were exploding in her heart.

Her mother and Dyadya Boris were walking into a shop. Oksana's mind raced. She couldn't let Dyadya Boris buy vodka and go to the apartment. He'd stay there for hours, or maybe all night, drinking and smoking and complaining. She wouldn't be able to get away from him to talk to Valentina and Babulya. She had to do something!

She darted in front of him. "Why don't you go out for a drink instead?"

His eyes narrowed. "Why? You don't want me to spend time with you and your mother?"

"It—it's such a special night," she stammered. "Why don't you finish the evening with another treat?"

"It's a lovely idea," her mother said warmly. "We haven't been to a bar in a while. We can sit and drink and laugh, like we used to in the beginning."

Dyadya Boris smiled. "A romantic evening just for us." Putting his arm around Oksana's mother's shoulder, he glanced at Oksana. "Finish your schoolwork. You know the rules."

"Yes, Dyadya Boris." Dutifully, she stood still as her mother kissed her cheek.

Hand in hand, her mother and Dyadya Boris walked off down the street. Oksana watched them go, her heart beating very fast. Once they had turned the corner, she flew across the street, dodging automobiles, not caring when the drivers honked their horns at her.

The alley Valentina had pointed at was dark and lined with rubbish bins. Light from the building spilled into the space, outlining two shadows who stood near the back. Valentina and Babulya!

Oksana rushed toward them. She hugged Valentina first, then Babulya. "You came for me!" She could scarcely believe they were standing here in front of her. They looked exactly the same. Both of them had on dark coats and fur caps. Babulya was smiling, but Valentina looked worried.

"Khusha, you're so thin!" Valentina said.

"Of course she's thin." There was a catch in Babulya's voice. "She hasn't been properly taken care of in weeks. Where did your mother and her man go?" she asked Oksana.

"To a bar. They could be there for hours. We have plenty

of time to pack my things, and then I can go home with you."
Home to Leningrad with Valentina and Babulya! She could
hardly wait to get on the train.

Babulya's smile fell. She glanced at Valentina, then back
at Oksana. Something in her expression told Oksana they
weren't taking her home with them.

"You don't want me." Oksana's voice broke.

"We do want you!" Valentina cried. "We wish you could
live with us, but . . ." She sent a helpless look at Babulya.

"My beloved girl," Babulya said, pressing her gloved hands
on either side of Oksana's face and forcing Oksana to look at
her, "there is nothing we want more in the world than to take
you home with us. But if you disappear, your mother will go to
the police, and where do you suppose they'll look? If you stay
with us, they'll find you."

Oksana felt cold. "You came all the way here to tell me no?
Why didn't you just write me a note instead?" She tried to pull
away from Babulya, but Babulya held tight.

"We aren't saying no," Babulya said. "We are saying we
have come up with a plan that will keep you safe. It will re-
quire you to be very brave."

Oksana didn't want to be brave. She wanted to be on a
train heading to Leningrad, with Babulya and Valentina on
either side of her, talking and laughing. But that wouldn't happen. The alley blurred, and she rubbed angrily at her eyes.

"I have a friend," Babulya went on, "a very dear friend who
sheltered me during the Great Patriotic War, when I was alone
and had no one to help me. She has been my friend for forty-
five years, and I would trust her with my life. I would trust her
with *you*."

"She lives in Uzbekistan," Valentina said. "She saved Babulya's life when they were our age, and now she's a grandmother with ten grandchildren, and they all live nearby, so you'd have plenty of friends straightaway—"

Oksana yanked herself free of Babulya's grasp. "I can't live with a stranger!"

Babulya knelt down to look in her eyes. "You already have. You lived with me."

Oksana didn't want to cry, but tears flooded her eyes anyway. How could she run away to Uzbekistan, a province she knew little about? To live with a woman she'd never met and where everything was new and different? She couldn't do it. She *couldn't*.

"I understand a little of what you must be feeling now," Babulya said gently. "I was your age when my entire family was killed. Right now, I imagine you feel as though you're alone in the dark. I promise you, you aren't. There are people who love you. And there are other people who want to love you, if you'll let them."

"Uzbekistan is so far away." Oksana's voice shook. "If I go, I'll never see either of you again."

"Maybe someday," Babulya said, "our country will change and we can travel freely, without fearing the government is spying on us. Until then, I will keep you in my heart and mind all the time."

Oksana let out a sob.

"My friend is an Uzbek and a Muslim," Babulya said. "You won't look like anyone else in her family, and I am sorry for that, for I know how hard being different can be. My friend Feruza and I came up with a story to explain your sudden appearance in her home—if you choose to go, that is."

"The story's close to the truth," Valentina piped up. "Feruza will say that you're the orphaned granddaughter of old friends of hers from the war. Lots of Ukrainian and Russian refugees passed through Uzbekistan back then. We'll pretend you're the granddaughter of one of them."

"Valentina had new identity papers made for you," Babulya said, pulling a booklet out of her purse and pressing it into Oksana's hand. It was an internal passport. "She went to your black-market man for help, and he made them for free— and another time, I would be scolding you for doing something so dangerous," she added, giving Oksana a long look. "Given the situation, however, I'm glad you worked for him!"

Oksana opened the booklet. There was her photograph, staring up at her, and the name *Tereshchenko, Klavdiya* neatly typed.

"You told me once you like the name Klavdiya," Valentina said into the silence. "I hope it's all right that I asked Comrade Orlov to give you that name."

Oksana thought of how frightened Valentina had been of her black-market work. Valentina had refused to get involved, or to go to Comrade Orlov's store with her. And yet, for Oksana's sake she'd found the courage to ask him for false papers. Valentina had done this for *her*.

And she thought of Babulya, coming all this way when it would have been safer to stay home and ignore Oksana's letter. They had done so much for her already, and still they were willing to do more.

Because they loved her.

And her mother didn't. Oksana didn't know what her mother felt for her, but it wasn't love.

"My mother will never love me enough." Oksana's voice cracked. "She's always going to choose a man over me. A *horrible* man," she added.

"There is something broken inside your mother," Babulya said. "I can't pretend to understand her, but I promise you that you are kind and clever and artistic and wonderful. You deserve to live with people who will love you."

If she went to Uzbekistan, how could she know this new family would be good to her? Babulya had said she'd trust her friend with her life, but what if this friend had changed?

"Hold out your hand," Valentina said suddenly to Oksana. She took off her father's broken watch and placed it in the center of Oksana's palm, folding Oksana's fingers around it. "When I feel sad or frightened, I touch this and I feel better. When you feel lonely, you can touch it and pretend I'm there with you."

Oksana shook her head no. "This is your most precious treasure."

"It's yours now," Valentina said.

Oksana gripped the watch. It did feel comforting. Even more comforting, though, was the knowledge that Valentina had given it to her because she didn't want her to feel lonely. Because they were best friends. Always.

She looked at the mouth of the alley. Beyond it, Volodarkovo Street was bright with lighted windows. The apartment was only a minute's walk away. She could go inside, and everything would go on as it had before. She'd be hit and belted and so frightened and angry all the time that she would turn into a shadow.

No, she knew she wouldn't stay with her mother. Deep down, she'd known ever since her mother had accepted the belt from Dyadya Boris.

She could run away to an orphanage or to Babulya's friend in Uzbekistan. Two choices. Only one, though, might include love.

"Thank you," Oksana said to Valentina, giving her a hug. She turned to Babulya. "I'll do it. I'll run away to Uzbekistan."

138

Valentina

VALENTINA'S HEART SQUEEZED. She was so happy that Oksana was going to run—and so sad because that meant they probably would never see each other again. She had to swallow hard.

"Excellent," Babulya said approvingly to Oksana. "You'd better go to your apartment and pack some things. It would look suspicious if you showed up at the airport without any luggage. Be sure to put some pillows under your blankets, so it looks as though you're asleep. We need to give you a head start before your mother figures out you're gone. And hurry!" she added as Oksana started to walk out of the alley.

Oksana spun around. "I can't go." She gasped.

"Why not?" Babulya demanded.

"I don't have a key to the apartment," Oksana said. "I had one, but Dyadya Boris took it back. A neighbor lets me in, if I'm not with my mother. So when I get my things and then leave the apartment, I won't be able to lock the door. They'll realize something is wrong right away, and they'll look for me and they'll see I'm not there . . ."

Her voice trailed off. She didn't need to finish, though, for Valentina understood what would happen next: Oksana's mother would telephone the police. They'd probably find her before her airplane even took flight. In order to escape, Oksana needed time to get out of the city and for her trail to run cold.

"I'll never escape from them." Oksana sounded as though she were having trouble breathing. "As soon as they get home, they'll figure out I've run away."

"We have time on our side," Babulya said. "There has to be a solution."

There was always an answer, Valentina thought. That was what her father used to say to her, when they were working on their experiments together. She had to figure out how to lock Oksana's door from the outside, without a key.

And then she knew.

She caught Oksana's arm. "I know what to do. But I have to go inside with you."

"You can't," Babulya objected. "What if someone sees you and remembers you when the police begin searching for Oksana?"

"Grown-ups usually don't notice children," Oksana said. "Let's go!"

Holding hands, they ran across the busy street, weaving between automobiles and ignoring the blare of car horns.

Inside Oksana's building, they walked several feet apart, pretending they weren't together. Oksana's apartment was on the third floor. After the neighbor had let Oksana into the apartment and gone inside her own place, closing the door behind her, Valentina hurried down the corridor and inside Oksana's common room.

While Oksana threw a few things inside a suitcase, Valentina raced to the kitchen, pulling out drawers until she found one that contained a jumble of pens, paper, and odds and ends. She took a pen, a rubber band, and piece of string.

After pushing the drawers back in, she helped Oksana lay a couple of pillows on the sofa, then spread several blankets on top of them. She thought it looked like a person sleeping.

"I wrote my mother a note," Oksana said quickly. "I said I had finished my schoolwork and gone to bed. As long as we can lock the door, she shouldn't check on me until morning."

"I can lock it." Valentina's heart hammered in her chest. She could do it. She knew she could.

Moving fast, she wrapped the rubber band around the dead bolt. She tied the end of the rubber band around a pen. After making a loose slipknot in the string, she pulled it tight around the tip of the pen. "Come," she told Oksana. Holding the string, she hurried into the corridor, Oksana on her heels.

Barely daring to breathe, she made sure the string was extended long enough so it would pass beneath the door and into the corridor. She closed the door. Crouched on the floor with the end of the string in her hand, she pulled to the right.

She felt the string grow taut—and then slacken. The rubber band must have come loose from the dead bolt.

Quickly, she twisted the doorknob. The door swung open. She was right: it hadn't locked. The rubber band had snapped, leaving the string dangling free.

"It didn't work," Oksana whispered. "What are we going to do?"

"I'll try again. I'll make it work this time."

Once again, Valentina rifled through a drawer until she

found another rubber band. This one looked newer than the first one. She wound it carefully around the dead bolt two times. Then she wrapped the string around the pen and left the pen hanging in midair. Clutching the string, she closed the door.

Her hands were shaking so badly on the string she was afraid she would drop it. She took a deep breath. Then she once more pulled the string to the right.

She felt it pull on the dead bolt. *Click.* The door was locked!

"You did it," Oksana whispered.

"Almost." Gently, Valentina tugged on the string. She heard the pen drop on the other side of the door. The string had gone slack in her hand. The pen was no longer attached to the string—she had pulled hard enough that the slipknot had come loose.

"When your mother gets home, she'll see a pen on the floor," Valentina whispered to Oksana. "But she'll probably think someone dropped it earlier. The rubber band should have come loose from the dead bolt, but I can't go inside to check."

"You're brilliant," Oksana whispered. "Let's go."

Valentina pulled on the string. Once she had all of it in her hand, she hurried after Oksana down the stairs. Once again, they dashed across the darkened street, running until they reached the alley where Babulya was waiting for them.

"Did Valentina's idea work?" she asked.

"Yes," they said breathlessly.

"Wonderful. You can explain it to me later. We must hurry." She pressed a few bills into Valentina's hand. "I'll take Oksana to the airport. In case anything bad happens, I want you to be far away. There's a bus stop down the street, past the big post office. When the bus arrives, ask the driver which bus to take to the train station. If I don't meet you at the station by dawn, assume the worst has happened and return to Leningrad without me."

Valentina swallowed hard. "All right."

"Good." Babulya looked at her, then Oksana, her expression softening. "It's time to say goodbye to each other."

Valentina turned to Oksana. She had to force the words out. "You'll always be my best friend."

Oksana flung her arms around her. "You're mine."

Valentina scarcely had time to hug her back before Babulya had taken Oksana by the hand. "Wait a moment before you come out," Babulya aid. "We don't want anyone to think the three of us are a group."

Valentina nodded. At the opening of the alley, Oksana stopped to look over her shoulder and wave. Then she followed Babulya into the street and vanished from view.

Valentina counted to ten, then left the alley. Her heart beat fast. Nobody was looking at her—were they?

The street was full of people and automobiles. A few yards ahead, Babulya walked alone. Oksana followed several paces behind.

Valentina turned to the left, the opposite direction Babulya and Oksana had taken. She passed a post office with a big clock. The bus stop was only a bit farther.

She waited at the corner. A handful of other people, mostly grown-ups and teenagers, stood there, too. None of them looked at her.

What if the bus driver didn't know how to get to the train

station? What if she couldn't figure out how to get there and missed Babulya?

Automatically, her hand went to her wrist. All her gloved fingers felt was the cuff of her coat sleeve. She'd forgotten—she'd given Oksana her watch.

A bus, belching exhaust, pulled up to the curb. Its doors opened with a hiss. Valentina climbed inside.

"Pardon me," she said to the bus driver, "does this bus go to the train station?"

"This is bus number five," he said. "You'll have to stay on until we stop at the children's clothing shop, then switch to a different bus."

"Thank you." She found a seat.

The bus lurched away from the curb. Valentina pressed her face to the window, watching the big buildings roll past. She was so tired. For the past three days, she and Babulya had been on the move constantly. They had left Leningrad secretly, early in the morning while it was still dark. Mama had stayed behind—she couldn't take time off from her teaching job, and someone had to remain to cover for them. Mama would pretend Valentina and Babulya were sick and home in bed. Every morning she would telephone Valentina's school to report her absence, and every evening she would cook a supper big enough for three people and carry it upstairs to their apartment. It wasn't a perfect plan, but it was the best they had been able to come up with.

After several stops, the bus jerked to a halt in front of a shop. Valentina peered through the window. Although the shop was unlit, she could make out the shapes of mannequins inside it. This must be the children's clothing store stop.

Outside, the night air stank of car exhaust. Valentina hopped from foot to foot, trying to stay warm. Finally, another bus pulled up. When she asked the driver, she learned that this was indeed the bus going to the train station.

It took another thirty minutes to reach her destination. Inside the station, it was dirty and nearly deserted. Valentina walked around the waiting area and peeked into the women's bathroom, searching for Babulya. No sign of her yet.

Valentina dropped onto a bench. Hopefully, Babulya would be here soon. Valentina wanted them to be far away before anyone realized Oksana was missing.

She wasn't certain how long she had been sitting there when a ticket collector came up to her. "You're awfully young to be here alone late at night, aren't you?"

Valentina sat up straight. "I'm waiting for my grandmother."

The ticket collector spat on the grungy floor. "Your grandmother ought to be more careful. You never know what sort of people you'll meet in a place like this."

"Thank you for your concern," snapped a woman's voice from behind him.

It was Babulya. She was giving the ticket collector the look she usually gave the lady from the third floor if she got too near their locked kitchen cupboard. "I assume," Babulya said, "your duties consist of dispensing tickets, not bothering young girls?"

Red-faced, he muttered, "Yes."

"Very good. I want two tickets to Moscow."

They went to the ticket counter. Valentina stayed close to her grandmother's side. Babulya must have done it! She had taken Oksana to the airport, or she wouldn't be here.

After Babulya had tucked the tickets into her purse, they walked to a platform to wait. Valentina leaned against her grandmother, wishing she could ask if Oksana was already on a flight and how she had seemed when Babulya had left her. But you never knew if someone was listening, so she had to settle with: "Is everything all right?"

Babulya patted her shoulder. "Yes."

That told Valentina everything she needed to know. Oksana was on her way! She would be safe, and loved, and she wouldn't have to be scared anymore. Valentina had to press her face to her grandmother's coat so no one would see her smile and wonder why she looked so happy.

Then she remembered she might not see Oksana again. Ever.

She had to blink hard so the tears wouldn't come.

Babulya squeezed her shoulder. "Distance between true friends doesn't matter when their friendship lives in their hearts," she whispered. "When you-know-who and I were going to the airport, I told her about how I met Feruza and lived with her until the end of the war. And can you guess what you-know-who said?"

Valentina shook her head no.

Babulya squeezed her shoulder again. "She said that you are *her* blackbird girl."

Something warm and soft spread through Valentina's chest until all of her was alive with it. "She's mine, too," she said.

■ ■ ■

The train from Minsk to Moscow grew more crowded at each stop, and soon passengers were packed so tightly together that Valentina didn't dare say anything to her grandmother other than, "I'm going to the washroom," or, "May we buy something from the food cart?"

At midday, they arrived in Moscow and had to wait at the train station until ten p.m., when they were allowed to board the night express to Leningrad. Valentina couldn't help thinking of the other time she'd taken this train, when she and Oksana had traveled alone to meet her grandmother. Automatically, her hand went to her wrist. Her finger grazed bare skin.

For a moment, she felt so far away from Papa that her throat ached. She reminded herself that Oksana needed the watch more than she did.

The train pulled into Leningrad in early morning. Valentina and Babulya took the Metro's red line to Avtovo. With her nose pressed to the glass, Valentina marveled at how the neighborhood hadn't changed since they had left. So much had happened since they had gone to Minsk that she felt as though the city ought to look different, too.

It was still dark; now that it was December, the sun wouldn't rise until past nine in the morning. The streets were choked with dirty snow. In the distance, the Neva River gleamed like a black snake, and in between the buildings flashing past, Valentina caught glimpses of canals.

As they walked from the Metro station to the apartment, Valentina's heart lifted. They were almost home! Mama must have left for work by now, but tonight they could tell her

Oksana had made it out of Minsk. If any of their neighbors saw them and asked why they weren't home ill in bed, they could make up a story about being well enough to return to work and school. They had done it!

They turned the corner. Up ahead was their apartment building. The street lamps were still turned on, and in their glow Valentina could see her mother, dressed in her hat and coat, standing on the front steps. Why was she waiting there? She ought to already be on the train, heading to her job.

Babulya grabbed Valentina's arm, yanking her to a stop. "Your mother doesn't want us to go home," she whispered. "She's sending us a message. Come with me, quickly."

They rushed around the corner, retracing their steps. Valentina's heart raced. What was wrong? Why couldn't they go inside?

"Stop here." Babulya halted in front of a shop window. She pretended to peer at the clothes on display.

"What happened?" Valentina couldn't stop herself from asking, even though she knew Babulya had no answer for her.

Her grandmother didn't reply. Valentina's eyes traveled over the red and blue frocks in the window.

"Do you think Oksana's mother found her?" she asked.

"Maybe," Babulya said crisply. "You'll be fine; don't fret. The authorities won't charge an eleven-year-old with a crime."

"Babulya, you must run!"

"There's nowhere to run to." Babulya adjusted her hat, the line of her jaw firming as though she were gritting her teeth. "Don't be upset, Valyushka. Some things matter more than my safety. Making sure you and Oksana are loved is one of them."

In the glass, Valentina saw a couple of people straggling past. Other than them, the street was empty. It was only seven o'clock: most of their neighbors were probably finishing their breakfasts before leaving for work or school. Suddenly, her mother appeared in the window's reflection.

"It's Comrade Popov," she said breathlessly. Valentina remembered him: the man with the spectacles, who was often in the communal kitchen watching everybody else with narrowed eyes.

"He's been asking about you ever since you left," Valentina's mother went on. "Just now he cornered me in the kitchen, saying he knows you've disappeared and you must be up to no good and he'll report you to the authorities."

Valentina clutched the satchel to her chest. It was all over. Babulya was going to prison. Mama, too, probably, for providing assistance. Oksana would be dragged back to Minsk, and she, Valentina, would be sent to an orphanage.

Babulya paled. "Where is he now?"

"In the kitchen. I knew you were supposed to come home today, so I went outside to watch for you. Both of you must get away from here as fast as you can!"

But Babulya shook her head. "Go back to the kitchen. Distract him. Cook him breakfast, argue with him, do whatever you must to keep him in that room. Valentina and I will sneak inside while you're with him."

"Do you think it's safe?" Valentina's mother asked. "He might catch you coming inside."

"Then you won't have done your work." Babulya nudged Valentina's mother on the shoulder. "Go, Galina."

Her mother took to her heels. Valentina watched her leave,

her hair streaming in the wind. What if Mama was right and Comrade Popov saw them entering the building?

"Babulya, we should hide someplace." Valentina plucked at her grandmother's sleeve.

"No." Babulya grabbed Valentina's hand. "We have to get inside our room so we can pretend we've been ill in bed for the past four days. This is our best chance, while your mama's with Comrade Popov. Come."

She strode along the pavement. Valentina scurried alongside her. Her heart banged against her ribs.

Together they turned the corner. Halfway down the street, her mother stood on the front steps of their building. Comrade Popov stood beside her.

Valentina gasped. There was no way she and Babulya could sneak into their apartment now. Comrade Popov would report them to the authorities, and the police would investigate, and soon they'd figure out the reason she and her grandmother had gone to Minsk—and what they had done there.

|39|

Oksana

OKSANA CLUTCHED HER suitcase. The airport in Tashkent was bigger than she had expected, full of people chattering to one another in languages she couldn't understand. Many of the women wore brightly colored dresses and small embroidered caps, with their dark hair either flowing down their backs or caught up in dozens of braids. Oksana saw a group of men in white tunics and loose trousers, and others dressed in the suits she was accustomed to. She couldn't take her eyes off the women; she'd never seen such bright colors before, and her hands ached to draw them.

Then she remembered all over again why she was here, and she was so nervous she could barely breathe. Would Babulya's blackbird girl be kind to her? What if she was caught with false identity papers? They had looked all right to her, but she didn't know what the authorities might notice. Perhaps Comrade Orlov's forger had used the wrong ink or had misspelled a word. An airport worker might realize the mistake, and then she would be sent back to Mama and Dyadya Boris, and they would be so angry—

She pressed a hand to her roiling stomach. She had to stop. Other passengers were starting to look at her.

Quickly, she turned away from the men and women milling about nearby. She stared at the floor, trying to make her mind blank so she wouldn't have to think at all.

"Excuse me," said a lady's voice in Russian, "are you Klavdiya Tereshchenko?"

Oksana continued staring at the floor. What if Feruza had forgotten about her? Or had changed her mind and didn't want her after all?

A hand touched her arm gently. "Excuse me," said the same lady's voice, "are you Klavdiya Tereshchenko?"

With a start, Oksana remembered that *she* was now Klavdiya. Still, she didn't say yes. Maybe this was a trap. Somehow the authorities could have traced her here.

Without answering, she looked up into the sweetest face she had ever seen. The woman was smiling, which made her black eyes crinkle up. Her skin was wrinkled and golden brown. She wore a red-and-yellow dress. An embroidered cap sat on top of her dozens of gray braids.

"I'm Feruza," she said. "I'm looking for a blackbird, Klavdiya."

It wasn't a trap. Only Babulya's friend knew about the blackbird girls.

"That's me," Oksana said. "I'm Klavdiya."

Feruza took Oksana's hands in hers and kissed them. "I'm so happy to meet you," she said. "Welcome."

■ ■ ■

Feruza lived in a small house on the edge of Tashkent. It was the same house she had grown up in, she told Oksana, and the same house Babulya had lived in more than forty years ago. There were so many people in the house that Oksana didn't know how she'd ever remember all of their names. There was Akmal, Feruza's husband, and their grown-up daughter, Zarina, and her husband, Nurmukhammed, and their three daughters, Sharifa, Khadicha, and Maftuna. The girls had stayed home from school today, to welcome her, and they seized her hands and, giggling, led her up to the attic, where they shared a bedroom.

"You can have the bed under the window," Khadicha said. She spoke in Russian, not Uzbek, for which Oksana was grateful. "And we cleared a space in the wardrobe for you."

"Thanks." Oksana had never seen a room like this before: the walls were painted white, the floorboards dark and varnished. Her bed was set in an elaborately carved wooden frame.

She peered out the window. A dusting of snow covered the ground. Beyond Feruza's yard, she could see dozens of other small houses and, far in the distance, the towers and big buildings of Tashkent. She thought of her paints and paper in her suitcase. Maybe sometime soon she could paint a picture of the city.

"It's beautiful," she said, and turned to see all of the girls smiling at her. Maftuna and Sharifa were little, but Khadicha was close to her age. Maybe they would become friends. She didn't seem to mind sharing her room with a stranger, and she had greeted Oksana by kissing her cheeks two times. Hesitantly, Oksana smiled back at the girls.

They ate supper in a big dining room. Oksana had never seen such food: a spicy stew filled with rice, meat, carrots, and onions; and noodles; and stuffed pockets of dough. She was so hungry she ate everything on her plate.

By then Nurmukhammed, Feruza's son-in-law, had returned from work, and he greeted Oksana by kissing her cheeks. Something inside her cringed when he touched her. She wondered if he hit his daughters.

But he laughed when Maftuna, the littlest at six, climbed onto his lap during dessert. He told a funny story about one of his clients, who had come to his office today but had forgotten all of his paperwork and had to go home to get it. After dinner, he sat in the parlor, and he and his wife, Zarina, played board games with their daughters.

Part of Oksana wished she had the courage to join them, but when they asked her, she shook her head no. She sat in a corner, watching Nurmukhammed and Akmal, Feruza's husband, who was reading a book and looked up sometimes to smile at his granddaughters. One time he smiled at her, Oksana.

Feruza sat next to her, reading a newspaper. Every so often, she smoothed Oksana's hair. "Are you tired, Klavdiya?" she asked.

She was, but she didn't want to leave the warm room filled with happy people. "No," she said, swallowing a yawn.

At last, it was time to go to bed. The girls washed their faces and brushed their teeth and changed into white nightgowns. They had a spare nightdress for Oksana, for she had forgotten hers at the apartment in Minsk.

Lying in bed was like floating on clouds. The grown-ups,

all four of them, went from one bed to the next, tucking in each girl and giving her a good-night kiss.

Oksana had thought they wouldn't come to her, but they did. "Good night," Zarina and Nurmukhammed said, and they each kissed her on the cheek. Akmal said good night, too, and after he kissed her, he said gently, "We are so happy you have joined our family, Klavdiya."

Tears pricked her eyes. "Thank you," she managed to say.

Feruza kissed her last. She brushed Oksana's hair away from her face and drew the blankets up to her chin. "Good night. May you have sweet dreams."

To Oksana's surprise, she did. At least, she must have, for she woke up the next morning smiling.

After breakfast, the other girls left for school and their parents went to work. Feruza said Oksana needn't attend school until next week, so she could have a chance to get settled.

At first, Oksana didn't know what to do with herself. She went from room to room, marveling at the dark carved wooden furniture and the white walls, so different from the concrete and steel she was used to. At last, she went up to the attic bedroom and got out her paints.

She had planned on sketching the view from the window, then painting it, but instead she found her thoughts turning to Valentina. She hated knowing she might never see her again.

But Babulya and Feruza hadn't seen each other for forty-one years, and they had still found a way to be friends. They had written each other letters. Feruza said Oksana couldn't do that, as the police were looking for her and might be monitoring Babulya's mail, just in case they suspected Babulya had helped her get away.

There had to be something Oksana could do, though, some way to tell Valentina thank you and to let her know that she was going to be all right in this new home.

An idea struck her, and soon she was lost in drawing. When she was finally done, she came back to herself and realized she was starving. Maybe it was time for lunch.

She looked for Feruza downstairs, but couldn't find her anywhere. At last, she took her coat off a hook by the back door and went into the backyard. Yesterday's snow had already melted. Several chickens were pecking at the ground, searching for feed.

Oksana approached a wooden shed. From outside she could hear someone moving about. Was it Feruza?

She peeked inside and saw Feruza standing at a table. Parts of a toaster lay scattered across its surface.

"Come along, now," Feruza muttered. She was tightening two metal pieces with a screwdriver. She must have heard Oksana, for she turned around and grinned at her. "You look surprised."

Oksana couldn't help thinking, with a pang, of her own mother in her elegant dresses and painted fingernails. "I'm not accustomed to seeing ladies use tools."

"I learned how to fix just about anything on the farm during the war when my father was away fighting." Feruza finished tightening the screw and set the pieces down. "Come inside, out of the cold." She hesitated, then said, "I saw the way you looked when Akmal and Nurmukhammed kissed you. I understand why you're afraid of men. Goodness, I would be, too, if I'd gone through what you have."

She looked into Oksana's eyes. "I don't hold with hitting

or violence of any sort. In this house, if we're angry, we talk."

Oksana fiddled with the buttons on her coat. She wanted to believe Feruza, but . . . she thought of her father, how red-faced he had gotten when he was mad at her, and how it had felt when he had pressed the tip of his cigarette into her skin. And Dyadya Boris, how quickly his smile turned to fury. And Mama, pale and trembling, taking the belt from Dyadya Boris's hand.

Oksana couldn't speak. She hitched a shoulder in a half-hearted shrug.

Feruza turned back to the table and picked up her screwdriver. "You'll believe me someday. Change takes time, Klavdiya. You won't always be afraid."

Oksana hadn't been afraid of Babulya or Valentina, after she'd lived with them for a while. Maybe Feruza was right.

"We are put on this earth to be kind to one another." Feruza began putting the toaster back together. "Human beings are Allah's language."

"I don't understand," Oksana said.

"People talk about miracles," Feruza said. "But there are miracles around us all the time that most of us don't see. Your friendship with Valentina, mine with Rifka—those are miracles. When we are kind and loving and generous, we become miracles ourselves." She gestured at the partially assembled toaster. "Rifka told me you're an artist. You must be good with your hands. Would you like to help me fix this? Once we're done, we can have lunch."

"All right." Oksana picked up a loose screw. She liked what Feruza had said. Maybe they *were* miracles, every single one of them.

As they fitted the pieces of the toaster back into place, Oksana glanced around the shed. It was shabby but comfortable. And the house was filled with good people, and the school she would start next week might have lots of friends waiting to be met. She looked at Feruza's sweet, wrinkled face. Best of all, this place had Feruza, and since Babulya loved her, Oksana knew she could trust her.

Oksana unbuckled Valentina's father's watch from around her wrist and set it on the table. "Feruza," she said, "would you please help me do something? It's for my best friend."

"Of course," Feruza said, and together they bent over the broken watch while outside the wind blew, but inside they were cozy and warm.

(40)

Valentina

VALENTINA STARED AT the front steps of her apartment building. She and Babulya had almost made it safely home, and now they wouldn't be able to get inside without Comrade Popov seeing them. From this distance, she couldn't hear what her mother and Comrade Popov were saying, but it was clear from the way they were talking in each other's faces that they were arguing.

"We must go," Babulya said. She hurried around the corner, away from their building. Valentina rushed after her.

"Where are we going?" Valentina asked.

"I don't know." Babulya picked up the pace. "There's no way we can bluff our way out of this. Comrade Popov will see us returning, and it will be obvious we haven't been ill at home. He'll report us to the authorities, and once they start investigating, they'll figure out we've been to Minsk. They'll put all the pieces together, and then . . ."

She let the words trail off. Valentina didn't need her to finish. She knew what would happen.

"Can't we hide somewhere and wait for him to leave for work?" she asked. "We can sneak inside while he's gone."

"Your mama said he was going to the authorities," Babulya said softly. "He was in his coat just now. He's probably on his way to report our disappearance. The police will check our apartment. We can't go back, in case someone is watching and sees us return."

For a moment, they didn't speak. Valentina felt like crying. What could they do?

Suddenly, Babulya stopped walking. "The courtyard," she whispered to Valentina. "We'll have to go through another building and sneak into the courtyard."

Valentina understood at once: an apartment tower on the street behind theirs shared their building's courtyard. Their building had a single door that led directly to the courtyard— and to a back stairwell. She used it herself when she took out the rubbish.

Leningraders had begun leaving their buildings. Soon the streets would fill with people.

"Come." Babulya seized her hand again.

Together they hurried down the street. The street lamps were still on, and by their light Babulya counted buildings under her breath. "Six, seven, eight . . . That must be it." She nodded at a massive apartment tower. Made of crumbling brick, it rose at least ten stories into the sky. "That's the building that shares our courtyard."

Valentina hoped she was right. Just then, a woman came out of the building's front door. Babulya hustled forward to catch the door before it closed. She held it open for Valentina. "Quickly," she said, and she and Valentina went inside.

In silence, they entered the lobby. Like theirs, it was lined with doors—the ones on the right and left probably led to stairs or communal rooms. A single door on the opposite wall might lead to the courtyard.

Together they crossed the room. Two men walked past without even glancing at them. Babulya opened the door. A wave of cool air rushed over them. Outside air. They had made it to the courtyard.

Without a word, they went outside. The hour was so early it was still dark, and the night's stars had vanished, leaving the sky black. Only the illuminated windows in the building opposite told Valentina that they had made the right choice— across the courtyard stood their apartment tower.

They rushed across the empty courtyard. Babulya yanked open their building's back door, and they ran up the stairs. Valentina could barely breathe. What if Mama couldn't distract Comrade Popov? What if he had already fetched the police, and they were waiting for them at the apartment?

At the sixth floor, they left the stairwell and rushed down the corridor. The overhead lights were left unlit during the day to conserve electricity, and in the gloom Valentina could scarcely see anything. But she didn't see any shadowy forms. The police weren't here yet.

Babulya unlocked their door. They hurried inside, with Babulya easing the door shut behind them. Valentina's mother had left a lamp on, which provided just enough light for them to see by. The curtains had been opened, the bed made, the table left cluttered with books and dishes. There was no indication that only one person had lived in this room for the last few days.

"Into your nightdress, quickly," Babulya said. "We must look as though we're ill in bed."

Valentina's hands shook so badly, it seemed to take her forever to unbutton her coat. Finally, she had it off and hung it on a hook. Then she ripped off her skirt and sweater and blouse. She shoved them under the bed. Babulya grabbed their nightgowns out of the wardrobe and threw Valentina's to her.

Hastily, they put them on. Valentina flung herself onto the sofa, sat up to grab the blanket hung across the back of it, and then lay down. Across the room, Babulya was climbing into bed.

Then silence. Valentina lay still, her heart racing.

Footsteps sounded from the corridor. Lots of footsteps. Valentina's eyes met Babulya's. Her grandmother managed a weak smile. "Let me speak to the police, Valyushka. You lie there and look ill."

The door opened. A young man stood in the entryway. A policeman. In the dimness, Valentina could see the buttons shining on his tunic. His eyes traveled over the room, stopping on Babulya. "Are you Rita Grigorievna Goldman?" he asked.

"Yes." Babulya sat up, clutching the blankets to her chest. "May I ask what the trouble is?"

"I'll tell you what the trouble is!" Comrade Popov squeezed around the police officer and came into the room. "You and your granddaughter haven't been seen in days, and your daughter won't give me a proper explanation of your whereabouts!"

"They've been ill!" Valentina's mother shouted from the corridor.

"Let's go into the apartment and clear this up," the police officer said.

They all filed into the room. In the pale lamplight, Valentina thought her mother looked nervous.

"The poor things have been sick in bed," her mother said. "Comrade Popov, surely you've seen me carrying their suppers to them every night."

Comrade Popov held up his hand. "They haven't been seen in the bathroom. They haven't been heard walking about this room. You know the walls are as thin as paper."

"Oh, for pity's sake!" Babulya appealed to the policeman, who was watching them without expression. "My granddaughter and I haven't been heard walking about because we've been lying in our beds. I hardly wonder our neighbors, the Kozlovs, haven't noticed us using the bathroom since their boys monopolize it."

The policeman aimed a stern look at Comrade Popov. "Making unfounded accusations is a serious matter."

Comrade Popov turned red. He muttered something under his breath, spun on his heel, and left the room, banging the door closed behind him.

Valentina's mother turned to the policeman. "May I help you with anything else?" she asked him politely. "My mother and daughter aren't well and need to rest."

"One more question," the policeman said. "Comrade Popov said you and your daughter recently moved here. Why did you come to Leningrad?"

Her mother folded her hands. "We used to live in Pripyat. My husband was one of the plant engineers at Chernobyl."

The policeman's gaze flew to her. "Was?"

"He was on duty the night of the disaster," Valentina's mother said quietly. "He died soon afterward."

The policeman shuffled his feet, looking uncomfortable. He glanced around the room. "All three of you live here?"

Valentina knew what he saw: a bed against the wall, a sagging sofa, a table crowded with dishes and schoolbooks and Babulya's sewing machine, and laundry hanging from the lines stretching from one side of the room to the other. The place looked desperately poor, even to her eyes.

"Yes," her mother replied. "It's the best we can manage."

The policeman took off his cap, turning it over and over in his hands. "It doesn't seem right," he said to himself. "The widow and orphan of a hero of the state being stuck in one tiny room."

Babulya lifted her chin. "I'm afraid it's all I could offer them. I've been on a housing list since 1968, but you know how it is."

The policeman nodded. "I'll have a word with your neighbor before I leave. He needs to understand he can't run to the police every time he takes a dislike to someone." He made a funny little bow. "Good day to you, ladies."

"Good day," Valentina's mother echoed, ushering him out.

Then she went to the table and scribbled something on a piece of paper. She held it up. *Sorry*, read the message. *Popov had already gone for police by time I returned from talking to you in the street. Held them off as long as I could.*

"You did well," Babulya said softly.

Then the three of them went to one another so they could embrace and say everything they needed to without saying a word—for the walls were thin, they knew, and they couldn't chance being overheard.

And that, Valentina thought, was that.

■ ■ ■

Only it wasn't. Five days later, they received a notice that Babulya's housing number had finally been called. A two-room apartment in the center of Leningrad was available. They would have to move in quickly or the place would be assigned to another family.

"Did the policeman arrange this?" Valentina's mother asked, rereading the notice.

"Perhaps it's a coincidence," Babulya said, opening the wardrobe door. "What does it really matter? Let's pack!"

During their final days in the apartment, Valentina listened for footsteps on the stairs all the time. She was afraid the police might have connected them to Oksana's disappearance. But the police never came. They must have decided Oksana was a runaway, she thought.

Although her mother and Babulya worried, too, they still played music in the evenings, after Valentina had finished her schoolwork and Babulya had put aside her sewing. Valentina's mother had borrowed a flute from the music department at her school, and she and Babulya played songs together. The music was so sweet it made Valentina's heart soar.

They moved into their new apartment on the last day of the year. Although Valentina was sad to leave her friends and teachers, her gladness outweighed her sorrow. Thanks to their new home's location, she would attend the school next door to the one where her mother taught. This place's rent was cheaper than their old room (again, her mother suspected the policeman of pulling a few strings in the local Communist Party on their behalf). Because the apartment wasn't as expensive, Babulya wouldn't have to work at the market anymore. She could sew clothes, which she liked, and, as Valentina's mother said, take a well-deserved rest for her weary bones.

Darkness fell early. The sky was black by the time they had finished putting their things away. Babulya turned on the lamps. Their golden warmth filled the large room that would serve as the sitting area, kitchen, and Valentina's bedchamber.

Valentina pressed her nose to the window. From here, she could see the bright, twinkling lights of Nevsky Prospekt, the most famous street in the city. It had been decorated in honor of the new year. When she had walked it earlier that day, she had seen its shop windows were crowded with books and chocolates and gifts and figurines of Grandfather Frost.

This new year wouldn't be like other years, she knew. In the past, her father had taken her to a children's show at a theater, where she and the other kids in the audience were given *podarki* gift bags, filled with candy and pictures of Grandfather Frost and the Snow Maiden. Her mother had spent the day cooking. They had eaten caviar with blini, and her parents had sipped champagne. Valentina had been allowed to stay up until midnight.

The best part, though, had been finding presents under the tree. Her parents had said that in other countries, people put trees in their houses to celebrate Christmas, but here it was to usher in the new year. She had always had several gifts waiting for her under an evergreen. She could still remember the crinkle of wrapping paper and the sharp scent of pine needles.

Nothing, though, was like before. There were no presents, no tree, no bag of *podarki*, no dish of caviar.

No Papa. No Oksana.

The colored lights of Nevsky Prospekt blurred. Valentina turned away from the window.

Her mother put an arm around her shoulders. "I'm sorry we don't have a tree this year." She kissed the top of Valentina's head. "You do, however, have a present."

"I do?" Valentina looked in the direction her mother pointed. There, sitting on the table, was a package.

"Go on, open it." Babulya stood in the doorway to the bedroom, smiling. "It arrived in the post yesterday. You didn't notice because you were so busy packing your things. Your mother and I saved it for today. We thought you'd like opening it on the eve of a new year and in our new home."

"I don't know anyone who would send me a gift," Valentina said.

Babulya raised her eyebrows. "Don't you?"

Oksana. No, it was too much to hope for . . .

It couldn't be, could it? Babulya had said there should be no contact between them for a long time, maybe forever.

Like someone in a dream, Valentina reached for the package. It was small and square, fitting in the palm of her hand. It was postmarked Uzbekistan.

Valentina's heart beat fast. It *was* from Oksana. She knew it, even though there was no return address. She tore open the package. A box tumbled out. With shaking hands, she opened it.

Inside lay her father's watch. The glass face had been polished until it sparkled, and the leather band had been rubbed with oil so it felt as soft as butter. The minute hand ticked as it made an orderly revolution around the numbers.

Joy flooded Valentina's heart. She couldn't speak. All she could hope was somewhere, thousands of kilometers away, Oksana could magically know she was thinking of her and thanking her.

A paper that had been rolled around the wristband fluttered to the floor. Valentina picked it up. There was no message. No signature. But she understood exactly what it meant.

It was a drawing of two blackbirds soaring through the sky, the feathers of their outstretched wings touching like a pair of clasped hands.

Author's Note

THE CHERNOBYL DISASTER was the worst nuclear accident in history.

In the early hours of April 26, 1986, the night-shift workers at reactor number four ran what was supposed to be a routine safety drill. What they didn't know was that the emergency alert system had been temporarily shut off to prevent it from responding to the test as if it were an accident. Turning off the alert system disabled the pumps that sent water into the reactor's cooling system. The reactor overheated, the temperature skyrocketing to five thousand degrees Fahrenheit, one hundred times its normal level.

At 1:23 a.m., the pressure burst the cooling system pipes. A second later, a blast ripped the one-thousand-ton roof off the building. Radioactive dust and debris shot up miles into the sky. Glowing lumps of metal rained down on the grounds of the power plant, sparking more than twenty fires.

Incredibly, there were no emergency plans in place at the nuclear plant. To prepare for disaster was to admit that disaster was possible, which went against Communist Party attitudes. At first, the government tried to keep the explosion a secret.

Therefore, the residents of Pripyat began that day, a Saturday, as usual. Despite the red sky and the ambulances and police officers and soldiers flooding the city, everyone continued about their business, certain that if they were truly in danger the government would rescue them. Children went to their half day of school on Saturday, little kids played outside, and gardeners weeded, unaware that their plants were coated with radioactive fallout. Some people sunbathed, and others fished in the river that ran through the city and past the plant, not realizing that anything they caught would be contaminated.

Soon, however, residents grew suspicious. Because the Soviet government had convinced the public how safe nuclear power was, though, many people thought folk remedies would save them. People ate cucumbers and drank milk, mineral water, or vodka, believing they would be fine.

By the next day, some residents began feeling ill, with nausea, headaches, dizziness, vomiting, and high blood pressure. Radiation had been spewing into the atmosphere for thirty-six hours. At last, the Soviet government ordered the city's evacuation.

Within hours, Pripyat became a ghost town. Residents' pets roamed the streets, searching for their owners. Firefighters remained behind to fight the blaze in the core of reactor number four.

Over the following days, the evacuation was broadened to

include more than one hundred thousand people. Eventually, three hundred thousand were displaced.

Soon thousands of workers, mostly soldiers, were brought in to clean up the contaminated areas. They were known as liquidators, and they spent months razing villages to the ground and covering them with fresh earth, washing off roads, and chopping down and burying entire forests. The woods that Valentina and Oksana drive through on their way out of Pripyat is known today as the Red Forest. The trees were cut down and buried, and eventually the area was replanted with a grove of pine trees, which are extremely small due to radiation.

Before the accident, Ukraine provided much of the food and grain supply for the Soviet Union. The reactor explosion, however, destroyed crops and farmland for at least one hundred miles.

Because millions of people in the Soviet Union depended upon the Chernobyl power plant for heat and electricity, the damaged plant continued to be operated. It was not until 2000 that the last reactor was shut down.

In the weeks and months after the disaster, workers hurriedly built a coffin-like structure over the ruined reactor. It took 206 days to complete the concrete-and-steel shell. Because the radiation risks were so great, builders could only work on it in five- to seven-minute shifts. It soon became clear that the clumsily constructed coffin could not last.

In 2017, after more than two decades in the making, a new structure was placed over the coffin. Known as the "sarcophagus," it is taller than the Statue of Liberty and is meant to safely contain the reactor for the next century. Hundreds of people from all over the world worked on designing, building, and transporting the thirty-five-thousand-ton structure.

Pripyat has never been resettled. Today it is a tourist attraction. Visitors can don protective gear and accompany a guide through the ruined city. Everything was left as it was in 1986, so Communist banners and flags still adorn buildings, although they are now in tatters. Windows are broken and gape like empty eyes; trees and vegetation have been allowed to run wild, so vines have overtaken many buildings. The amusement park that Oksana thinks of going to with her friends still stands, although its metal rides are rusted. The animals that its owners were forced to leave behind have died, but many of their descendants have gone feral and today run in the streets of Pripyat.

■ ■ ■

Immediately after the accident, wind carried radioactive dust across Ukraine, over the Baltic states, and into Scandinavia. Sweden began to suspect that there had been a nuclear disaster in Ukraine. Initially, the Soviets denied it. As more and more countries began accusing them of covering up an accident, Soviet officials realized they had to come clean. At nine p.m. on April 28, more than two full days after the explosion, the government finally announced the disaster on national television.

Parents were frantic to send their children out of harm's way. Unfortunately, however, there were no evacuation plans. In fact, there was a suspicious shortage of airplane, bus, and train tickets. The prevailing opinion was that the government deliberately withheld tickets in order to prevent a mass exodus from affected areas.

Many children, however, managed to get to safer places. One of them was my dear friend Victoria Belfer. Much of *The Blackbird Girls* was inspired by her family's experiences during World War II and the Chernobyl disaster.

After the nuclear accident, Victoria's parents managed to get one airplane ticket. They sent Victoria to live with distant relatives in Tashkent, Uzbekistan. By the autumn of 1986, however, the relatives could no longer care for Victoria, and she was moved again, this time to Kremenchug, Ukraine. Finally, after living away from her parents for a year, she returned home.

When the Soviet Union collapsed in 1991, Victoria's parents and grandparents filed to leave the country on humanitarian grounds. As Jews, they had suffered religious persecution for generations. Although they were permitted to leave Ukraine, initially no country would accept them, and they became stateless citizens. They lived in Italy for a year before the American government approved their paperwork. They moved to my hometown, Niskayuna, New York, and I met the girl who would become my lifelong friend.

I also met the rest of her family. Her grandparents Valentina and Yefim Khirge inspired the character Babulya and are two of the most resilient and courageous people I have ever known. Her mother, a talented music teacher, was also kind and brave. Sadly, she later died of leukemia, a common affliction for those who have experienced radiation poisoning.

I am grateful and fortunate that Victoria and her grandparents shared their memories with me. Despite the Nazis, bullies, and cowards they faced, they also met people who helped them. It is my hope that Valentina and Oksana's story reminds us there are many good-hearted people in the world—and even when we have to look hard for them, they are always there.

Resources

—

IF YOU ARE experiencing emotional or physical abuse at the hands of an adult or another young person, please know it is *not* your fault. You did nothing wrong; you are not bad. You deserve to be treated with love.

One of the most important things you can do is **TELL AN ADULT YOU TRUST.** This grown-up might be a relative, a neighbor, a teacher, or a guidance counselor. Many teachers and school psychologists have gone through training to help children who are experiencing abuse. Remember, you are not alone; there are many people who care about you and who can help you.

Many organizations are devoted to stopping child abuse. For more information, please visit the websites listed below:

❯ **CHILDHELP.** This nonprofit aids victims of abuse: childhelp.org.

❯ **THE AMERICAN PSYCHOLOGICAL ASSOCIATION.** This organization provides helpful resources about abuse, including education and prevention: apa.org/pi/families/resources/understanding-child-abuse.

❯ **CENTERS FOR DISEASE CONTROL AND PREVENTION.** This agency seeks to educate the public about abuse and violence: cdc.gov/violenceprevention/childabuseandneglect/index.html.

If you need help, you can also call the **NATIONAL CHILD ABUSE HOTLINE** at 1-800-4-A-Child (1-800-422-4453).

Further Reading

—

IF YOU'D LIKE to learn more about Chernobyl or life in the former Soviet Union in the 1940s and 1980s, I recommend the following books:

NONFICTION:

Alexievich, Svetlana. *Voices from Chernobyl: The Oral History of a Nuclear Disaster*. Translated by Keith Gessen. Normal, Ill.: Dalkey Archive Press, 2005.

Bellamy, Chris. *Absolute War: Soviet Russia in the Second World War*. New York: Knopf, 2007.

Hautzig, Esther. *The Endless Steppe: Growing Up in Siberia*. New York: Crowell, 1968; HarperCollins, 1987.

Ingram, W. Scott. *The Chernobyl Nuclear Disaster*. New York: Facts on File, Inc., 2005.

Kort, Michael G. *The Handbook of the Former Soviet Union*. Brookfield, Conn.: The Millbrook Press, 1997.

Manley, Rebecca. *To the Tashkent Station: Evacuation and Survival in the Soviet Union at War*. Ithaca: Cornell University Press: 2009.

Plokhy, Serhii. *Chernobyl: The History of a Nuclear Catastrophe*. New York: Basic Books, 2018.

FICTION:

Hesse, Karen. *Letters from Rifka*. New York: Puffin Books, 1992.

Lasky, Kathryn. *The Night Journey*. New York: Puffin Books, 2005.

Whelan, Gloria. *Angel on the Square*. New York: HarperCollins, 2003.

Yelchin, Eugene. *Breaking Stalin's Nose*. New York: Henry Holt and Co., 2011.

Acknowledgments

—

I HAVE WANTED to write this story for more than twenty years. At a sleepover in ninth grade, a new friend told me she had survived Chernobyl when she was a little girl in Ukraine. That friend's name is Victoria Belfer Zabarko, and we are still friends today. No words can do justice to the love and respect I have for her. I'm grateful to Victoria and her grandparents, Valentina and Yefim Khirge, for sharing their experiences with me.

From my first phone call with Kendra Levin, I knew I wanted to work with her. Frankly, I knew I desperately wanted to work with her. I'm thankful to Kendra for her guidance and insightfulness, and her ability to ask the right questions. Because of her, *The Blackbird Girls* became the story I had hoped it could be. I'm so fortunate Kendra is my editor.

Gianna Lakenauth is as clever as she is kind. Her comments always helped me see this story from a different angle. I'm grateful to everyone else at Penguin, especially Ken Wright, Nancy Brennan, Aneeka Kalia, Janet Pascal and the rest of the copyediting team, and the marketing team at Penguin Young Readers, particularly Venessa Carson, for their genuine enthusiasm for this book. Many thanks to Shreya Gupta for a breathtaking cover. I'm especially grateful to Maggie Rosenthal. Working with her has been a delight.

Every day I'm thankful Tracey Adams is my agent.

Volunteering to unpack boxes at an SCBWI conference for the opportunity to meet her is one of the best decisions I ever made. Tracey believed in me—and this story—when I was at the lowest point of my life, and I'll never forget it.

While I was drafting *The Blackbird Girls*, my husband was diagnosed with cancer. One Sunday morning, Mike felt strange; five days later, doctors discovered he had a ten-centimeter-sized malignant tumor. For the following year, Mike underwent grueling treatments: chemotherapy, daily radiation, major surgery, more chemotherapy, another surgery. Even when Mike was at his sickest, he enjoyed hearing about this story, and I could not have written it without surviving the highs and lows of cancer. I will always be thankful Mike is my love, partner, and best friend.

Our daughter, Kirsten, had just turned nine when we received her dad's diagnosis. As we struggled to get through the next year, Kirsten became incredibly strong and resilient. She inspired many parts of this story. I'm so proud to be her mom.

My parents, Lynn and Peter, are both wonderful and tough. Without them, I couldn't have managed my family's journey with cancer, let alone finished writing this book. My mom has read each of my manuscripts before anyone else, and her comments are invaluable. After Mike was diagnosed, a week didn't pass without her bringing over a pot of home-cooked soup, which was often the only food he could stomach. Every Monday night, she cooked a delicious dinner for us. My dad ripped out the bushes in our front yard that we didn't like and planted new ones; he stained the back deck; and he showed me how to handle the household repair work that had once fallen to my husband. Most importantly, he and my mom cared for Kirsten when Mike and I could not, and they made her feel safe and loved.

My brother, Paul, was a constant source of support. He checked on me all the time, sent us care packages, and drew pictures of Kirsten as Wonder Woman and Mike as Superman. I'm glad I'm his sister.

Many thanks to my dear friend Chin-Lin Ching, MD, for her expert advice on cigarette burns.

I'm thankful for my family and friends, especially Deb, Janie, Richard, Julie, Matt, Mark, Bekah, Lucy, Amy, Alissa, Kate, Kim, Dan, Lili, Mike, Nicole, Stephanie, Randi, Melissa G., Michelle, Allison, Mary, Elizabeth, Cathy, Serena, Toni, Carl, Pam, Jim, Leslie, Chris, Adam, Sharon, Anne W., John, and Astrid. My friend and fellow writer Sara Raasch sent us gifts, frequently checked on us, and planned a writing retreat that I desperately needed. My daughter's fourth grade teacher, Marion Kramer, cared not only about Kirsten's education but also her emotional well-being, and helped her navigate the scary, confusing world of being a child with a critically ill parent. My rabbi, Scott Nagel, counseled and prayed with us, and every time I entered Congregation Beth Ahabah, I remembered that my home isn't only where I live with my husband and daughter.

To all the readers, writers, teachers, librarians, educators, and bloggers: thank you.

Most of all, I'm grateful to writing itself, which gave me light during a dark time.

My cup runneth over.